Faded Perfection

Beautifully Flawed Book Two

CASSANDRA GIOVANNI

SHOW N'OT TELL PUBLISHING
CONNECTICUT

Show n'ot Tell Publishing

Connecticut, USA

This is a work of fiction. Names, characters, places, and incidents are products of the author's imagination. Any resemblance to actual persons, living or deceased, events or locations are wholly coincidental.

PUBLISHER'S CATALOGING-IN-PUBLICATION DATA:

Giovanni, Cassandra

Faded Perfection

ISBN: 978-0692689424

Cover Art: Gio Design Studios © 2016

Printed in the United States of America

Prologue

I'd never seen the man that stood in front of me, but somehow I knew that look. My skin crawled as he looked back at Adam and me. He opened his mouth to speak, and all I could see was the movement; all I could hear was white noise. I felt Adam's hand go slack in mine, and the world spiraled back at me. The force of the realization knocked the breath I had been holding out of my lungs. I struggled to breathe as the words pounded into my brain and shattered my soul.

"There's nothing we could do for him."

Him. Bobby. Gone.

My head jerked back in slow motion as I heard Adam's knees hit the floor. The hospital droned, but all I could hear was Adam sobbing at my feet with his fists pounding into the ground. I realized I was still staring at the doctor unblinking as my brain struggled to catch up—as I struggled to get air.

In my mind I was trembling, screaming Bobby's name, ripping at my hair. In my head, I lost it. In real life, I was standing doing nothing. Not even breathing.

The doctor's eyes trailed down to Adam and mine followed.

Reality jolted into me and everything suddenly was going too fast. Adrenaline rushed through me as I pulled Adam into my arms, a broken shell of a person, something I desperately wanted to be but couldn't. The noises bore down on me now, pulsating into my skull as I tried to grasp on to Adam as the beehive that was the hospital exploded in my brain.

"Tara?" I finally asked.

I looked at Adam in my arms to the doctor. He swallowed.

More bad news, but it wasn't *that* news.

"We aren't sure yet. She's comatose."

I nodded as I pulled Adam to the chairs where he continued to shudder. I closed my eyes as I tried to block out the noises around me. My senses burned with the imagined stench of death, the sound of sobbing and the buzzing of machines as the person on the other end struggled to live...or died. The worst part was the emptiness I felt growing within me; a black hole that fought to consume me, one that already seemed to have devastated Adam.

Then I heard it—the running—a heaved breath as two sets of feet stopped in front of me.

"Oh. God. No," Vickie's voice hit an unbearable pitch.

"River!" she screamed in my face. "Where's my son?"

I pried open my eyes, and the look on my tear-stained face told her the truth.

"No!" she screeched as I tucked my head into Adam's shoulder against the sound. "No!"

Her wails softened against the fabric of a shirt, and I knew Alec pulled her into his arms.

So we crumbled. A broken family even further broken by the lack of the one thing that held it together: Bobby.

Adam's sobs finally softened, but I felt the silent tears still continuing to stain my shirt. His, or mine—I couldn't tell.

It didn't really matter.

So we break

as we take God's mistakes

for misguided perceptions of fate.

• FADE BURN

Chapter 1

I sat there with Adam's head in my lap, running my fingers through his hair until the tears stopped, and his breathing slowed. He was asleep, and I didn't know how to feel anymore. He flinched at my touch when he thought I'd blame him, but now it seemed to be the only thing holding him together...semi-together. He still blamed himself, and I didn't know how to fix it. I'd always been able to help Adam, and now I didn't know how to because I was just as broken. Sighing, I moved his head onto a pillow and stood to get some air. Once outside the apartment I sunk to the floor with my back against the door separating Adam and me.

I was so close to losing everything I loved. Bobby was dead; Tara was lingering on the edge of darkness, and Adam...I didn't know what would happen to him. His grief was overpowering. It felt like all the air has been sucked out of the earth, and I was suffocating from it while drowning in an ocean of pain.

I struggled to feel as my eyes bore into the faded wood door across from me. I might never see two of my best friends walk out that door again. I'd certainly never see

Bobby walk out it again. Finally, I bowed my head to my knees and sobbed. There was no one there to comfort me, but I wasn't sure that was what I needed. Adam needed me to be strong, so I would be—at least when he was watching.

My phone vibrating in my pocket pulled me out of my sadness.

"Hello?" I answered.

"Duckie?" Dad's voice was a shock to my system, and I had to take a deep breath.

"Daddy...Daddy," my voice cracked as a fresh set of tears streamed down my face. "Bobby—"

"I know—don't say it."

"What do I do?" I asked through hiccups. "I don't know what to do."

"Where's Adam?"

"Asleep."

"You need me, Duckie?"

"Yes," I replied, my voice as weak as I felt. "But Mom will kill you."

"Nothing is worth your pain—especially not a stupid tattoo. How's Adam handling things?"

"He's screwed up," I replied. I thought back to the hospital. He hadn't said a word. He handed me the keys to the GLI and curled up on the back seat. Then when we got home he stared at his cell phone until he admitted his guilt—that he thought the whole thing was his fault.

"We all are. None of us saw this coming...none of us could imagine..."

"I don't know if I can fix him...it's like he's not even

there. He sobs, but doesn't speak—he holds me, but only to hang on."

"I know this won't make things better, but it's only been a few days—eventually everything will settle."

My head dipped back against the door, and I closed my eyes. "I don't think you're right."

I heard his car start. "I'll be there as soon as traffic allows. I love you, Duckie."

"I love you, too."

I hung up the phone and stared at Bobby's door again before standing and going to it. Bobby's hands touched these surfaces. It was the only thing left, pieces of him, scattered memories. Our childhood. Twenty years of happiness and he molded himself into a part of who I was. Now I was torn in two. I needed to stay strong for Adam, but I wanted to crawl in the same hole Bobby would be buried in. The overwhelming pain of loving Bobby washed over me again, and every touch remembered sliced a part of me away. Each laugh that echoed through my skull was a memory of intense happiness suddenly overruled by intense pain.

"River?" a groggy Adam asked from behind me.

I looked over my shoulder to where he stood in the doorway, and my tears stopped. I wondered if it was because there were none left.

"Hey," I replied as I let go of the door knob.

"I heard you talking?"

I held my cell phone up. "It was Dad."

"Your dad?"

I nodded.

"He heard?"

"He's coming," I said.

"Now?"

I nodded.

"We need one good parent here," Adam said as he stepped forward and closed the gap between us.

He pulled me into his arms and buried his face in my hair, muffling his words. "I don't think I'll ever be the same again."

It was the one thing that pained me as much as the loss of Bobby—what if Adam couldn't ever be Adam again?

What if I could never be River again?

Chapter 2

Every day passed in slow motion as we waited to put Bobby in the ground. This day was the wake, which reminded me this would only be half of it. I squeezed my eyes shut as my stomach rolled. The Beckerson's opted to have the wake in the morning since icy conditions were the norm this time of year in New England and no one wanted— I stopped the thought before I could finish it. Instead, I rolled over in bed, blinking my dry eyes until they adjusted to the morning light. Adam sat in the chair beside the window staring at his bass guitar laying in his lap. When I sat up, his gaze shot up to mine, and my body numbed how hollow I felt. I watched as darkness moved across his eyes, making them cold. I pulled my knees to my chest, watching as he stood and placed the guitar on its stand before leaving the room without saying a word. My forehead dropped to my knees as the tears I kept in swarmed my eyes. I heard the coffee pot begin to trickle, but I stayed there, staring at the motionless guitar until the tinkling of water against empty glass slowed and the smell of coffee filled the apartment.

Part of me wanted to cry, but another part of me felt there were no tears left. I took a deep breath before heading into the living room where Adam leaned against the island watching the pot fill. He didn't acknowledge me, and I turned into the bathroom, stripping off my clothes and turning the shower on as hot as I could bear. The heat burned my skin, pushing into my aching muscles but not touching my heart. My skin was red when I got out of the shower, but I still felt so cold. I pushed the thought of the chasm that seemed to have opened between Adam and me overnight out of my mind as I searched through my makeup drawer for anything waterproof. My eyes rose to the mirror. My skin lacked any color, besides the purple circles beneath my eyes, and I realized I just didn't give a shit. I inhaled, wrapping the towel tighter around myself before walking out of the bathroom. Adam was already in his suit, and my coffee sat on the island in a travel mug. The air felt low of oxygen as I stared at him sitting on the barstool with his back to me.

I wanted to say something, but nothing felt right. There was nothing I could say to fix the rift of pain suddenly dividing us. Instead, I turned into the bedroom and went to the closet. The first thing I saw was the sparkling dress– the one Adam brought to me for our special night. The night that ended in tragedy. I never did get to know what was so special about that date. The metal of the dress' hanger squeaked against the rod as I shoved it aside a bit too roughly and found a black sweater and pencil skirt.

Bobby always liked my pencil skirts.

When I came out Adam nodded at me before handing me the coffee. We left the apartment and as we turned we stopped, staring at Bobby's door. My skin prickled, and I blinked my eyes to keep away the tears that threatened to make their presence known. Adam's hand found mine, and he squeezed it. I glanced over at him, and he leaned to kiss my forehead. A small hint of heat warmed my body, but we remained quiet as we moved down the stairs, to the car and drove to the funeral parlor.

The parking lot was still empty, but what struck me most was the stark white house in front of us. I stared at the building as I tried to come to terms with the finality of what was before of us.

Bobby wasn't coming home.

Adam's head buckled to the steering wheel and his arms trembled against it. "I don't think I can do this."

"We have to."

The truth was, I didn't think *I* could either.

He shook his head as his knuckles turned white against the red leather. "River, I...just don't think I can hold it together."

"Who said you had to?" I asked, reaching forward and putting my hand on his elbow. I didn't quite know how to comfort him. Touches like this seemed as hollow as my heart.

He looked up at me and swallowed. "I can't show them any weakness."

I knew how he felt, and I needed to do anything to fill this gap between us. I needed to make an effort to close it. I leaned my forehead against his, tangling my fingers in the back of his hair as he closed his eyes.

"This is for Bobby, not for them," I said, reminding myself of them same. "We have to do this for Bobby."

Adam nodded, cupping my face with his hands as his eyes fluttered open. "For Bobby."

~~~

The hours of the wake slid by slowly and not a word was exchanged between Adam and his parents; not even once everyone left and calling hours ended. Adam and I stood in front of the casket, numb from the day's events before he nodded at his parents, placed his hand on my back and guided me towards the door. I felt the tension in my muscles releasing as we reached the door, but I knew it wasn't right. The blowout at Thanksgiving over our matching tattoos, then not being invited to Christmas or New Year's seemed petty compared to the gravity of what our families were now facing.

"You're not going to say anything to them?" I asked under my breath as he moved to open the door for me.

"There's nothing to say," he replied with his tone hard.

"Adam!"

He shook his head once and nodded outside. When I didn't move, he lowered his head saying, "You didn't speak to your mom, did you?"

He was right, and my cheeks burned as I moved out the door he held open for me. We walked feet apart, and when we got into the car, I sank into the seat, crossing my arms.

"Please," Adam said as he started the car; "don't be mad at me."

I heaved a sigh, rubbing my forehead before replying, "I'm not."

"Then why are you sitting there like that?"

I sank deeper into the seat, closing my eyes. "Because today sucked. Every day this year has sucked, and I don't see it getting any better."

I heard Adam breathe in deeply, and my stomach sank at my sharp response. I slipped my hand into his as he drove, but the fissure was still there.

Chapter 3

I stared out the window of the car as we made our way onto the Mass Pike back towards Framingham. The day before couldn't have ended sooner. When we got home from the wake, I went straight to bed and despite sleeping solidly through the night, my whole body ached. This was it. After today...I stopped the thought as I tipped it back against the back of the GLI's racing seats. Adam's blinker was the only noise in the car, clicking as we reached the exit. His coffee sat untouched in the holder, and I glanced over at his tired face. Where I slept far too much, he was sleeping far too little, and it showed in his dull, red-rimmed eyes.

"You should drink your coffee," I said as we sat at a four-way intersection.

"Huh?" Adam asked, looking over at me, eyes wide as if he forgot I was there.

"You look exhausted," I said, nodding to his coffee. "It's probably getting cold."

Adam sighed, taking the cup and drinking some before returning it to the holder as the light turned green. We sat in silence, each of us finishing our coffees just as we reached the already crowded church.

"Maybe I should've gotten a double shot," Adam said as he parked the car, and his hands tightened on the steering wheel. "Today's going to be a long day."

"It was a double shot," I said, leaning over and kissing his cheek. "Maybe I should've asked for a triple."

Adam laughed, and the sound echoed through the car until I found a sad smile on my face. It seemed so unfamiliar in the silence and cold that settled in over us.

"Hopefully, it kicks in soon," he said as his thick brown lashes fluttered over his cheeks. He leaned back against the headrest before letting his head roll to his shoulder, so he was looking over at me. "Tara's parents will be here today. They apologized for not being able to make it yesterday."

My jaw tightened as I turned to look straight ahead. Adam's eyes burned into me, and my cheeks flushed as my stomach tightened.

"Yeah," I replied, looking down at my chipped finger-nails. They hadn't been painted since Christmas when Tara decided to give me a manicure.

Adam's hand went over mine, stopping me from picking at the red paint. "Do you want to see her today? Her parents said they moved her to a different area of the hospital."

I shook my head before finding the words. "I think today's going to be a bit much as it is."

"You haven't seen her since the accident."

I bit my cheek as I thought about the many reasons why I never wanted to walk into that hospital again. "I don't think I can."

Adam's fingers, calloused from years of playing guitar,

slid under my chin and turned me to face him. His eyes were soft as he replied, "I don't really want to go in there either, but I think we need to."

I knew he was right, but I couldn't do it. "Not today."

"Okay," he replied as he leaned forward and kissed my forehead. I closed my eyes, wishing we could stay wrapped in each other's arms instead of leaving the safety of the parked car. Adam pulled away, his thumb brushing my cheek as his eyes raced back and forth over mine. As we got out of the car the cold air knocked into my lungs, and a shiver ran through me as I looked up at the church. Adam walked around the car, and his breathing was a pale white plume in the air as he popped his peacoat collar and held his hand out for me.

"Ready?" he asked, glancing over at me as I placed my hand in his, shaking my head. He gave me one of those sad smiles I was now becoming accustomed to. It was a smile that didn't reach his eyes; more of a flinch than anything. I missed the cocky one. "Me neither," he said. "This isn't the way I thought I'd say goodbye to him."

"Did you ever think we'd say goodbye?" I asked as our feet crunched against the frost on the gravel. People nodded in our direction as we passed them, but we didn't stop to talk to anyone until we reached the door where the priest took Adam's hand in both of his.

"Your parents are in the back," he said, dipping his head. "I'm sure your father already let you know we'll be meeting back in that corner shortly. You'll be carrying the casket with him, your uncle and Bobby's godfather. Once the service is done, you'll come back up and carry the casket out to the hearse."

I felt Adam's free hand trembling in mine as he nodded at the priest. No words left his lips. What could he say?

"Do you want to see your parents?" the priest asked, and the trembling abruptly stopped.

"Sure," he replied, and his voice cracked at the end as he glanced over at me. His Adam's apple rose and fell before we turned and walked towards the room his parents were in. It was tucked in the back of the church, hidden away from prying eyes, but we could still hear Vickie's sobs far before we reached the door.

I put my hand on Adam's forearm, cocking my head as I looked at him. "I'm proud of you. I know it's hard for you to face them."

Adam breathed out through his nose, and I leaned up to kiss his cheek. I could feel the corner of his lips move up in a small smile against my mouth, and I felt my heart beat quicken. Maybe we could be okay after all of this. We both stared at the wood door for a moment before Adam stepped forward and lifted his hand to knock. He stopped short when his mother's sobs formed audible words.

"I just don't understand," Vicky said through hiccups. "Why was it, Bobby? I don't understand why—my baby...now all we have is Adam."

Adam's face didn't change as his hand hovered mid-knock over the door. His eyes were hard and cold; the only display of emotion was the tightening of his throat. The words were nothing compared to the tone of her voice—the tone that said she wished it was *Adam* and not Bobby they were putting in the ground. Uncomfortable tingles rushed up my spine to my neck and face before rushing down my arms and numbing my body. This was another family feud, but it wasn't one I'd be able to fix. The words were unforgivable. I squeezed my eyes shut.

As if we weren't all broken enough.

Adam's fist squeezed tighter before he dropped it and slipped his hand back into mine. He turned, walking just ahead of me, so I couldn't see the look on his face as he led me through the hall that went to the pews. I stopped in my tracks as we reached the entrance, and he turned to face me. His head hung as he looked at the floor. I took his face in my hands, and his eyes squeezed shut, wrinkles spreading from the corner of them and through his forehead.

"Adam?" I said, pressing my forehead to his. I wanted to say she didn't mean it, but I couldn't force the lie to my lips.

He put his hands on my wrists, his whole body trembling. "I'll crumble after, but I'll need you to put me back together," Adam said, and his voice cracked as tears formed at the corners of his shut eyes.

"Always."

Adam's eyes opened, staring at mine, and he rubbed the tears away before pressing his lips hard against my forehead. "I have to carry the casket."

I let my fingers run through his as he walked away, and the feeling of his touch warmed the icy parts of my soul. I wrapped my black shawl tighter around my shoulders, fighting a cold that was nonexistent—a cold caused by the absence of part of who I was. My heels clicked against the granite floor as I passed the endless rows of mourners, and the room echoed with my movements and the soft moans of those shedding tears. My heart flowed silently down my cheeks as I finally reached the row with my parents. Dad stood and pulled me into a hug. His arms clutched tightly around me as if I might disappear.

"It'll be alright, Ducks," he said into my ear, but I could tell from the crack in his voice he didn't believe it either.

He hadn't even heard what Vickie said.

"The Beckerson's are destroyed," I said, knowing he wouldn't understand the depth of the statement. I knew they'd never be the same again. Adam's parents would be lucky if he ever spoke to them again. They were losing two sons, not just one.

Dad held me out at arm's length, and I realized the pressure the situation put on him as well. His eyes had dark circles beneath them, and red lines coursed through the white, just like Adam and I's.

"You'll hold them together," he answered with a stern nod of certainty.

My breath caught in my throat, and my chest tightened as I shook my head. "I can barely hold myself together."

"You're stronger than us all," Dad said, and his voice was solid as if he believed it.

I didn't. How could I put this back together? It was shattered.

"Adam's parents..." My voice drifted as I tried to think of the words. "He just lost his brother—his best friend, the only person in his family that he ever felt loved him...and they just proved," my eyes fluttered against the fresh set of tears; "they just proved they don't love him."

"Riv, you know that's not true." Dad's brows furrowed over his eyes. "What could they say to make you think that?"

I looked at the ornate ceiling before forming the words. "It was more the way it was said than the words."

My eyes drifted back down to Dad's, and he bit the inside of his cheek. "Did Adam?"

"Yes, he heard."

Dad's eyes locked on mine. "You have to be strong for him, Riv."

The air broke from a hollow cry, and my stomach dropped. I fought the emotions tumbling around in my mind; pain, hurt, and most of all rage. The sound grew closer, and Dad moved me in between him and Mom. Alec placed Vickie next to Dad, and I watched as Dad patted Alec on the back. Dad's anger showed in his eyes as Alec whispered to him, but he responded with a curt nod, pulling Vickie into his arms. Alec took a deep breath before leaving his wife behind and walking back down the row. Dad sat down with Vickie crying on his shoulder, but his hand found my knee. Mom's arm wrapped around me, and she kissed my cheek. I didn't pull away or react. She didn't bother whispering everything would be okay. We were all faced with the fact it wouldn't be. Bobby was dead, and to Adam, so were his parents.

The organ's voice boomed across the ceilings and off

the granite floors, signaling us to stand. I swallowed before Mom's hands found my elbow and lifted me. At that moment, I was thankful for her because I wasn't sure I had the strength to support myself. Everyone turned towards the door where the casket was being led in, and Mom guided me to do the same. Adam and Alec were on either side of the dark black lacquered box, followed by two men I didn't know.

Adam's eyes stared emotionless and straight ahead, but I could see the wet lines cascading down his cheeks. His movements were almost robotic as the procession moved forward while Alec was barely holding it together. His shoulders racked with a sob, and his face contorted as he tried to contain his pain and carry the weight of his son. The sea of people echoed the movements of the casket until we were facing the front of the building where the priest stood in his stark white robes. The men laid the casket in front of him and moved back into the crowd. When Adam reached me I pulled him into my arms, and he whispered in my ear, "A part of me is dead."

His head tucked in my shoulder as my hands wrapped under his arms and my fingers dug into the jacket at his shoulder blades. Mom's soft touch on my back let me know we needed to sit, and I loosened my grip on Adam until we were staring at one another again. He nodded and we sat, his fingers entwining with mine. His parents moved to the other side of him, but his eyes remained on the black box in front of us. I watched as Alec's hand reached for Adam's knee and squeezed. Adam's eyelashes fluttered at the touch.

He didn't move otherwise, and Alec's lower lips pursed as he tried to decipher the reasoning for Adam's reaction. He slowly removed his hand and let a breath out.

He'd find out soon enough.

The priest's words echoed through the church, but I couldn't decipher their meaning as I stared at the black casket. I went through the movements, following the people around me without actually understanding what was going on. I stood, knelt, sat and tipped my head in prayer, but my eyes never moved off of that black mass.

Bobby was gone.

When the service ended, and Adam moved to go back up to the casket I couldn't pry myself away from him. Adam didn't try. His eyes met mine, and he realized just as I did, that I was not leaving his side. Adam moved my hand to his arm, and we walked up together where he stood on his side until the casket lifted and we moved forward. My heart beat slowed as we made our way to the door, but with each step, it felt as though the door was further away instead of closer.

"You okay?" Adam asked, and his voice brought me back to. Sparks dotted my vision as I inhaled, and my nails dug into his jacket. I stumbled, and Adam's body tensed against mine. "River?"

"I'm all right," I replied, and the door was suddenly opening in front of us. The cold air woke my system as we made our way to the hearse, and I knew I was shaking uncontrollably. I stepped back as Adam helped slide the casket inside. He turned as soon as it was in and pulled me into his arms and his hands pressed my head to his shoulder.

"I love you," he said as he pulled slowly away and wiped my face.

I shook my head, closing my eyes as more tears coursed down my cheeks. I couldn't control them now. I tried to reply, but my voice caught in my throat. Adam's chest rose as he looked over his shoulder at the hearse's engine starting. We didn't say anything as we walked passed it on the way back to Adam's car. The silence continued to the cemetery, where Adam helped place the casket over the empty hole in the ground. I stood back, alone, listening to Vickie's sobs from the car she refused to get out of as I watched. My mind raced through empty thoughts as I tried to keep breathing.

How they managed to dig a hole in the middle of winter.

How heavy the casket must be.

How Vickie cried so loudly.

How I felt like vomiting into the hole.

How I felt like crawling into the hole and never coming out.

Adam's eyes met mine as he walked up next to me, and the thoughts ceased, replaced by the sound of our breathing as we stood and the crowd began to thicken around us. A man handed us each white roses, and the priest came to the front of the casket, a bible pressed against his torso that he fanned open, before holding his free hand out and looking at the gray sky above us.

Again, he spoke, but I heard nothing. My eyes locked on the casket. On Bobby.

When the priest was done, Adam's hand on the small of

my back indicated it was time to step forward. My eyes fell to the hole beneath the casket, and the temptation to crawl into it returned as the rose in my hand dropped slowly onto the surface. Its white color was a harsh contrast against the shiny black, and my stomach rolled so hard I gripped it in an attempt to keep the coffee in. We pushed to the back of the crowd, and I fought the urge until we neared a tree. I dropped Adam's hand and rushed forward, the coffee coming out as tears streamed down my face. Adam's hands ran over my spine as the contents of my stomach emptied. In the background, I heard someone say something about a lunch to follow, and I turned to face Adam, who shook his head.

"Thank you," I said as he wrapped his arms around me. Adam's body tensed, and I heard the sound of the casket being lowered, and then the metallic sound of dirt running off of shovels. My stomach clenched, but there was nothing more to come up. Adam's hands moved over my arms until our fingers entwined and we walked back to the plot. It was just him and me, staring at the newly placed dirt as the voices behind us faded into nothing.

His body trembled, and his foot struck out as he screamed, kicking the dirt. The scream turned into a sob as he crumbled to his knees beside me. The anger from his parent's vile words dissipated and all that was left was the agonizing pain of loss. It was all consuming; anger and pain now mingled until I felt like nothing was left.

I wanted to crumble beside Adam.

I wanted to scream and claw the ground.

To demand God give back our souls.

Adam had been strong for me during the ceremony, and now I needed to be strong for him. I fell beside him and pulled his shuddering body into my arms. Silent tears rolled down my face as I sat rocking him. My bare legs prickled with the cold, dead grass beneath us, and I wasn't sure if the cold was creeping in and making me numb, or if it was the gravity of the situation sinking in. Adam's body stopped trembling, and I was able to compose myself as he pulled away. His gentle hands found my face, and his eyes bore into mine.

I watched as his parched lips parted, and he spoke, "I don't think I'll ever be able to forgive them...do you think Bobby would blame me?"

"I don't blame you," I replied, squeezing my eyes shut as another wave of emotion rolled over me.

"But would he?" His voice cracked.

I opened my eyes, and his brown ones looked almost black. "Maybe...that's why he got in that car that night, wasn't it? Because he saw how cruel they were."

I wished he hadn't seen the truth of their personalities. Then we wouldn't be here now. Adam's eyes flashed, and I knew he felt the same.

"Adam?" I began, and his eyes drifted up to mine. "I know it's not enough, but I love you."

His lips twitched, and he pressed them hard against my forehead before kissing my nose. "It's always been enough."

He began to stand and pulled me up with him. For a moment, we stood and stared down at the turned over ground littered with white roses of those that chose to leave them on the surface instead of beneath the ground with Bobby.

"We should see Tara," I finally said.

"Are you sure?"

"We owe it to Bobby," I replied.

I didn't think I was strong enough to stare at my best friend sitting in a coma, hooked up to a zillion machines, barely hanging onto life. What was worse was the ache in my chest when I thought of what I would have to tell her when they pulled her out of the medical coma–if they could. Adam's hand drifted from my shoulders down to my lower back as he leaned forward and took one white rose from the pile.

"He'd want her to have one," Adam said, but I couldn't respond. The best I could do was a sound similar to that of someone drowning.

Adam didn't push for more, and his hand slipped into mine as he guided me away from a part of us we would never recover.

Chapter 4

My skin prickled, and the hair on my arms rose as Adam parked the car at the hospital. It looked more like a hotel than a place where people went to die. The car continued to idle, turbos cooling as we sat in silence. I fought the urge to tell Adam to leave–to go anywhere but here and never return again. Adam's blank expression and heaving chest indicated he must be thinking something along those lines too. I rubbed my sweaty palms against my skirt as my muscles bulged with the urge to run away. They tightened further when I heard Adam take a deep breath, and his keys jingled as the car's motor finally ceased.

"We can do this," Adam said as he stared at the white rose sitting on the dashboard. He reached for it, and my eyes ran from the rose up his exposed forearm to the once pressed but now wrinkled white button-up to his pale face. He licked his lips, and I watched as he swallowed. "We can do this."

A shiver ran through my body, and I closed my eyes as I trembled. The warmth of Adam's palm cupping my chin caused my body's jerking to softened, and I opened my eyes.

"Okay," I said, reminding myself we needed to do this for Tara. "Let's do this."

Instead of rushing in from the rain like the last time we arrived at the hospital, we slowly walked up the steps hand in hand. The day was already fading, and the air was crisp again as if it might snow. The world was still a frozen waste-land from the weather that caused the accident, but now it was dotted with ugly patches of brown and gray sand. The beauty of the storm was showing its true, harsh and disgust-ing colors. Adam's gaze was locked on me as we stood in front of the door and my breath came out in a misty ball as he opened the door. When we entered the warmth, the stag-nant air hit me and filled my lungs. I felt it stop there as I fought the urge to gag and run back the way we came, but Adam's hand found the small of my back and gently pushed me forward. His hand remained on my back as he pulled his cell phone out, looked at a text and signaled with his chin to the silver doors in front of us.

"We should take the elevator," he said.

I nodded, afraid to open my mouth and let the air of death into my lungs. It was irrational, but all I could feel around me was death, pain, and loss. It was palatable as if I breathed it into my soul and now it was a part of me; a part of me I could no longer change or remove. I stepped into the elevator, and Adam moved behind me wrapping his arms around mine and resting his head on the top of my own. I tried to concentrate on Adam's breathing behind me, but the red numbers flashing the floors drew me in, and I found myself watching them as they slowly flicked by. Each one jogged a breath out of me as we moved closer and closer to Tara in God knew what state. When the door opened, we didn't move. Instead, we stared down the dull white hall as the noise of machines flickered in and out.

Another couple stepped into the elevator and looked at us expectantly.

"What floor?" the man asked.

I shook my head as if I could rattle my brain back into functioning. It didn't work, but Adam seemed to be still able to function because he stepped around me and stuck his arm out so the elevator wouldn't close.

"This is us," Adam said more to me than the man as I stood holding my elbows.

Adam cocked his head at me, his eyes searching mine, and I swallowed before I forced my legs to move forward. Once they were moving, I couldn't stop them, because I knew If I did I'd dart back onto the elevator and hit the ground floor key until it broke. Adam's footsteps jogged up behind me as I stopped and stared at the door in front of me.

This is it.

I kept my eyes down as my hand clasped around the cold knob and then let the door slowly swing open. My eyes found the bed where Tara lay, black and blue with an intricate web of wires dancing over her embattled skin. I could feel my lip trembling as I stood there without breathing. Bobby hadn't lived, but I couldn't imagine Tara was alive from the way she looked. My stomach rolled.

Bobby probably wasn't recognizable.

I lurched into the room and grabbed the trashcan by the

bed, burying my head in it as my stomach heaved but nothing came out. There was nothing left in my stomach after the cemetery. Again, Adam's fingers ran over my back, trying to comfort me as the tears streamed down my face and into my open mouth. I put my hand on the bed for support and jumped back screaming as my hand touched Tara's cold, lifeless one.

Adam grabbed my shoulders and whipped me around before I could look at Tara.

"River!" Adam's hands shot up to my face and held it there. "Calm down."

Bobby's face flashed in my mind, but it wasn't his. It was purple and blue; his lip was busted showing his teeth as his unseeing eyes bulged.

Oh, God.

I could feel myself screaming, but I couldn't stop it. My reaction should've been this way when the doctor told me Bobby was dead. I was coming apart.

"River!" Adam's voice knocked into my head. "You need to calm down!"

The screaming that once was inside my head and was now coming out of my mouth turned into a strangled sob.

Adam's voice cracked. "Please, River! Please, calm down."

My head jerked back as I opened my eyes, locking them on him. I sensed there was a crowd of nurses at the door, but I kept my eyes on him.

His eyes raced over my face, panicked. "That's it, breathe."

"This was a bad idea," I said, and my voice sounded as raw as my throat now felt.

"It's okay. We had to do it sometime, now turn back around slowly," Adam said, and his hands slipped down my body to my elbows, applying pressure to make me turn.

"I can't, Adam," I whispered. "She's...God...how's she still alive?"

"*God*, that's how."

I closed my eyes and turned slowly. My eyes flickered over her, and I clasped them shut again.

"Is there any part of her that's...normal colored?" I asked, and I wondered if he heard me because I could barely hear myself.

"Not that I can see," Adam said, his voice catching as his hands tightened on my arms.

I opened my eyes again and looked at her fully. Next to her hand was the white rose. I blinked several times before reaching forward, my hand hovering before I swallowed and wrapped it over hers.

"Tara, girl...I need you to wake up," I said, keeping my eyes on her hand. I glanced over my shoulder at Adam. "How can she survive this?"

Adam's gaze was locked on Tara's face, and his thick lashes moved in rapid succession against his cheeks as he shook his head. "She has to."

Chapter 5

I cracked my aching eyes open, blinking them as if it would help the dryness that set in when all the tears were gone. I cried myself to sleep in Adam's arms after seeing Tara, but now the space beside me was empty.

"Adam?" I asked as I sat up, cursing as pressure pushed hard against my temples. I squeezed my eyes shut as I placed my hands on my temples, rubbing them as if it would help the horrible ricocheting in my head. I fought the urge to throw up yet again as I stood, putting my hand on the headboard as I rocked on my feet. "Adam?" I called again as I stumbled forward. I made my way to the bedroom door expecting to see him on the couch, but he wasn't. My heart started beating to match my headache. "Adam!" I said, looking around the empty apartment as my breathing heaved.

I heard a soft moan from the kitchen and rushed towards the island, sliding on my socks around it. I grasped the corner to slow myself as Adam came into view slumped against the cabinets with an empty bottle of SoCo. I bent down and tilted his head up. I knew he bought the bottle for New Years, but he hadn't touched it until now.

"Adam...Did you drink that whole thing?"

"Head hurts," he said. His words slurred as his head fell forward into my chest. "Hold me."

"Come on," I said as I attempted to pull him up.

"Head hurts," he repeated, supporting his weight against mine. My head still pounded, but I was too busy concentrating on not dropping him to focus on it.

"Can you somewhat walk?" I asked as I leaned against the counter.

His head rolled from side to side. "Sure."

I doubted his response, but somehow we managed to stumble our way to the bedroom where I dropped him on the bed and collapsed next to him. The pounding in my head rushed back, and I found myself breathing rapidly as the waves of pain squeezed against my skull.

"You okay?" Adam asked as he cuddled into me.

Not really.

"You shouldn't have drank that whole bottle," I replied.

"Mhmm...tell me about it," he said, tucking his nose in my neck and letting his alcohol filled breath wash over me.

I gagged, turning my head away from him and staring at the wall of guitars. I wished he chose to play one of them to distract himself instead of getting drunk, but I imagined it was easier to open the bottle and tip the liquid into his throat to numb his mind. A part of me understood the urge to drink, but for me, it just wasn't strong enough. I sighed as I turned and wrapped my arms around him, letting my hands drift over his arms until it lulled us both to sleep.

When I woke my eyes didn't hurt as much anymore, but the feeling of weight inside my chest hadn't lifted. I rubbed my face before rolling over to see Adam sitting by the window. His face was painted in pale moonlight, and his eyes filled with the sadness that seemed to have become a part of us. He didn't stir as I crawled out of bed and moved towards him. His chest rose as he sighed and moved to pull me into his arms. He rested his head on my shoulder, and his arms snaked around mine until our fingers were intertwined. "How do we move forward?"

I let my body sink deeper into his arms. "We just do."

"You say that as if it's the easiest thing in the world," he answered, and his chest rumbled with a sarcastic laugh.

I swallowed and pulled away, looking down at him as I turned in his lap. "I didn't say it was going to be easy."

"Riv," his eyelashes fluttered; "I didn't mean it like that."

He pressed his fingers to his temples, and I felt my heartbeat slow as I watched him struggling to explain how he was feeling. I put my hands on his shoulders, letting my thumbs brush his neck now stippled with a heavy five o'clock shadow.

"I know... I just don't think there's a secret to getting over this," I replied, letting my shoulders rise and drop before continuing; "I don't know there *is* a way to ever get over this. We just have to move on from it."

Adam's hands dropped over mine, and the warmth of his touch spread up my limbs until I felt a small smile tugging at my lips.

"We have each other," I said.

Adam's eyes drifted from my lap, up my body until they met mine. "That's all we've ever really needed, isn't it?"

He licked his lips, and I felt the inevitable pull of my body towards his. He lifted his hand and let it caress my cheek, before slipping it behind my neck and moving me towards him until our lips touched. It started with a soft kiss, but desperation sunk in as I leaned my body closer, and his hands drifted down my spine to grip my hips. His lips crushed into mine, spreading them, so his tongue met my own. I tangled my fingers in his hair as he moved my legs and stood, carrying me to the bed without his lips leaving mine. I pulled away gasping, and he tucked his head into my neck, his tongue washing over my bare skin as he slipped his hands under my shirt and then lifted it off. I knew we should talk, but words were always useless with Adam and I. Instead, I let the physical consume me and settle the pain that rose inside my soul. For that moment, it overrode the doubt that all we needed was one another.

Chapter 6

I looked down from the book I was reading to my cell phone vibrating against my leg. Reading was my only reprieve from the violent and painful thoughts catapulting around my brain, and the number on the cell phone brought them all rolling back over me. My jaw clenched as I stared at the number.

"They've called me twenty times today," I said, and it was not an over-exaggeration; proven by the fact the screen flicked to MISSED CALLS 25. "How many times have they called you?"

Adam looked up from his tablet, his finger hovering over the screen as he exhaled. "Enough times."

His cell phone began buzzing across the coffee table and both our eyes went to it before he continued playing what I could only assume was Angry Birds from the sounds emitting from the device. "I guess she should've thought of what she was saying before she said it," Adam said as his finger slid across the screen.

I leaned forward and kissed him. "I'm sorry."

He looked up, and his jaw clenched before he replied, "It's not your fault they'd rather have me dead."

My throat tightened. I wanted to deny his words and tell him it was all a misunderstanding, but I didn't feel like it was. I heard what she said and the way she said it.

All we have is Adam.

"If they didn't care, they wouldn't be calling," I said, running my fingers through his hair, so his eyes fluttered shut. They opened as his cell phone vibrated yet again, tittering on the edge of the coffee table it finally reached.

I looked at the ceiling before grabbing it and swiping my finger across the screen. "Hello?"

"River?" Vickie's voice hammered into my skull and sent my skin prickling with unease. The anger built in my body, and I felt myself begin to tremble as Adam's eyes raced over my face. It seemed he was as unsure of what I was going to say as I was.

"Yes," I replied.

"Adam won't return our calls," she said.

"I'm sorry to hear that. We're both not interested in talking to anyone right now."

Especially you.

"Even your mothers?" Vickie asked, reminding me that several missed called were from Mom. Her voice was innocent as if never did anything wrong.

My fists curled causing my nails to bite into my palms. "Right now, we need space and time."

"Why?"

My voice was shaky as I repeated her question, "Why?"

"Yes, darling," she said, and my whole body tensed at the strange mix of soft word and hard tone. "Why?"

I swallowed as I looked straight ahead, and Adam leaned into my line of vision. He put his hand on my knee and squeezed, mouthing the words *hang up.*

"We have our reasons, Mrs. Beckerson. We'd appreciate it if you gave us some space," I replied, and I was shocked how I held my calm when I wanted to yell at her; to tell her what a shitty parent she always had been. But she was still Adam's mother, no matter how cruel she was to us. I wondered how he dealt with it his whole life when I could barely manage to deal with his parents for more than a ten sentence conversation.

She heaved an exaggerated sigh. "How long do you need?"

"Adam will reach out to you when he's ready. Until then, we'd appreciate our privacy. Goodbye, Mrs. Beckerson," I said. I pressed the end button before she could reply and leaned back to look at the ceiling.

I watched Adam stand from the corner of my vision, and I closed my eyes as his bare feet padded against the hardwood. I held my breath as I heard the refrigerator open and a cap unscrew. My body tensed, and my nails went in my palms again, this time so hard my skin shifted beneath them.

Please don't be that bottle.

Adam didn't drink before, well, not other than at special events. In the week and a half since that phone call, Adam consumed more Southern Comfort than all the years I knew him added together. I fought the rolling in my stomach as he sat down beside me.

"You okay?" he asked, and I realized my chest was heaving. "River?"

I breathed out slowly. "I don't know."

Adam put a bottle of water on the table, and my tensed muscles loosened. Maybe I was just overthinking his drinking. He put his hands on my neck, his thumbs tucking beneath the edge of my hair as he leaned forward.

"Me either," he replied. "Sometimes I wish they were different people, and I didn't feel this way about them. I mean, shouldn't we all be supporting each other right now?"

I felt my shoulders rise beneath his hands as I licked my lower lip. "They don't know how to support other people..." I swallowed before continuing; "They'd just drag us down."

My body numbed as I watched a tear roll down his face, catching in his scar and splitting in two. As his eyes searched mine, I knew the answer to how he handled his parent's abuse and even how I handled it. It was one in the same.

The thing tearing us apart was the very thing that held us together–Bobby.

Chapter 7

Two weeks.

Two weeks had passed since Bobby left us, and although my life felt frozen, I continued moving forward. I visited Tara every day for an hour or two and read books to pass the remainder of the time, but I needed to return to real life. I took a deep breath as I picked my cell phone up off the charger. The voicemail now flashed full, and I wondered if there were any from Mom on there, or if they were all from Vickie. I grit my teeth at the thought as I stared down at Adam lying in the bed curled into a ball with his pillow pulled to his chest.

I wondered how he was comfortable.

I doubted he was.

I knelt down to pick up the empty bottle of SoCo from beside the bed, and walked to the door, picking up my stilettos as I did. I glanced behind me at Adam, my pulse rushing through my ears before going into the kitchen and dropping the bottle in the recycling. I gazed down at the handful of empty bottles of liquor and closed my eyes as I ran my hands through my hair. Adam was not dealing with the loss well, or at all really. I mentioned I was going back to work today, but I wasn't sure he heard—or, what scared me the most, that he cared. I took a shaky breath as I slipped my shoes on and then headed to the door, grabbing my coat and slipping it on before looking back at the bedroom.

He'll be okay. It's only been two weeks.

I closed my eyes, pinching the bridge of my nose before turning out the door. I kept my eyes on the red tips of my shoes as I walked down the hall and to the stairs. I hoped Adam would get out of bed and not just to go to the liquor store. I shook the thought from my head as it started pounding.

"You can do this," I said to myself as I began walking forward.

I wasn't sure I could. I was going back to work—the place I met Tara, and the place Bobby found an internship for me. My chest tightened as I opened the driver's side door, slipping into the car and putting the key in the ignition. The car roared to life, but I found myself pressing my forehead against the steering wheel as my grip tightened and the leather squeaked. I couldn't stop the memories from rushing in.

Bobby had come to my dorm room with a paper in his hand, and one of those killer sideways smiles. He had waved it in my face as I shook my head and nodded for him to come in. My dorm mate had bit her lip as she stared at him, and I had rolled my eyes.

"You know how you were saying you needed an internship?" Bobby had asked as he sat on my couch, throwing his arm around me as I sat down beside him.

I curled my legs under myself as I cocked my head at

him. *"Yeah, but they're all full. If it's this impossible to get an internship in Boston, how am I ever going to get a job?" I asked with a frown. I narrowed my eyes as a huge smile spread across his lips. "Why do you look so excited?"*

"This," he replied, pushing my knees down and placing the paper on my lap. There in the middle was an advertisement circled in red marker with three explanation points. I looked from the paper to him and furrowed my brow as he raised his and nodded at me. "Go ahead, read it! It's perfect for you!"

I had read it as his fingertips ran over my shoulders. He had been right; it had been ideal for me. It had turned into the best thing that had happened to me. While my peers were struggling to find any job at all, I already had one lined up a year before I even had my degree. That had all been because of Bobby. He had been looking for months for an internship for me without me even knowing.

I still had the paper saved in a journal I kept during college. I looked across the city in front of me. I wasn't sure how I was going to make it through this day, but I had to. There was no point in getting lost at the bottom of a bottle with Adam. Then there would be no way to save either of us.

I needed to stop thinking.

I slipped a CD into the player and ratcheted up the volume, letting the screaming of Ollie Sykes sink in. I needed this. The heavy rhythms coursed through my body, thrumming through my chest and I let go, piece by piece.

When I parked the car and turned it off the silence engulfing the car caught me off guard, and I found my fingers wrapping tightly around the steering wheel. I watched as my knuckles turned white before letting them drop to my side. My stomach fluttered; empty except for the coffee I consumed on the drive in. I took a deep breath as I tried to steady the dizziness coming over me.

I can do this.

I got out and walked to the door.

I can do this.

I yanked it open and slipped inside the office building, walking up the short set of steps and into the lobby before turning right and walking into the marketing firm I called home for four years now. The warm air of the building hit me, and I found I was sweating as I stuck my head in Jesse's door.

"River!" my boss said, standing and coming around his desk.

I stepped forward, and his hands fell onto my shoulders.

"I'm glad to have you back," he said with a weak but warm smile. "How are you doing?"

I looked up at the ceiling before letting my gaze return to him. I returned the smile, or at least I attempted to. "Okay, I guess."

"Listen, you don't have to work the whole day. If you need to ease back into it, I'm fine with that." Jesse's blue eyes darted over my face as he tried to judge if I was okay. His chest rose with a suppressed sigh before he let go and walked back to his desk.

"I appreciate the offer, but I think I'll be fine," I said, sitting down in the seat he nodded to.

"Alright, then I need you to work on the branding for

Alexis' Grove. It's a new restaurant in town," he said as he pushed a project folder in my direction.

I opened it and looked at the company's profile briefly. "I think I can handle this."

"That's my girl. We need to have a shoot scheduled in the next two weeks for advertisements, and we need to develop a solid slogan and logo for them. Something that speaks to the rustic Italian feel they're going for. You'll also want to get in touch with their interior designers."

I shut the folder and gave my first real smile in weeks. "I'll get right on it."

Jesse winked at me before turning back to his computer. "That's my girl."

I stood and turned, but froze as my eyes landed on a cubical overflowing with flowers.

Tara's cubical.

I pressed my eyes shut and counted to three as the temperature of the room seemed to rise with my pulse.

"River?" Jesse's voice yanked me out of another flashback as Tara's smiling face flickered and changed into the battered and bruised one it was the last time I saw her. My eyes found the red tips of my shoes again. It seemed they were one of the only things that would get me through the day.

"I'm good," I replied, but my voice cracked.

"You sure?"

I nodded but kept looking down as I moved towards my office. When I walked in I was greeted by the scent of the flowers that also sat on my desk. I picked up the vase and set it on the table near the window without bothering to open the card. They were all the same. *Our deepest sympathies for your loss* or *You are in our thoughts during this difficult time.* I set the project folder down before sitting and placing my elbows on my desk as I let my head sink into my hands.

I can do this.

Can't I?

Chapter 8

I looked up the stairs of the apartment building, my hand gripping the railing as my chest rose to my chin. Going back to work exhausted me. Between catching up on 1,000 plus emails and dealing with people again, my head was spinning. Too many people I didn't know now knew me as the *girl who lost her best friend*, and their words, much like their cards, left me feeling as empty as the false sympathetic smiles they threw me. Not to mention the personal invasion of space with gentle squeezes of my shoulder. I thought about going to see Tara, but the day had been enough as it was. I hoped her mom would understand. I turned to the elevator instead of the stairs I used religiously. I was too tired to walk any further. The ride up felt too long as my mind moved from the stress of work to Adam. I rubbed my palms against each other as the elevator numbers changed from one to two and then the door slid open. I stepped out and looked between the two doors on either side of the hall before closing my eyes, breathing in deeply and turning to our door. As I reached into my purse for my keys the door swung open, and I stepped back, jaw slack as Adam smiled at me.

"Hey!" Adam said, stepping forward and kissing my forehead before heading to the stairs.

"Hey?" I replied as I blinked hard at his back. He looked cute in his black flannel button-up over a teal shirt and jeans. He was even clean shaven. "Where are you going?"

He didn't stop or turn; instead, he held his keys over his head and jingled them. "Boy's night out!" he replied, and before I could answer he turned the corner and disappeared down the second set of stairs.

I stared at the empty stairwell, rubbing my arms as I whispered, "It's not Thursday yet."

My eyes drifted to the door across the hall. The emptiness I somehow managed to forget at work began to fill me as I stared at the wood and imagined the happiness that once occurred behind it. I dropped my arms as my hands clenched at my sides. Adam left me to suffer in my silence, and I realized I had no friends aside from Adam, Bobby and Tara. I never thought I lacked in the friend department. Girls generally didn't stay loyal to me because of my friendship with the Beckerson boys. Throughout high school, I became used to girls using me to get at them and eventually I just gave up on relationships with the same sex. Adam and Bobby were always enough, and Tara had been a pleasant surprise, although her motives had to do with Bobby too. She was just always clear what her intentions were, and I was all right with that since they didn't involve Adam. I swallowed as I turned into the apartment, shutting the door behind me and putting my forehead against the wood door. I should have been happy at Adam's abrupt return to the real world, yet the smile hadn't met his eyes. I still saw the flat, emotionless glaze that settled in since that night. I turned, pulling my jacket off and staring at the mirror next to the empty coat rack. Beneath the mascara, silver eye shadow and cat eyeliner was the same gaze.

Empty. Emotionless. A hollow shell.

I wondered if Adam saw it too. I put my jacket on the coat rack. If he did, he didn't care.

~~~

Even though I left work, I brought my laptop with me and continued to work until my eyes wouldn't stay open any longer. I checked the time as I fell into bed –1:45 AM. The tension left my body as I pulled the crisp sheets into a cocoon around me. My dreams consisted mostly of pitch black since Bobby passed, and it was the only relief I felt from the same inky darkness overwhelming my soul.

Bang!

My eyes snapped open, and my chest heaved as I blinked several times and sat up on the bed.

There it was again; someone was slamming on the front door, and they were laughing. I grit my teeth as I glanced at the alarm clock—3:07 AM. I picked my sweatshirt up from the floor and yanked it over my head before grabbing my glasses and shoving them over my eyes.

"Let me in, River!" Adam said from behind the door he was still slamming on.

I pulled it open with so much force that the person holding Adam dropped him. "What the fuck?"

I pushed Adam off of me, and he latched onto the door frame.

"Sorry, Riv," Mark said as his eyes widened. "We didn't expect him to get *that* loaded."

I glared at him, and his hand went to the back of his shaggy head of hair. "I should, err...get going."

"Maybe next time you could stop him before he's so cocked he can't stand?" I asked, my heart pounding hard against my ribs.

Adam looked up at me, puppy-brown eyes making my stomach turn. "Don't be mad at them, Riv."

"Don't you dare *Riv* me, Adam Beckerson!" I said as I yanked him into the apartment and slammed the door in Mark's face. I knew Adam made the decision to get drunk, and I shouldn't be mad at Mark. They couldn't control him any more than I could. I was madder at myself for letting him go without warning them how alcohol was suddenly his crutch. Adam stumbled forward and faced planted on the couch, and I felt my body tremble as I sat down on the one stair leading into our living room. I put my head in my hands, chewing on my lip.

I should have taken the look in Adam's eyes for what it was worth. It meant one thing—the bottle of SoCo wasn't far behind. My hands moved over my face. Would Adam be able to get over this, or would SoCo be his only way out of his pain?

Time. That's what he needed.

I stood and went to put him in a more comfortable position, remembering from classes in high school to put his head out so he wouldn't swallow his vomit if his stomach revolted against the alcohol. I kissed his forehead before moving to the chair Bobby and Tara cuddled in on Christmas. I pulled the blanket off the back of it and wrapped it around myself as I watched Adam until I fell asleep again; until the darkness once again consumed me and quieted my soul. What was left of it, anyway?

Chapter 9

I curled deeper into the lounge chair, pulling the blanket tighter around myself before my eyes shot open. There it was, the smell of bacon and coffee brewing. My stomach growled as my eyes focused on the now empty couch. I yawned and wandered to the kitchen. I stopped at the island and stared at Adam's back as he poured pancake batter onto the bacon greased pan.

"Adam?" I asked as I stared at the anomaly across the island from me.

He turned to face me and my breath caught in my throat. He hadn't had a hair cut in some time, but he styled his hair this morning in a way that enhanced everything about him, especially that lip ring. The bad-boy-crooked-grin was on his face as he looked back at me.

"Hey, love," he said.

Dreaming. I have to be dreaming.

My fingers curled into my palms, and my nails bit into my flesh. I wasn't dreaming. I blinked at him a few times before running into his arms and wrapping my legs around him.

"I totally just got batter on your ass," Adam said, his voiced muffled as his face buried into my hair.

I stared down at him in a black band tee stretched in all the right places, and my heart fluttered out of control. There he was. Adam was staring back at me. His eyes were warm, and tender; staring at me like I was his world.

"You'll just have to do something about that, won't you?" I said, biting my lip to contain my smile.

My Adam held me against him, and his hands moved, so my body slowly slid through his arms and against him. Heat flushed through me as my shirt rose against his body, and his spatula-less hand slid up my spine, his warm fingers brushing across my bare skin. One eyebrow raised as he looked down at me through my bangs.

"I love it when your hair is all messed up like this," he whispered, and his breath washed over me.

I closed my eyes and breathed in the scent. Clean–spearmint and sexiness—none of the nasty liquor I was accustom to.

My eyes fluttered open as his hand moved to cup my chin, thumb resting against my lower lip. His brown eyes rushed over my face, taking in the flow of my hair, down my cheeks and finally to the lips he so softly embraced. He lowered his mouth to mine and his lips brushed against me with an excruciating and delicate passion that set all of my nerves on fire and my heart into palpitations. It was too gen-tle when all I felt was the desperate need for every piece of him to be a part of me. I pushed back, pulling him tighter to me and the spatula fell to the ground as his other hand came up to cradle my face. I lost my breath then, caught in the way his hands held my face so gently when our lips were so desperate for each other. His tongue pushed into my mouth, dancing on mine until the smell of burned pancakes filled the room and choked the air we were barely breathing. My feet found the ground again, and Adam turned to the stove, shoving the pan to the cold side as he swore. I stood back, my hands going over my swollen lips as I giggled at his red face. He turned slowly back to me, running his tongue across his teeth before raising any eyebrow and pulling me back into his arms.

"What. About. My. Breakfast?" I asked between kisses as he lifted my legs back around his waist and carried me towards the bedroom.

"I think. We. Need. Dessert. First," Adam replied as he navigated the furniture.

He placed me on the bed as his kisses trailed up to my neck and down my bare shoulder.

"Isn't it a little early for dessert?" I gasped as my hands buried in his hair.

His hands slid down my body as his eyes met mine from my shoulder.

"Is it?" he asked, fingers tangled in the string of my underwear as he gently tugged at it.

The air caught in my throat as his fingers skimmed over my inner thigh. I couldn't make any sound other than a gasp as I shook my head. I watched as he moved down my body, kissing the tattoo on my hip before slipping the tank top over my head.

~~~

"Do we have to go to work today?" Adam asked as he rolled over and wrapped me in his warmth.

I smiled and closed my eyes again. "Maybe go in a little late? After you finish making those pancakes?

My phone began ringing, and I felt Adam's weight shift over me as he reached for the phone, and then his chest heaved as he looked down at it. "It's the hospital."

I lurched forward, grabbing the phone from his hand and touching the screen just before it stopped vibrating. "Hello?"

My eyes searched the room for a clock that would tell me what time it was. How long had we been?

"River Ahlers?" the voice on the other end asked.

"Yes?" I answered, and a cold sweat began to build on my brow.

"We have some good news. The doctors decided to pull Tara out of the coma today. She's fully awake, and she's asking for you."

The room spun. Tara was up. This phone call wasn't bad news.

"Seriously?" I choked as the tears began to stream down my face.

"Yes, visiting hours are until six today, but she's adamant that she wants to see you as soon as possible."

"Has anyone told her about—"

"The gentleman driving the car?" My rapid breathing must have signaled the woman to keep going. "Yes, her parents did about two hours ago, but short term memory can be a bit slower to recover depending on the situation. Since this was drug induced, her recovery should be faster. Just be prepared that you may have to explain it to her again."

I blinked hard as I absorbed the information. Tara had been awake for hours. She was told Bobby was dead, but she might have to be reminded? I felt my body numbing at the thought of having to relive telling her over and over again. *Please don't be that bad.*

My brain kicked back into gear and happened on the first reasonable question. "She's been awake for hours?"

"Yes, should I tell her you'll be coming?"

I looked around the room again and then gave in. "What time is it?"

"7:30," the women answered, and I put my head on my knees.

"I'll be there in forty minutes," I said.

I hung up the phone and looked at Adam. His fists formed balled at his sides, and I realized he wasn't going to be coming with me.

"I can't go, River," he said, his eyes racing over mine. "I don't ever want to go to that hospital again. After seeing Tara in there after the funeral...I just can't."

Alone. I would be alone as usual.

"I don't want to go either, but this is for Tara– and I need you," I said, but my voice faded as I watched him go to the window and place his head against the pane of glass.

A part of me understood how hard this was for him, but another part of me raged with anger. For the first time in over three weeks, he was sober, and he still couldn't stand by and support me. Maybe the alcohol had less to do with our drifting than I thought. I shook the thought from my mind as I looked down at my hands. Adam lost a part of him in that hospital, and I needed to understand what that meant to him. If Tara weren't at the same hospital, he would be by my side. I knew it.

"It's fine," I replied, glad he wasn't facing me to see my expression. "I get it."

"I'll go when they move her to rehab. I promise," he said, his voice muffled by his arm.

"Sure," I replied as I stared at him. The photographer inside of me begged me to grab my camera and capture the moment. His face was framed by the light streaming in the window, but the dividers in the panes sent shadows over just the right places making him look as sad as he was. I unfolded my legs from under me and walked up to kiss his bare shoulder. "I'll be back in a few hours."

He put his chin on his shoulder, and I leaned up to quickly kiss him goodbye, but instead his hand cupped my chin, and his lips raced over mine, leaving me breathless.

"That's not fair," I said when I managed to pull away.

"Can't be mad at me anymore, then?" he asked, and his eyes danced over my face. The sadness still there.

I reached up and ran my fingers over his stubbled chin. "Who said I was mad at you?"

His brows rose into his forehead in disbelief. "I know you pretty well, and I know your voice—I've memorized every tone you've ever used with me. That tone you just used was your I'm-pissed-but-I-don't-want-to-tell-you tone."

"No, that was the I'm-pissed-but-I-totally-get-where-you're-coming-from tone," I replied.

He turned to face me, holding my arms as he lowered his forehead to mine. "I got the important part right. The 'I'm pissed' part."

I laughed, biting my lip. "So you know I'm not anymore then?"

Adam leaned down and kissed me once more. I kept my eyes closed as he pulled away and his lips hovered over mine, his breath warming my cheeks.

"I hope not," he replied.

I shook my head and opened my lids slowly. "You're really good; you know that?"

His gaze fell before coming back up to me. "Just remember that the next time you're pissed at me."

"Fine," I replied, but instead of moving like I knew I should I remained there.

"You don't want to go?" Adam asked, moving my bangs away from my eyes.

"I've been going every day...I just kept it from you," I said as I put my hands on his shoulders. "I think I'm just in shock. I didn't think she was going to wake up..."

"I know you went," Adam said, and my head shot up.

"How?"

"Tara's parents have been calling me...trying to convince me to come in. They thought because I was so close to Bobby, being his brother, that it would be good for her.

Maybe they thought she would mistake me for him—too bad they don't know I don't look like Bobby at all," he said, his forehead wrinkling as he continued; "Not that she could see me."

"Maybe they just thought she could use another friend," I replied with the squeeze of his hand before I went to get dressed. When I looked back at Adam, he was sitting in the chair by the window leaning forward on his knees with his fists clenched. I closed my eyes as I turned towards the exit.

I wondered if when I got back, he'd be sober.

Chapter 10

When I reached the hospital, I found myself frozen as I listened to the engine idle. I slammed the car into park and placed my head on my hands as my body heated up. It was mid-February, yet I felt like I was sitting in Hell. I gazed over the steering wheel up at the brick building. It was just a building, so why did I feel the urgent need to vomit?

I sat back in my seat as my mind reeled with memories. The Swarovski-encrusted dress wrinkling against my skin as Adam crumbled in my arms—the god awful screeching sound of Vicky's sobs against the incessant buzzing of medical equipment. I had somehow buried them in the back of my mind, and in an instant I understood how Adam would be driven to drink, especially if he couldn't forget as quickly as I did. I couldn't fathom why I was being affected like this now when I visited Tara countless times. I let my breath out slowly as I tried to rationalize the situation. I didn't know how Tara was going to be, and handling her recovery, Adam's descent into possible alcoholism and my grief along with everyday life seemed daunting. *She'll be okay.*

I took one deep breath and got out of my car, slamming the door behind me and concentrating on my feet as I walked in the building. I kept my eyes down as I walked up the stairs I knew all too well and with each step the hollow hole that formed inside me grew. Bobby could have been the one in the coma; the one waking up—but he wasn't. At least Tara was, though. I gave my name at the guest check in and took a seat as I waited for admittance. Tara's mom, Becky, came down the hallway and wrapped me in a hug that squeezed my tiny rib cage smaller than I thought possible.

She held me at arm's length with a huge smile on her face. "She's doing well, but let's talk before you go in."

I nodded, and we took a seat back in the chairs. "How did she handle..."

Becky looked up at the ceiling as her shoulders lifted. "I'm sure they warned you her short term memory could take some time to recover. Her whole recovery could take anywhere from six to twelve weeks, but the good thing is the medical coma kept her injuries from escalating. She shouldn't have any long-term side effects."

I swallowed. "Will she ask me about Bobby?"

Becky placed her hands over mine. "It's possible. She seemed aware of it when she woke up–I'm not sure how, but she did."

"Okay," I replied, taking a deep breath before standing. I went to her room and poked my head into it. Tara was looking through a cosmetic bag with a frown on her face.

"Hey." I broke the silence as I let myself in the room.

She smiled up at me and her face the first time I saw her

after the crash flashed in my mind. I blinked it away and smiled back down at her, mostly healed.

"Aren't you going to hug me or something?" she asked with a cock of her head.

I wrapped my arms around her and squeezed once before sitting down on the edge of her bed.

"So," Tara began, putting her hand over mine; "how have you been?"

I blinked at her, my mouth only forming odd gargling sounds as I tried to fathom her attitude.

"You're oddly calm," I managed to say.

"I'm awake, and I'm grateful for that."

I shook my head as I wondered if she already forgot Bobby wasn't going to wake up. The tears started tumbling down my face without control and Tara pulled me into her arms, now far thinner than before. She hiccuped, and I knew she was crying too. We sat like that for more minutes than I liked to remember before our combined sobs softened and we pulled away laughing.

"He'd be so pissed; you know that?" Tara asked as she wiped her face with the back of her hand.

"Yeah, and why is that?"

"He'd hate to see his girls so sad," she replied, and I had to take a deep breath to keep from falling back into tears again. *She still knew.*

"Yeah, you're right," I said as I squeezed her hands in mine.

"So, how's Adam?"

The hollow in my heart returned, and I looked down at

our hands. "It's been rough. He's been drinking a lot, but yesterday he was sober–so hopefully that's a good sign."

Tara bit the inside of her cheek, and her eyes flickered as she struggled with some thought. She shook her head, and it seemed to pass. She smirked as she replied, "Bobby's going to kick his ass if he doesn't stop."

My body tensed as I looked at her. Maybe she thought he was in another hospital bed. I fought back a wave of nausea. I couldn't tell her, not without breaking down completely again.

"He should be more concerned about me kicking his ass," I replied instead, giving her a weak smile.

Tara ran her fingers running over the sheets pooled around her lower body, staring at the red bag that had been pushed aside when we hugged. "Speaking of kicking asses– I'm going to kick my own if I can't figure out how to put mascara on–*or* which one of these is mascara."

I laughed, taking the cosmetic bag and opening it up. I held the black tube and a tiny mirror up.

"Together?" I asked.

"Together," she replied, and the corner of her eyes wrinkled with determination.

Chapter 11

I tightened the tie around Adam's neck as I looked up at him. He hadn't drank in a week, and he was going back to work. I didn't know how he managed to sit around the apartment for so many weeks, but I figured he was probably playing music, although I hadn't seen him play since he almost destroyed his guitar. I blinked hard as another thought rammed into my brain, *or he was so drunk it didn't matter.* A part of me was beginning to feel normal again, and I didn't want to weigh it down with the thought of the fact there was still a chilled bottle of Southern Comfort in the refrigerator door. My stomach tightened as my eyes focused back on Adam. I could still feel the missing pieces of me pulling away as I walked out of our apartment past Bobby's empty apartment, or down the hall at my work past Tara's empty cubicle. When I got home Adam was there with a smile on his face and that helped to make the week feel more manageable.

"I can do this," Adam said as he touched his forehead to mine.

"That's the same thing I told myself all day the day I

went back to work," I replied, leaning up on my toes and kissing him.

His hands slipped up to cup my face. "I'm not as strong as you, River."

"When you come home, I'll be here," I replied. A shaky breath rattled passed his lips, and he nodded. "Besides your kids miss you."

Adam's eyes moved passed me, focusing on nothing in particular as he nodded again. "I miss them too."

"See–at least you won't be stuck in an office all by yourself with a bunch of smelly flowers," I replied, scrunching my nose as I slipped on my high heels.

Adam's face paled, and his hand stuck in his newly cut hair. He asked me to cut it short on the sides and leave the top long, and his hands now disappeared in the slicked back top. "Flowers?"

I slipped my hand into his as we walked out the door together. "I asked Principal Michaels to make sure you didn't have to deal with any of those. You'll be okay, I promise."

Adam shook his head as we started down the stairs. "You're always taking care of me now. Isn't it supposed to be the other way around?"

I kept my eyes ahead as my heart hammered against my chest. "It goes both ways."

Adam smiled as he opened the door, and the winter air bellowed into the warmth of the building. I pulled my scarf up further as we walked out the door.

"I'll make dinner tonight, okay?" he said, reaching over and rubbing my arm as I shivered.

I smiled up at him, swallowing as my mouth went dry. I didn't know if he would make it through the day, let alone want to make dinner at the end of it.

"Sounds fabulous," I replied as I fought the urge to look at the sky and pray it would happen.

"What do you want?" Adam asked as we reached our cars and he turned to face me.

"I think there are some meatballs in the freezer, and I could go for spaghetti," I said.

"And garlic bread?" Adam added as he tucked my hair behind my ear.

"Even better," I replied, trying my hardest to keep the fear out of my voice as I glanced up at him.

His eyes were red, and I knew he didn't sleep much the night before. He leaned down, kissing me before pressing his lips on my forehead. The hollowness flashed in his eyes before retreating as he whispered, "Love you."

"Love you more," I replied as I opened my car door and sank into the seat. I waited for him to pull out before shutting my eyes and leaning my head back. I needed to have faith he could do this.

I knew he could.

I opened my eyes and put the car into gear.

I wasn't sure I could handle it if he couldn't.

~~~

The first two hours of the day I spent looking at my phone over and over again. Finally, at the third one, I stopped looking, but anxiety continued to play with my mind. My body flushed with heat as I told myself everything was going to be okay. At hour four my body finally relaxed, and I was able to get some work done. I sent the final print files for the restaurant and booked the models for my next shoot. I stood to stretch, looking out the window at the busy Boston street. Three blocks away Adam was busy teaching his students. I smiled to myself as I sat back down, pulling my apple out and biting into it just as my cell phone rang. The song from Fade Burn made my eyes prick as I looked down at the picture of Adam.

This couldn't be good.

"Adam? What's wrong?" I asked, and my voice pitched as I looked down at my apple, one bite mark out of it. I swallowed the gritty piece in my mouth, feeling it move down my throat as I waited for Adam to response.

"I...I don't know what I was thinking," he said, and I heard him curse under his breath.

"I don't understand," I replied, my heart hammering too hard against my chest. I rubbed my hands across my collar bone. He didn't sound bad.

"I just...I fucked up, Riv. Can you get me?"

"I need you to explain," I said as the urge to vomit rolled over me as my body went cold. What had he done?

"I brought..." I heard him grit his teeth, and a trash can go skittering across a tile floor. "I drank–not a lot. But...now I'm afraid I smell like booze, and I can't drive if I smell like booze–but I can't go back out there when...I don't...God, I'm so fucked up."

I pressed my fingers into my forehead. "Where are you?"

"In the bathroom. I dumped the bottle out, but now I still have a bottle. Riv, I don't–" his voice cracked; "I don't know what to do. I love my job."

"Stay there. I'll pick you up. Make some vomiting sounds intermittently."

Adam didn't respond.

"Adam?" I asked.

The line was quiet for another moment before he asked, "Do you hate me?"

"No," I replied, biting my lip before continuing; "I'll be there in a little bit."

"Thanks, Love."

I nodded, forgetting he couldn't see it before hitting the *End* button. I closed my eyes, looking up at the ceiling. "Taking Bobby wasn't enough?" I asked someone I was having trouble believing existed.

I let my head fall into my hands as I took three deep breaths and then stood, grabbing my purse and heading to Jesse's office. I rubbed my damp palms against my skirt before bracing myself against the door and peeking my head into the room. "Hey."

"Hi!" he replied, looking over his reading glasses at me. "What's up? You seem upset."

"It's Adam. He decided to go back to work today...and I thought he was ready..." I answered, heaving a sigh; "he just called and...well...he wasn't."

Jesse took his glasses off and nodded. "Alright," he said, cocking his head and giving me one of those looks that said he understood, even when I didn't say anything. "Don't take it too hard on him, though."

"I'll try," I said before turning to leave.

"River," Jesse said, and I looked over my shoulder. "Don't take it too hard on *yourself*."

I bit my lip before offering him a pained smile. "See you tomorrow."

He nodded, breathing through his nose as his eyes raced over me. I turned, staring out the door and my mind flashed to Adam the night Bobby died. Adam's was arm linked in mine as we walked out these same doors; our laughter bouncing off of the vestibule as he swept me into his arms before racing to the car in the rain. I stood frozen with my hand on the crash bar as I stared at the sunny day outside, a horrible juxtaposition to the clouds in my mind and the tears I felt dripping down my cheeks.

When I got to the school, the kids were still outside for recess. Several of them jumped up and waved as I walked up the steps. I smiled back and acted like nothing was wrong. I was becoming way too good at pretending.

"Hi there, River!" the secretary said from behind her glass. "You know the drill!"

She passed the clipboard, and I shook my head. "Adam called because he's stuck in the bathroom—sick to his stomach. Do you know if Principal Michaels is available?"

She looked at her computer screen, typed quickly and then nodded. "His office is the first door on the right."

I was a horrible liar, and I felt my hand trembling as the buzzer sounded letting me know I could proceed. I grit my teeth before walking through and turning to the office where Principal Michaels was opening his door.

"River, nice to see you!" he said.

I raised my shoulders up, nodding up the stairs to where Adam's classroom was. "Adam called me on his cell phone—he's not doing too good. It seems I may have brought home the flu going around at my work. I came to pick him up. I hope that's okay?"

Principal Michaels nodded. "Better at home than sharing it with the kids here. Crazy how these things wipe through places of work and schools."

"For sure," I replied.

"Well, the next time I see you, hopefully, it will be under better circumstances."

"Agreed," I said. "I should probably get him."

I turned to the stairs and headed up them, only letting the breath I was holding out once I made it to the top.

He bought it. Thank God.

I headed down the hallway towards the sign for the restroom, and my heels clicked against the marble floors, echoing through the corridors in a way that made the hair on my neck stand up. I always hated it, but at that moment, the noise seemed compounded. I didn't want to draw any more attention because my heels sounded like a rhino was rampaging in the hallway. I reached the door and prayed it was him in there and not someone else. I gulped in air, feeling it sear into my lungs before I knocked.

"Adam?" I asked.

"Riv?" he replied, and I heard the door unlock.

I stepped into the bathroom and looked at him. His hair wasn't slicked back anymore and instead fell in his eyes as he yanked at his tie. His hands went into the air, forming fists before he rubbed the back of his neck, squeezing his eyes shut. "I'm sorry. I just—"

I shook my head, cutting him off. "Where's the bottle?"

Adam took it out of the sink, and I put it in my purse before nodding to the trash can. "You're going to want to put your head in that and make convincing vomiting noises. You already look like hell."

"Thanks," he mumbled, and I raised an eyebrow at him.

"Vomiting noises," I said as he grabbed the trash can and pulled the half-full garbage bag out of it.

I smirked at him.

"What?" he asked as he dropped it on the floor. "I don't need to actually be vomiting, do I?"

I shrugged, pursing my lips and he glared at me. "Ready?"

His eyes froze, looking down at the empty garbage can in his hands as he licked his lips. "I thought so."

I squeezed his elbow as I opened the door. A part of me understood. Another part of me was screaming. I was already used to telling it to shut up, though.

Chapter 12

I wished I could sleep but I couldn't. The first few weeks after Bobby left us sleep was the only reprieve from the darkness hanging over me. It had alluded me since I went back to work, though. My mind never seemed to shut off, and if I did fall asleep, I wasn't able to rest. My dreams were horrible images. I squeezed my eyes shut and my mouth watered with the urge to gag. I planned on working instead of sleeping, but my whole body hurt and I couldn't stop thinking.

Thinking.

Thinking.

Adam's not going to get better. Work is going to make this worse.

I rubbed my eyes again as I tilted my head back and let my inhales come one at a time. I felt the eyes on me but stayed the way I was.

"I know you're not sleeping, River," Adam said, and his voice sounded raw from his slumber. I listened to his footsteps, counting them and knowing when he would arrive in front of me. "You never sleep anymore."

I opened my eyes and stared up at him. Behind his frame, I could see the clock on the wall. Three AM.

He was right. I didn't sleep anymore.

I was a virtual zombie.

And he was a drunk.

I wondered what Bobby would think of the monsters we became in the days following his death.

Forty-five days.

Ten hours.

Five minutes.

Thirty seconds.

"So," I said, my throat parched.

Adam shook his head before going into the kitchen. I didn't move as I listened to the sound of the fridge opening, and a bottle unscrewing. My lip trembled as I fought the tears. I counted his steps, expecting them to go to the bedroom and jerked forward as they stopped in front of me again. I looked at the bottle of water he held out to me, and he widened his red eyes expectantly.

"Come on, Riv. I can tell you're dehydrated. Your lips are cracked."

"No," I began, but as I did, I felt the skin tear and blood trickle down the middle of my lip. Adam sat down next to me, handing me the bottle before letting his hand settle on my thigh. I took a sip, licking my lips with the dampness from my mouth. "Thank you."

He nodded, pinching the bridge of his nose as he opened his mouth, but no words came out. After a moment, he spoke, "Listen, about yesterday."

"It's fine, Adam. I know this is hard on you. I know how hard it was for me to go back to work. I imagine it was worse for you," I said, looking over at him.

He shook his head, leaning on his arms as he looked over at me. His chest rose as he continued. "We need to talk about it, River– or at least I do." I nodded, and he continued. "I'm not going to make an excuse for my actions, River…" his voice faded, and he sunk back into the couch. "I'm sorry if you feel like you're fighting this alone."

I took another sip of the water, holding the liquid in my mouth before swallowing. I looked ahead before draining the bottle and staring at the empty plastic in my hands. I hadn't said it. I hadn't even allowed myself to feel it, but suddenly that emotion crashed into me, and I found myself squeezing my eyes shut.

"Do you hate me?" Adam asked for what seemed like the millionth time since Bobby's departure.

I turned to face him, shaking my head. "No, of course not. I'm just…scared of what we're becoming–of the road, you're traveling down. What if you can't shake this? What if that bottle is the only way out? I don't know if I can handle that."

Adam leaned forward putting his hands on either side of my face, and I let my hands settle on his wrists. "I'm trying, River. How long before you give up hope?"

That wasn't the response I wanted. I wanted him to tell me it was a momentary lapse of judgement, and it wouldn't happen again. I locked my eyes on him; placing my hands on his cheeks as my thumbs caressed the dark circles under his eyes, and I said the words he needed to hear, "Never, Adam. You're the only thing keeping me together."

But now I felt like every part of me was falling apart.

If he couldn't keep it together, how would I?

How would *we*?

Chapter 13

I rubbed my eyes, yawning as I stared at the computer screen. The edges of my vision dimmed, and I blinked hard. Even with the open window behind me the florescent lights were making my eyes go buggy. I heaved a sigh before digging in my drawer and pulling out a snack bar. As I took a bite, I felt eyes on my back, and I turned slowly to find Jesse leaning against the door frame with his arms crossed.

He stretched his left arm out, his sleeve pulling up to reveal a shiny, over-sized watched. Even from the distance between us I could see the Z on the side bolt. "Two thirty and that's what you're eating?"

I rolled my eyes as I chewed slowly before swallowing and giving him a broad smile. "Yum."

Jesse blinked at me several times before standing straight and nodding over his shoulder. "Let's go."

"Where?" I asked as my vision finally brightened back up.

"Lunch. It's a good thing we have similar work styles, except my wife tends to yell at me when I don't eat right–so I'm saving you while you're saving me. Let's go," he said, and as I opened my mouth, he shook his head. "No, no way out. You've been producing a lot lately, and I know that it doesn't mean you've become more efficient– no offense. It means you're working too much."

I narrowed my eyes at him but gave in when his shoulders slouched in disappointment that I wasn't following instruction. I breathed in before I hit control alt delete and grabbed my purse from below my desk.

"Where to?" I asked.

He shrugged, looking over at me with his hands in his trouser pockets. "What do you like?"

"Honestly?"

He nodded.

"Burgers and fries–curly fries."

Jesse laughed to himself as he pushed the door open for me. "I should've figured."

"What will your wife say about you eating right?" I asked as we walked to his BMW.

He shrugged as he unlocked the door. "At least I'm eating."

My eyes dropped to my hand on the door as I wondered if Adam ate the sandwich I made him every day, or if he left and...I shook the thought from my head. He wasn't drinking at work. He wouldn't do that again.

"You okay?" Jesse asked as I slid into the passenger seat and buckled in.

"Huh?" I asked, looking up at him.

"You look like I said something wrong," Jesse replied, cocking his head at me as his blue eyes darted back and forth over my face.

"Just worrying about Adam," I said, sinking into the cold leather seat and pulling my purse closer to myself as I shivered.

Jesse nodded and then flipped some switches on the dash. "Leather is good, except in the winter it's freezing–but that's what they made butt warmers for. As for the summer, you just burn your flesh off–instant suntan."

I couldn't help but laugh, and I gave in smiling. "Thanks for tearing me away."

"There's a burnout factor, and I want to make sure it doesn't happen. I've got big plans for you," he said, winking at me as he put the car in gear.

"Do you now?" I asked, glancing over at him as he grabbed a pair of aviators tucked beneath his sun shield and put them on his face.

James Bond. I pulled my lips into my mouth as I stifled the giggle. Adam was right about that, but Jesse felt like a father figure to me. He was someone I looked up to, and while I knew he was soft on the eyes, I wasn't attracted to him.

"I sure do, but it's in the works, so as a good professional, I shouldn't have said anything," he replied.

I rolled my eyes. "Piquing my interest. You know I'm gunning for an officer title."

Jesse's hands tightened on the steering wheel as he turned into traffic. "Actually, you've never said anything about that."

I pulled my lower lip in. "I know how hard it is to get one– but you can't blame me for dreaming, right?"

"I don't think it's a dream. I believe that's a goal, and I'm glad I know about it now. After all, I do have some say in that," he said. "I am CEO after all."

"Yeah, I haven't forgotten. You see there's this huge plaque on your door, but it does say Chief Executive Officer," I paused, pulling my shoulders up as I pursed my lips. "Good thing I went to business school–otherwise I'd have no idea what you actually do. Oh, wait..."

"Ha ha," he shot back. "I keep people like you in line."

"Is that what you're doing by making sure I eat?"

"Hey, if no one else is doing it–" His words caught in his throat when he glanced over and saw my face.

I looked down at my hands as my chest tightened and made it hard to breathe.

"I didn't mean it like that, River," Jesse said as we stopped at a light. His jaw tightened. "So Adam...?"

I bit my lip. "Is the reason I'm so efficient lately. I don't know," I replied, putting my fingers against my forehead. "I'm either working or worrying about him...or Tara."

"Sleeping?"

I laughed at the thought. "What's that?"

I watched Jesse out of the corner of his eye as he pulled into a local pub known for fantastic food. He pushed his lower lip out with his tongue as if he was trying to figure out what to say. "Burnout factor, Riv. You still need to find time for you."

I don't even know who I am anymore.

"And eat, right?" I replied.

Jesse smiled over at me before turning the car off. "Speaking of which, I'm hoping you like this place."

"I haven't been, but I'm excited to try."

"Perfect," he said as we walked to the entrance.

"So what big plans do you have for me?" I asked as he signaled for two and the host grabbed menus before leading us to a table.

"Ah," Jesse said as we slid into the booth across from one another. "See I knew I should've kept my mouth shut. One thing that I'm not good at as a CEO."

"It's good to keep your employees informed," I replied as a waitress walked up.

We ordered sodas before falling into a comfortable silence as we looked at the menu.

"How do you feel about splitting some mozzarella sticks?" Jesse asked, keeping his eyes on the menu. My stomach growled the response, and I felt my face flush. "I'll take that as a yes."

"Are you ready?" the waitress asked as she smiled at us.

We placed our orders, and the comfortable silence became uncomfortable. I tapped my fingers against the leather of the booth before speaking, "So do you worry about what your wife eats?"

Jesse rubbed his chin. "Not really– she's a health freak, so I know she takes care of herself. If she were like you or I, on the other hand, I probably would have to text her every day at the same time to make sure she ate–and if she didn't respond, text her again a few hours later. AKA what happened to *me* today."

Adam didn't text me at work anymore. I swallowed, playing with the straw of my drink. He never really did before, though, so I knew the sinking feeling in my stomach to be misplaced. I just couldn't shake it.

"Have you seen Tara lately?" I blurted out. I wasn't sure if that was out of line. I pressed my eyes shut. I was trying to think of anything else, and I landed on Tara of all things.

Jesse breathed in through his nose. "I haven't. You?"

"No," I said, looking down at the mozzarella sticks that just arrived. "I guess I'm not that great of a friend. I was going every day before she woke up, but now it's harder. I know that probably doesn't make sense, but she keeps forgetting what happened and why she's at the recovery center. It's hard to see her like that...and then to have to replay telling her Bobby's gone over and over..."

"Has Adam gone with you?" Jesse asked, not touching the food. I let my eyes rise to his and I shook my head. He didn't speak for a moment, and the silence waded around us as we stared at one another. "Why don't we go together?"

I felt the tears pricking at the corner of my eyes as I nodded, unable to speak.

"These look great," Jesse said, and the conversation broke into something easier. We talked about clients, laughed about some of the ridiculous things they asked for and enjoyed one another's company until both our plates were bare.

"I can't believe I ate all that," I replied, sinking into the seat.

"You sure you don't want dessert?" Jesse asked, smirking at me as he signed the receipt.

"No, but thank you for this. I needed it," I replied as we stood and headed for the door.

"I know," he replied as we reached his car. He glanced over the top at me. "You ready to see Tara?"

I let my eyes fall to the shiny red paint of the roof before looking back up. "Yeah, I think it's about time I did."

"I was thinking the same thing."

~~~

I bit my lip as I stared at Tara looking out the window of her room. She looked small and frail and despite the fact her cuts and bruises were faded you could still see their outlines, reminding me of why she was here. Jesse stood beside me, shaking his head as a choking sound came from his throat. He rubbed his forehead, now deeply lined with wrinkles.

"I don't know how you did it," he said, and his voice trembled.

"Did what?" I asked.

"Came in here right after it happened. She still looks..."

Like death. The words faded from his lips.

"I didn't handle it well," I said as my eyes drifted to where the white rose sat, now dried and brittle, exactly where Tara was staring.

"You're handling it well now," Jesse replied, his eyes locking on mine.

I inhaled, my shoulders rising as I chewed on the inside of my lip. "I guess. You're just lucky you're not inside my head."

"Why? What's going on in there?" Jesse asked.

My stomach tightened as I fought the tears pricking in my eyes. "I just miss my best friends. All of them...gone in one night. I can't really talk to her about anything right now — she's too fragile."

Jesse nodded. "I'm sorry you feel so alone, but I don't want you to feel that way. We have services available–"

I cut him off with a shake of my head. "I'll be fine."

"You're strong, River, but if you need someone to talk to–you should," Jesse said.

Everyone thought I was so strong, but I felt so weak. Still, I shook my head.

"Ready to go in?" Jesse asked, placing a hand on my back.

I nodded, and we headed into the room.

"Hey girl," I said, and Tara's head moved to look at me.

"River! You brought Jesse!" she said, putting her hands on the arm of the chair. Her face turned red, and I watched as she struggled to figure out what to do next.

"Sure did. You can stay right there if you're comfortable. Jesse and I will sit on the bed," I said, and I watched as she pulled her hands into her lap. She gave me a forced smile, and I knew she was frustrated.

"Still haven't figured out how to walk yet," Tara said, and her brow furrowed as she looked around the room. She rubbed her forehead, and I watched as her chest rose up. "Where am I, River?"

I glanced over at Jesse, and his jaw was tight as he locked eyes with me. I stood back up and went to her side, putting my hands over hers. "You're in the recovery center, remember, a few weeks ago there was a car accident."

Tara's eyes fluttered against her cheek, her head rolling to the side as she fought the memories. When her eyes opened, they were wet. "Oh, yeah. How's Bobby doing?"

I glanced down at my hands over hers, and I could feel my knees shaking as I wondered if I should just walk around the subject or if I should answer her. I didn't know how her parents did it, and I didn't know if I could do it. I squeezed my eyes shut.

"Jesse!" she said, and my eyes snapped open. "You're here too!"

"Sure am," Jesse said, and I stood to sit next to him, looking at the ceiling.

"How are you?" she asked him, cocking her head. She was wearing light pink lipstick today and mascara. I wondered if she remembered how to put it on or if someone helped her.

"We miss you at work. Things are a bit boring in the cube's without you—or so I'm told. It makes me wonder what kind of trouble you brew up. I guess we'll just have to discuss that when you get back to work, though."

I smiled at Tara. "It sounds like someone's a snitch. I can't believe this guy didn't realize you were the cause of all the trouble. I thought you had the word trouble tattooed on your forehead."

Tara tipped her head back and laughed; honestly laughed. All the parts of me that went cold when she asked me about Bobby warmed back up as Jesse's laughter, along with mine met up with hers.

"Must be super boring without me," Tara said, and her eyes went down to her feet. She wiggled her toes beneath her slippers. "They've been doing therapy with me now–trying to get me to remember things. It's just super frustrating. I mean I remember how to do a Gantt chart for work, but I can't figure out how the hell to walk."

"Must mean you remember all the crappy things," Jesse replied, elbowing me.

I felt my stomach sink. Not *all* the crappy things. My eyes drifted to the white rose as Jesse began filling Tara in on the projects she would need to help with when she came back and updating her on what he heard for office gossip–which wasn't much.

"Did I miss anything?" Jesse asked me, and I shook my head. He knew more office gossip than I did. I kept to myself before the accident, but now I rarely wandered away from my office. Jesse rubbed his hands on his slacks, looking down at his watch.

"You've been quiet, Riv. How's Adam?" Tara asked, and she blinked at me expectantly as my jaw worked but no words formed.

"Great, he just went back to work–" I replied, leaving out the *and got loaded while there* part.

Tara's brow furrowed. "Why was he out of work? Was he in the car too?"

I fought to keep the emotions off of my face as I took a shaky breath. "No, he was just out for a bit."

"He took a vacation? And you didn't take one with him? Riv, you've got to lighten up!" Tara said, and she fluttered her eyelashes at me.

"You'd swear work was her ball and chain," Jesse said as he winked at me.

Tara's laugh filled the room once again but this time, I found it hard to join in.

"Well, we should probably be going," Jesse said, and I tried to keep the relief off of my face as I stood to give Tara a hug and a kiss.

"I promise I'll be back soon," I said in her ear.

It was a promise I intended to keep.

Chapter 14

The days began to blur into one another, and I was never quite sure what day it was. I realized I was working my life away, but I just didn't know any other way to deal with what was happening. I stared at the computer screen, my vision darkening at the edges, so I had to flick on the desk lamp to try to decrease the effects of the harsh lighting above me. I heaved a sigh as I looked down at my watch. Friday. It was already Friday.

And it was...

"Crap!" I hissed as I shut my Macbook and shoved it into my purse.

Ten minutes was all I had to get to Webster. That was not going to happen. I pulled my cell phone out of my purse as I rushed out of the building, stopping at the door as I looked over my shoulder. The cubicles were all empty. It wasn't like anyone else stayed at work until almost seven on a *Friday*. Even Jesse's office was dark.

I needed to get a life.

I shook my head before turning back out the door and texting Dad.

Running Late. About thirty minutes out.

What a lie. If I were lucky, it would take forty-five–going seventy-five the whole way once I was out of the city. I grit my teeth as I tossed my purse into the car and cranked the engine on, turning the music up as I watched the light change to green. I concentrated on getting out of the city in one piece, and when I hit the highway, I hammered on the gas. Rush hour ended hours before, and the way out of Boston was mostly clear. I glanced down at the speedometer before sighing as I lifted my foot off the pedal.

Ninety.

The world sped passed me, but I felt frozen in the car as if I was no closer to getting to where I needed to go. I let the numbers dip down to seventy before hitting the cruise control button. In truth, I looked forward to my weekly meeting with Dad. What I didn't expect was the constant lie I told him about Adam. The scenery rushed passed me until I came to the exit, turning the music down as I pulled into the commuter lot.

Dad stood outside his car, leaning against the hood with his arms crossed. "Ducks!"

I got out of my car, and he wrapped me in a hug.

"I thought you weren't going to make it," he said, and I felt my neck flush up to my cheeks as my chest tightened.

"You know me. I get distracted," I replied, shrugging as we moved to his car.

He shook his head, gray eyes darkening. "No, you're never late."

I breathed in, looking at the ceiling of the car as I held

my purse against my chest. "That's because of Adam. He's the one who's always early," I replied.

I pulled my phone out of my purse and looked at it. Nothing. But Adam knew Friday was my night out with Dad. I felt my throat tighten. That was why he hadn't texted...all day. I shook the thought from my head.

"Speaking of which, how is Adam?" Dad asked as he put the car in gear.

The bubbling lie surfaced so easily from my lips. "Adam's fine, Dad."

I still hadn't convinced myself of those words, but I hadn't seen Adam drink anything in weeks. So I wasn't positive it was a lie.

"And you?" he continued, looking at me out the corner of his eyes. "You like tired."

"I'm fine, Dad."

Now, that– that I knew was a lie.

"Is it safe to assume you were working?" Dad asked as he put the car in park, his hand on the shifter as he glanced over at me.

I bit my lip, shrugging. "Hoping for that big promotion, you know?"

Dad looked down at his watch, his eyes narrowing. "Working yourself to death won't get you that."

I rubbed my neck. "I'm good, Dad. I promise."

"You should bring Adam next time," he said, and his eyes raced over my face.

I smiled, nodding as my stomach twisted in knots. I fought against the wave of nausea as I wondered what Adam was doing, and if he would be willing to come if I asked. My voice was normal as I replied, "Sure, why not?"

Dad's lips lifted into a smile, and I realized he believed me.

When had I learned to cover my emotions so well?

Chapter 15

I parked my car next to Adam's and turned it off. My eyes moved to the apartment building in front of me, and my hands fell into my lap. I stretched them as I realized just how hard I gripped the steering wheel as I drove. Despite the ridiculous volume of my music, my mind still wouldn't rest between thoughts about work, Tara, and Adam. I got out of the car, and the warm Spring air hit me.

Spring.

It was Spring. February melted away, and life was moving forward, even though I was stuck in stop, go. I shook my head. That didn't even make sense, but that's what my life was. It just kept going even though I wanted it desperately to stop. Every week followed the same pattern. On weekdays, Adam and I barely spoke because I got home well after dinner and he ate without me. Sometimes we watched television together, but most of them time he fell asleep, and I opened my laptop to keep working. Friday's I went out with Dad and Adam did God knew what. Saturday somehow changed to boy's day, and I figured it had something to do with the fact Adam didn't want to be around me for an entire day. I swallowed at the thought, the stairs looming above me as I stared at them. Sunday's I went to visit Tara before grocery shopping, and maybe a part of me crammed both things together because *I* feared spending a whole day with Adam. It seemed the crevasse between us was turning into a gapping canyon. So much had changed in just three months.

I realized I was still staring up the stairs and standing like an idiot in the lobby. I inhaled and then began the ascent, taking each step slowly. My feet tripped over the top step as my eyes drifted to Bobby's apartment. I rubbed my hand over my face as I moved to my door, opening it and tossing my keys onto the table beneath the mirror. My makeup was gone, and the dark circles under my eyes were apparent, only enhanced by the mascara left on my lashes.

"Adam?" I asked, looking around the dimly lit apartment. The lamp beside the couch was on, but Adam was nowhere to be seen. I poked my head inside the bedroom and saw Adam sitting in the chair on the balcony. His chin was tucked into his chest, and an empty bottle lay at his feet. I walked up to him, swallowing as I picked up the SoCo and fought the urge to chuck it. As Adam breathed out, his alcohol filled breath washed over me and nausea built inside of me. I thought he was doing this, but now I had proof. I looked around the room and saw his wallet on the dresser. I began to tiptoe towards it, and then gave up, knowing he was out cold, so any noise I made wouldn't wake him. I picked up the beat leather bi-fold and held my breath as my pulse rushed in my ears. My eyes closed as I opened it and then looked down at the thin white receipts jammed into it.

I pulled them out, looking at each of them before sinking to the floor. The little pieces of paper rained down around me, settling on the hardwoods as my chest heaved up and down.

Bruce's Booze

Corner Package Store

And countless others. Their names blurred together as my hands gripped tightly against the soft leather. I had proof Adam had a problem. One I didn't have a clue how to handle. I gathered up the receipts and shoved them back in his wallet before placing it back on the dresser and changing. My eyes moved over my shoulder to Adam as I reached the door of the bedroom.

What would I do now?

Sleep? I scoffed at the thought before closing my eyes and turning into the living room. I couldn't sleep when all I could think of was Adam. Despite the fact we spent so little time together he was all that consumed my thoughts.

I settled on the couch, and my eyes moved to the door. On the other side was the hall, and at the other end of the corridor was the empty apartment Bobby's parents were still paying rent on. My thumb went to my mouth as my eyes moved to the bowl on the side table next to the door. The keys glinted in the light.

The apartment needed to be cleaned out sometime. Why not now?

I could feel a part of me screaming as my stomach clenched even tighter and my fists went into balls as I stood. My feet moved as my brain wound the words *don't do it* over and over again. Still, my fingers wrapped around the hard edges of the key as my free hand grasped the doorknob and pulled it open. I stood staring at Bobby's door as the metal that would allow me into it bit into the palm of my hand.

Someone had to do this, and it sure as hell wasn't going to be Adam. I breathed in and closed my eyes, only opening them as I exhaled and put one foot in front of the other. The key was hot from the heat of my body as it shook its way into the door knob. The metal clunked, and the wooden door swung open, leaving me staring at the empty room once filled with happiness. My eyes rushed over it as my mind flashed with memories, and my feet somehow continued in–all the way to Bobby's bedroom door. My chest constricted and stars popped in my vision as I swung it open. I found myself blinking rapidly as my eyes wandered the room, stopping on the dresser where frames contained pictures of Adam and me, Bobby and me, the three of us, and then Tara and Bobby. My feet yet again propelled me forward, but I stopped as I breathed in, choking on the air.

My body warmed as my chin trembled and I breathed in again.

There it was again.

Bobby. The room smelled like him.

My eyelashes fluttered against my cheeks as the scent encircled me. Bath and Body Works' Twilight Woods. The cologne we picked together when we were twelve. For fifteen years he'd worn it, even after Tara told him she hated it.

My eyes opened and moved to the hockey jersey hanging half out of a drawer–exactly where he left it that morning. My knees shook, and I found myself sitting on the bed staring at it. I reached forward, and the worn fabric embraced me as I brought it up to my chest. I pursed my lips together as the tears gathered and I pulled the jersey over my head, engulfing myself in his scent–it was embedded into this clothes despite constant washing. In my memories, his laughter carried through the room. It wasn't the first time I wore one of his jerseys. I closed my eyes and curled into a ball on his bed.

"So you remember it too?" Bobby's voice reached my ears, and the darkness behind my lids drifted away, parting until it was him and me in the tree house. I sat up on the bed, looking at him as he smirked at me from the edge of it. "See the thing is, I imagined it like this–you know? You practically naked;" his teeth ran over his bottom lip as his eyes ran up my legs, barely covered by my sleeping shorts. "in my jersey."

He moved forward and his hand cupped my chin as his thumb caught a tear. "You weren't crying in my fantasies, though. You cry so much now, Riv. I don't want you to cry."

I closed my eyes as my vision blurred from the weight of them, burdened by the false warmth of his touch.

"I've lost myself just as much as I've lost you," I whispered, trying to memorize the feeling of his soft hands against my skin. So caring and loving when everything seemed so cold now. "All my dreams are shattered without you."

Bobby's hands reached for my face, turning it, so I was looking at him. He was beginning to waiver in and out, and panic burned its way up my throat.

He was going to leave.

But this was so real.

"Please don't leave," I said, and the tears and clenching of my throat made the words as physically painful as they were emotional.

"I thought all my dreams shattered when I found out Adam was with you–and it was over for me–that I didn't have any more chances. My dreams realigned, though, Riv–they changed, refit into even better dreams. I expect you to do the same," he said, and he was fading faster; his body just a wisp and his touch a mere warmth with nothing substantial behind it.

"But Adam–"

"You'll figure out what to do, it might be hard, but in the end, it will work out. You and him are what's left of me. Remember that. Together you make me whole," he said, and his lips reached for my cheek, sending heat through my body as he disappeared.

"Bobby!" I yelled, and suddenly I was sitting straight up in the bed sobbing, the warmth of his lips against my cheek a stinging pain. I leaned back, pulling my knees to my chest and cried until the darkness consumed me.

This time, Bobby's warmth didn't return.

Chapter 16

Monday.

Tuesday.

Wednesday.

Thursday.

Friday.

Each day moved into the other, and I only slept a few hours at night. I often found myself wandering to Bobby's apartment. I swallowed the lump in my throat. Bobby hadn't returned to my dreams and loneliness dug into me as I slowly worked my way through his things, fighting against the constant barrage of memories. There were times where I just couldn't bear the tole of dealing with my emotions, and I turned to work instead. It was one of those nights. I stared at the door for an hour before deciding I just couldn't handle it that day. I always had work to do anyway. I pulled my Macbook from my purse and sat on the couch, crossing my legs as I placed it on my lap. I typed in my username and password.

Access Denied. Contact System Administrator.

Maybe I typed my password wrong. I typed it in again.

Access Denied. Contact System Administrator.

I grit my teeth as I typed it in over and over with the same results.

"What the fuck!" I said as the screen displayed the error message.

I jumped as Adam leaned against the door frame, arms crossed as he looked at me on the couch.

"What time is it, River?" he asked as he stood, coming to sit next to me.

I looked up at the clock. "One AM."

"And why are you trying to sign on to your work computer?" he asked as he pushed the laptop closed and pulled it off my lap to set it on the coffee table.

"I can't sleep," I replied as I pushed my fingers into my tired eyes. My lack of sleep had nothing to do with not needing it.

I felt his arm around my shoulder. I gave in, placing my head in his lap.

"I can't ever sleep," I said, too tired to fight him or wonder why he wasn't completely loaded right now. I knew he had alcohol somewhere in the bedroom. There was no other reason a twenty-five-year-old man would go to sleep at eight at night.

"I know," he said, and his voice was soft as he ran his hands through my hair. "That's why I had Jesse block your rights during non-business hours."

I shot up, yanking my body out of his warm arms. "You what?"

Part of me was pissed, and another part of me longed for the warmth his arms just gave me. My chest tightened, not because of the fact I was mad, but because I realized how badly I missed something as simple as him holding me. The angry part of me took over, now more agitated because of the fact he withheld this part of himself from me so very often now that I needed to miss it to realize it.

Adam blinked at me, his lips in a flat line. "You don't need to be working past seven at night or on the weekend."

"It's not night anymore," I said, crossing my arms.

His lips twitched at my smart comment before going back into the thin line. "Or before seven in the morning."

I sucked in a breath through my nose.

"You're welcome," he replied as his brows raised into his forehead underneath his too-long hair.

I sighed as I settled my head his lap, being mad at him was futile when his eyes were clear. I needed his arms more than I needed to work. Hell, I didn't need to work. I needed him, and he was here. My muscles relaxed for what seemed like the first time in months.

"Let's go in the bedroom?" Adam asked, and before I could respond he swept me into his arms to carry me in. He placed me on the bed and crawled in beside me. I rolled over to put my head on his chest, and his hands swept through my hair. The panic that overtook my mind twenty-four hours a day began drifting away with each caress.

"Thank you," I said as I fought the collapse of my mind.

"You're not alone, River." He kissed my forehead, and the soft darkness consumed me.

Chapter 17

The weekends were the hardest because I couldn't work. Adam made sure of that when Jesse restricted the rights on my computer, but that didn't mean he was there for me any more than before. Saturday I thought he might stick around, but when I woke he was already putting coffee in a thermos. He kissed my head before going out the door and leaving me in the empty apartment with nothing much to do. I made my way over to Bobby's and drowned myself in memories. When I couldn't take it anymore, I walked the few blocks to Starbucks and spent an hour with a coffee before heading to the bookstore. I practically bought out half of the bargain section before going home and falling asleep ten pages into the first book. Sunday came, and I asked Adam if he would go with me to see Tara. Just like I did every Sunday, and his response was unchanged. He had something to do.

Of course, he did. I nodded, kissed him and then left, crying on the drive to the recovery center. When I arrived, I stood at the threshold of Tara's room, and my body reacted instantly; my nerves causing my skin to crawl with a tingling sensation as my eyes burned. She looked like herself now, albeit a paler, more intense version—but she wasn't covered in the bruises that made the contents of my stomach come up. My stomach still shifted in unease as I stared at her sleeping in the bed. The windows were open, casting a cool spring breeze over her and wafting her long hair across her face as the sun cascaded over her frame. I swallowed, my nails digging into my palms as I finally stepped into the room. I sat down beside her, wondering if I should wake her up. I could only bear to come once a week, because by the end of the visit I was hollower than when I woke up that morning. It seemed impossible, but each time it was the same. We talked about the same things because she was still struggling to remember anything from her short-term memory. She would get frustrated, but at least now she knew where she was and why she was there. She was still having trouble remembering what happened to Bobby, though, and that was the part I dreaded the most. I managed to get around the conversation during the handful of times I visited since she woke up, but I knew eventually I needed to face my fears and tell her, and keep telling her. That was the only way she was going to remember.

I reached out and slid my hand under hers. My stomach fluttered as I moved my lips, suddenly parched. "Hey, girl. It's me again."

I watched her face, looking for any sign that she was going to wake up. My body relaxed, and I sat back in the chair as I looked at her. I could never tell her what was going on if she was awake.

"It's been almost three and a half months since I heard

Bobby's voice..." I coughed as I fought back tears. "It hasn't got easier... I wish I could talk to you –really talk to you...or anyone." I closed my eyes tighter. "I'm trying to be strong for Adam. He's..." I paused as I choked on the word. "Drinking. I think he's more of the functioning drunk. When I wake up he smells like booze...so I guess he's drinking at night, but I don't know for sure."

I pulled my head up as I took a deep breath, letting my eyes go back up to her face. "He had Jesse block my computer rights last week. Now, I have no excuse not to sleep." I looked at the ceiling. "I still don't, though. Sometimes I just sit and stare at the wall."

I put my head in my hands, pinching my nose between my palms as I stared at her comfortable breathing. "I don't feel anything anymore, but I feel it. God, everything's so fucked up. I'm so hollow...empty. I feel like my soul has been sucked into the ground where Bobby is. I just...I just want him back. I want everything back. I want you to be able to talk to me about these things." The tears hinged my eyelashes now, blurring her. "Tara, I don't...I don't know how much more of this I can take. I'm watching Adam self-destruct, and he's disappearing as fast as I am. But no one knows I'm disappearing. They all think I'm doing amazing for what's happened, but I'm dying, and there's no one to save me."

I heard steps behind me, and jumped, glancing over my shoulder. I didn't want anyone to know the things I told Tara when she was sleeping because this wasn't the first time I'd done this. I stared at the empty door frame, my brows furrowing. There was no one there. I shook my head before turning back to Tara, and her eyelashes fluttered against her cheeks.

She squeezed my hand as she woke. "Hey," I whispered. "Sleeping in the middle of the afternoon– that's the life."

Tara laughed as she pushed herself up. "Sure would be if it wasn't because I'm so tired from doing normal things."

I put my other hand on top of hers. "How's the walking coming?"

Her upper lip curled in the corner as she heaved a sigh. "I can't do it yet. You'd think since it's so easy a baby can do it that I would be able to figure it out."

I cocked my head at her and forced a smile to my lips as I replied, "They get to crawl first, though."

"Thank God the therapists haven't had me do that. Can you imagine that?"

I chuckled to myself, and she slapped my arm. "So how long were you being a creeper watching me sleep?"

"Not long," I replied, and my face burned with the lie. Especially seeing I was talking to her...even creepier. If only she knew how fucked up I was.

She raised an eyebrow. "If you say so. How's Adam?"

Her eyes fogged, and I knew what was coming next as she shook her head, her chin trembling as her brain no doubt fought against dark memories.

Probably drunk again.

"Good," I replied.

She smiled, and the fog disappeared. Whatever memory she was fighting was tucked away. "He calls me every day."

I leaned forward, my eyes narrowing. "He what?"

Tara used her hand to symbol a phone and put it up to her ear. "Calls me."

"Every day?" I repeated, and my voice was as breathless as I was. My chest constricted.

Her eyes widened, and she slowly nodded. "I wish he'd just come, but he says it's too hard–something to do with Bobby."

She blinked hard, and her hand squeezed mine so tight I flinched. "Tara?" I asked.

She shook her head as if she could rid herself of the thought. "Sorry, I still get confused about things. I miss Bobby."

Me too. "I know."

My eyes drifted to the dried, brittle white rose on the window sill. Her body trembled, and my eyes shot back to her. She put her hands to her face, pulling her knees to her chest and I stood.

"It's okay, girl," I said as I sat on the edge of the bed, rubbing her back as her body wracked with a sob.

A part of her knew.

A part of her was fighting.

And I knew exactly how that felt.

She leaned up, and I pulled her into my arms, rocking her in my arms until her sobs quieted. She pulled away, wiping her eyes. "I don't know what that was about...it's like there's a hole in my soul."

I pulled my lips into my mouth as I nodded. Maybe we

couldn't talk about it, but somewhere inside of her she understood. Somehow that made it easier.

"Thank you," Tara said, squeezing my thigh; "for being here for me. Eventually, I'll figure this all out and be able to go home."

"Any news on when they'll let you go?" I asked. I wondered if that would be better or worse for her memories.

"Depends." Tara bit her lip. "I have to remember a bit more — I'm still having breakdowns like that, so I'm not allowed to be alone. As soon as I'm allowed out, can we please get Starbucks and go shopping?"

"Of course, but you don't have to wait for Starbucks–next time I come I'll bring you some — okay?"

I watched as her shoulders slouched, and her lips pushed out. "I don't know if they'll let me have caffeine–might stimulate me to remember too much at once or something."

I squeezed her hand, now entwined with mine. "They make decaf."

Her lip twitched. "What's the point of coffee if it's decaf?"

I rolled my eyes, leaning forward and kissing her cheek. "That's what I get."

"You're silly, Riv," she replied, and her smile sent tingles of warmth through my body.

"I should get going. Have to make the boy dinner," I replied as I pulled my phone out and looked at the time. It was almost six o'clock, and Adam hadn't even texted to see where I was. I wasn't sure if I needed to make him dinner, or if I was avoiding the inevitable Bobby question.

"Tell him I want *him* to bring me the Starbucks. I need some eye candy," she replied. "He's not as good as..."

She bit her lip, and her eyes faded once again before she let them come up to mine. The warmth seemed to have disappeared.

"See you soon," Tara replied, and I nodded before turning out of the room.

~~~

When I slipped into the apartment it was dim; lit only by the light in the bedroom and Adam's shoes sat by the entryway. I closed the door behind me, inhaling through my nose as I leaned my head back. I counted to three before slipping off my shoes and walking to the bedroom with them in my hand. I could see Adam sitting on the balcony, and I knew from the way he was sitting he was asleep.

Don't look, River. It's not worth it.

I shook my head as I slipped off my clothes and grabbed a pair of yoga pants and one of Adam's t-shirts. I stared at the mirror as my whole body started to shake and tears streamed down my face. I needed him to be awake, to talk to him about the battle I saw in Tara's eyes–to ask his advice on what to say to her. I turned towards the balcony and made my way out to sit across from him, my vision blurring as I pulled my knees to my body.

His chin was buried in his chest, and a half empty bottle of liquor sat his hand at his side. I shook my head as I looked up at the sky, the salt of my tears sliding over my lips.

Slipping.

We were slipping into our crutches–his in the bottle and

mine in my silence and work. My eyes drifted down, and I leaned forward to pull the bottle out of his limp hands. I held it in mine, staring at the amber liquid before sliding my head into my forearms as my mind spun.

"We're masochists for watching each other with anyone but one another."

"So why do you torture me, River?"

My eyelashes fluttered with the weight of the water on them as the memory kissed me and faded away. A bottle like this led to that...and now, now it was ripping my heart apart.

My lips trembled, and my chest heaved as I stared at the bottle. I hated the way it tasted.

I hated it.

But now it was tempting me.

I needed something—anything to quench the undying thirst; anything to seal the hemorrhaging in my heart.

My eyes slipped through the bottle to Adam's frame, magnified by the empty part of the glass and it slid through my hands before tittering on its side until it toppled over. I watched as the alcohol rushed out, and then trickled it's last drops over the cold metal grates. When my eyes lifted, Adam's bloodshot eyes were locked on me. He blinked at me but didn't say anything. His eyes looked passed me and then fell to his hands as his lips twitched. I swallowed before standing, and as I passed Adam his hand wrapped around my wrist.

His voice was hoarse as he whispered, "No."

I looked down at him and shook my head. I wanted to ask why, but nothing would come out.

I didn't feel anything.

He seemed to know that.

He tightened his grip, pulling me down into his lap. I closed my eyes, burying my head in his wrinkled button-up as he ran his fingers through my hair, kissing the top of my head.

"I'm sorry," he whispered.

Me too. But the words never left my lips.

Chapter 18

How do you admit someone has a problem? It was a question that plagued my mind all day at work. Usually, I used work as the device to help me forget everything.

Like Adam was using alcohol.

My jaw clenched as I opened the door to the apartment knowing it would be empty. Adam's car wasn't in the lot, so I knew he wasn't home. But there was still a part of me that hoped something was up, and his car was in for service, or anything really, that meant he was home and not off somewhere getting loaded. I sank into the couch, kicking off my heels, and tipped my head back, putting my chilled hand to my overheated forehead. Then again, it appeared he didn't have a problem getting drunk here either. Adam had a problem, and I had my own. I couldn't even begin to grieve over Bobby when I was grieving over the implosion of my entire life. I barely made it through the day at work because my body ached. The part that hurt the most was my chest. It was tight, making it hard to breathe and the air conditioning didn't seem to be working. I boiled at work, even in my car with the air blasting. I glanced down at my watch, and a shiver ran through my body. Adam hadn't texted all day, or to indicate that he wouldn't be home, but I was late– wicked late in fact. I squeezed my eyes shut. Maybe he came home on time and then left because I hadn't. Maybe his drinking was partly my fault. I rubbed my throat as pain coursed up it, and I went to get a drink of water from the kitchen.

This could be my fault.

I filled a glass and gulped down the contents before leaning against the counter and watching the water dripping from the faucet.

Or this could all be in my head, and Adam was just out practicing with the band. I knew they were getting paid to perform now because Adam left the checks on the entryway table for me to deposit. Maybe all that plus working with the kids every day was just wearing him out. Maybe that's why he was going to sleep so early every night.

I turned to face the living room. There was one way to find out. If he was going to drink in the bedroom, then there had to be a stash there. My feet propelled me to the room, and my hands formed fists as I glanced around the immaculate room. Where would I even begin to look?

My eyes drifted to my guitar case, and then up to the wall where my guitar was mounted. My fingers tingled, and I was tempted to abort the mission and pick it off the wall to play it. That would be more soothing than finding a bottle or more in that case. My gaze dropped back to the worn leather case leaning against the wall. But there could be nothing in it–then I could play and have peace of mind.

I swallowed hard. Or there could be at least ten bottles of SoCo. I rubbed my sweaty palms against my slacks as

I walked up to it and then leaned down to flick the brass buckles open. I closed my eyes as I lifted the lid, opening them slowly to stare at the red velvet fabric. My stomach rolled, and my breath rattled in my chest as I stared at the half empty bottle. It wasn't ten, but as I fell back on my ass and dropped my head to my knees, I knew one thing for sure.

It was one too many.

I hadn't realized exactly how accurate it was when I said Adam was a functioning drunk. Every night it was the same thing. He came in the bedroom and drank away the day. I looked up at the dark Boston sky– or maybe he didn't. One half empty bottle didn't mean that.

I let my chin drop to my chest as my hands tangled in my hair.

No, but hiding it was a strong indicator it did. And the receipts. And the booze breathe.

I pulled my cell phone out of my pocket. Seven, and Adam still wasn't home.

Where are you? I texted him before going to the contact list.

"Hey, Ducks, everything okay?" Dad asked.

I was quiet. What was I going to say?

"Ducks?" his voice deepened, and I realized he was probably panicking.

"Sorry, I just need someone to talk to."

"About?"

"Adam...I think he has a problem."

"A problem?"

I rubbed my hand over my face. "Yeah, he's drinking a lot..." I began and then the words rushed out in a uncomprehending stream; "And I found all these receipts and a bottle hidden in a guitar case and he smells like booze almost every morning, and he leaves me alone so much of the time;" the words slowed, and I swallowed as I admitted, "God, I feel so alone."

Dad was quiet on the other end, and I pulled the phone away from my ear thinking I accidentally hung up. His face was still on the screen with the seconds ticking away above. I put it back to my ear and heard him suck in a deep breath.

"It's been a rough year," Dad managed to say.

I leaned over the balcony, staring at the spot where Adam's car was supposed to be. "What am I supposed to do?"

"When did it start?" Dad asked, and I looked up at the darkening sky, biting my lip.

"Since the day after Bobby died...so almost four months," I replied, and I fought the burning pain in my throat as I thought about that.

Everything seemed to have happened so long enough.

"Give it some time...maybe try to have a conversation with him about it to let him know you're concerned—but stay level headed," Dad said, and I could hear his fingers tapping against something in the background.

I watched as Adam's car pulled in, and my body was stuck going from hot to cold as I wondered what he was doing that he wasn't home. Level headed. I didn't feel level headed anymore, and I wondered from the way he said it if

I *ever* was about anything besides work. I knew how to talk to people at work, but that was a skill I acquired. Talking to Adam used to be easy.

Used to.

My life used to be perfect, and I took that for granted. I wondered if this was punishment for that.

"Okay," I finally replied.

"River?" Adam called from the entryway, and I closed my eyes as my chin dropped back.

"Adam's home," I said, my voice quiet.

"I love you, Ducks."

"Love you too," I replied as I inhaled and then stepped back through the window. "In here."

Adam came in the bedroom, loosening his tie and his eyes were tired. I fought the urge to glance at the guitar case that hid his secret. I swallowed as the realization hit that he chose *my* guitar case. Had he wanted me to find it? My whole body rushed with tingles, and I realized I was staring at it, unblinking.

"What were you doing on the balcony?" he asked as he began to unbutton his shirt. "And you're still in your work clothes."

My head jerked up, and my eyes met his as I blinked the dryness away. "I could say the same for you?"

Adam slipped his shirt off, his muscles rippling as he balled it and threw it into the laundry bin. "Parent teacher meetings."

"Ah," I said, nodding as I bounced on the balls of my bare feet.

"Did I forget to tell you?" he asked, his hand rubbing the back of his neck as he stared at me.

I swallowed, my face turning red as my eyes ran over his abs. I was supposed to be mad at him, but he looked so model-like shirtless in black pin-striped slacks. "I may have forgotten—"

"Or tuned me out," Adam replied with a wink as he slipped the pants off and grabbed a pair of pajama pants from the dresser. "You going to get into something more comfortable?"

This was what made things so hard. He acted so normal when he came home. I breathed through my nose as I looked down at my loose gray sweater, long necklace, and black boot cut slacks. "Yeah."

"Good," he said, sitting at the edge of the bed and leaning back on his elbows. "I get to watch just like you watched me."

My chest rose up to my chin as I narrowed my eyes at him. It was only half a bottle. I shook my head before I began to undress, and then I was suddenly in his arms.

"Another thought," he said into my ear before letting his lips caress the curve of my neck.

Talk to him.

But my brain wasn't keeping up with my body, which was currently on fire as his fingers slipped under my shirt. Then my brain was thinking again, but it wasn't about talking. The shirt slipped over my head, and Adam's hands moved up my spine as I twisted, so my legs were on either side of him. I could feel the smile on his lips as they moved down to my chest, kisses warm and soft.

Chapter 19

Adam successfully distracted me, so I never brought up what was on my mind the night before. I closed my eyes as I snapped the backdrop in place and then pulled the gold fabric over it as I began to drape it. Then I moved on to setting up the lights, umbrellas and other equipment I needed for the shoot. I was tired today like I was every other day and I hadn't slept the night prior, which was also like every other day. I fought the fatigue in my arms as I adjusted the fabric. A smile came to my face, at least today it was because Adam spent the whole night with me. Tingles shot up my spine as I inhaled.

"You don't have anyone to do that for you?" a voice asked from behind me.

My body tensed. Thinking about *that* with *him* behind me was awkward. I turned slowly, knowing exactly who it was, and it wasn't someone I wanted to see. "What are you doing here, Alec?"

For the first time since I was a child, using his first name came easily. Maybe it was because I just didn't care what he thought of me anymore.

"You've blocked our calls," he said, stepping forward

into the direct light of my setup. Bobby and Adam's father aged in the months since the funeral. Deep lines creased his forehead, and marionettes pulled the thin lips he shared with Adam down. His blue eyes raced over my face as he stepped closer, and I saw the dark shadows beneath them. He looked like he slept about as much as I did.

"Yes, we asked for space," I replied, turning my back on him.

Rude, River. I grit my teeth. I may not have cared what he thought, but I still had a conscience.

He closed the gap between us, and his large frame cast a shadow over me. I pressed my eyes shut as I tried to remain calm. "We've given you a lot of space, River."

I turned slowly, my chest rising as I breathed in. "It's still not enough time."

"What exactly did we do?" Alec asked as he looked down at me.

I clenched my jaw. How could I be level headed with exactly what had been said and done? I inhaled deeply, softening my eyes so I wouldn't look like a total bitch. "Look, Alec — we overheard a conversation at the funeral...and it rubbed both of us wrong. Please don't make me repeat what was said–you have to know–"

"Yes," Alec replied as he closed his eyes and rubbed his temples. "I don't know that's what she meant."

I went to my tripod and began adjusting the settings.

"Listen, River, Vickie and I have our problems. I'm not saying what she said was right–"

My hand numbed against the grip I now had on my tripod as I stared at him. "You could've–"

"Should've—would've, none of that matters now. You know that as much as I do," he interrupted, and as I glanced over at him, his shoulders slumped.

I looked down at my tripod and released my grip. I stretched my hand before asking, "Why did you come here?"

"You're the last connection I have to *both* of my sons...and some things need to be taken care of."

My stomach dropped at the final words, knowing he meant the apartment, Bobby's things– and whatever else. I was slowly working on organizing the items into boxes, and I didn't want anyone else to touch them. I knew where they needed to go–what Bobby would want. I doubted anyone else would.

"River Ahlers?" the model I selected came into the room.

I put my clammy hand to my forehead, its cold icing down my mind as I looked around Alec. "Yeah, come on in. I'm just finishing setting up, and we have to wait for Valerie and a few other models."

My gaze returned to the stone of a man in front of me. He looked lost as he stared down at me, large arms tensed and eyes tired. "Please, River."

"Obviously, I have a shoot to do;" I began, the harsh words not matching my soft tone as I watched his shoulders slump. "This one should take about two hours once Valerie gets here. She's the owner of the store and needs to style the models. You can stay if you want, and then we can get dinner or something."

"What about Adam?" Alec asked, his brows furrowing.

I pursed my lips. "He has work, and he's just getting back on his feet. I don't want to burden him with this right now."

Alec's blue eyes deepened, just like Bobby's did when he was upset. "So it's true?"

"What?" I asked, tipping on my toes as the other models entered the room and started chatting. I fought the hard blinking of my eyes.

Alec stepped forward and lowered his head so only I could hear what he said. "He's drinking."

Dad.

My body tensing appeared to be answer enough, and his eyes dropped from mine before he nodded to a chair in the corner. "You don't mind?"

Yes.

I shook my head, signaling with my hand for him to sit down. "Of course not."

I was glad to have my tripod for the shots because there was no way I could hold my camera without the stabilizer going nuts trying to compensate for my shaking hands. I concentrated on the models, positioning them, adjusting them and trying to get them to look as natural as possible.

"Listen," I said to them as tightness clenched my chest. The shots were not going the way I wanted them to today. "We're going to do this a bit differently. I know this is probably going to seem odd to you, but I'm going to talk to you throughout this whole thing—and I don't mean I'm going to be telling you how to stand. I want you to really *feel*. What I'm getting right now is empty; hollow. I need to see something *real*."

The confusion set in on their faces, just like it did with other models that were new to my style. It made me feel like I was insane for doing it, but sometimes I just needed to; otherwise my photos were static. In marketing, we needed photographs that pulled at people's emotions, and standard models didn't always know how to do that. I inhaled, letting the air rattle in my lungs before I gave them a smile.

"So Joey, any hot dates lately?" I asked.

He raised an eyebrow and the girls around him broke into laughter. I snapped the shot. Then another as I asked ridiculous questions, or simply just got to know the people in front of me. I arranged them, and rearranged them, asking them questions as I went along—pulling out their souls to place them on my digital screen.

I clicked the final picture. "That's it, guys!"

"That was seriously cool," Joey said as he slipped off the leather jacket Valerie had put on him. "I've never actually interacted like that before."

"It's the only way I'm able to get the shots I want."

"Perfection is all River will accept," Alec said, standing and coming towards us.

"I can seriously not wait to see those pictures," Valerie replied as she took the jacket from Joey, her eyes on Alec. "And who is this?"

"I'm sorry," I began, my face reddening at how unprofessional it was to have him there.

Alec stepped forward, sticking his hand out and giving Valerie a smile I used to see Bobby use to seduce girls. I swallowed the ball forming in my throat. They were so similar.

"Alec Beckerson, proud father... of her boyfriend," he replied, the smile twitching only slightly.

"Ah, the handsome fellow in the salon shots," Valerie said, nodding as she dropped his hand. Her eyes ran up and down his body as she appraised him. "You have the same lips, but other than that you don't look very alike."

"Looks more like his mother."

Valerie stiffened at that, seeing the band glittering on his hand.

"Very lucky woman, I'm sure," she said before turning to me. I felt faint from watching the interaction, mortification driving my head down. "When can we expect some initial advertisements?"

"In two weeks we'll have the entire campaign for your new line available to you," I answered.

"Perfection is what I'll expect!" she said as she tossed the jacket in her trunk before snapping it closed.

"I can help you with that," Alec said, and she nodded, watching him pick it up and carry it out.

"You'll let me know if he gets divorced, right?" she asked before following him out.

I watched her back fade before sitting down on the prop chair. *Holy God,* I thought to myself as I looked at the empty room around me. I closed my eyes as I counted my breathing. *Alec was Bobby thirty years from now.*

My eyes popped open as the dread closed my throat.

Except he's dead.

I stood, busying myself with cleaning up. Alec came in just as my backdrop stand gave in and threatened to take me out with it.

"Whoa!" he said as he rushed into the room, reaching me just in time to help me keep it from toppling over. "You really do this by yourself all the time?"

I huffed, chewing the inside of my cheek as the fabric backdrop slid onto the floor. "Usually, I'm smart enough to take the fabric off first," I replied as I leaned forward and stuffed it into a ball before throwing it in my bin.

He looked down at the stand, unscrewing the final piece to make it collapse cleanly. "I'm sorry I threw you off kilter."

I shook my head. "No worries, that's my life now."

He tensed at the comment. "You seem—"

"Harder?"

"Sad."

I stopped, my hand hovering over my lens cap. "You too."

We finished packing everything in silence.

"Any suggestions on where to eat?" Alex asked as he shut the trunk of my car.

I pulled out my cell phone and texted Adam.

Eating out with a client. Be home a little later. Can I get you something to eat?

I didn't expect my phone to buzz almost instantly.

I'll miss you. A burger and fries?

I smiled before replying.

And a shake we can split?

Perfect was the quick response.

"Looks like Adam's having a good day," I replied as I tucked my phone back in my purse. "He wants me to bring him home a burger and fries, and I could go for one myself—you?"

I watched as Alec's blue eyes brightened. "Glad to hear it, and I'd love that myself."

"Meet you at Vanek's?" I suggested. Alec nodded before sliding into his BMW.

I inhaled through my teeth as I watched him merge into the traffic along the city street before pulling out myself. I cranked up the Bring Me the Horizon CD as we moved along. Alec seemed different; not the cold, arrogant man I grew up watching Bobby admire. He seemed sad and as if what happened took him down a notch. I parked behind him, and I grabbed my purse as he opened my door for me. His lips tipped in a weak smile, causing my stomach to rise before plummeting. For the first time I saw the resemblance between Adam and his father; the sadness I knew I couldn't remove flickered through his eyes, weakening the smile on his lips and he heaved a sigh.

"Please don't hate me, River," he said. "I know I've been a shitty father."

I shook my head as I stood. "No, you weren't."

"To Bobby."

I bit my lip as I glanced over at him. He held the door for me, and I gave him a small smile that I hoped was reassuring.

He didn't need to feel any crappier than he already did. This was hard enough.

"I wish I could make it up to Adam now," Alec said, and the cracking in his voice showed he truly meant it.

I looked at the ground, waiting as the hostess grabbed us menus and showed us to a booth before I answered, "I can't help you with that right now."

He nodded, looking down at his menu but not opening it. "I'm sorry. I know I'm saying that a lot here, but I feel like I have to say it to *you.*"

"Why me?" I asked, smiling at the waitress as she filled two glasses with water.

"Anything else I can get you to drink?" she asked as she placed a basket of freshly made potato chips in front of us.

"This is fine," I replied.

"I'm good too," Alec said, and when the waitress left he continued. "I know we haven't treated you fairly either."

"You were never *that* bad," I replied as I flicked through the menu. I wasn't really hungry, and I was pretty sure this conversation was going to drive away any appetite I did have.

"River, my wife hasn't been a very nice person to you—or Adam, for that matter."

My eyes rose to meet his. "Especially Adam."

He scratched his blond head, where his hair was beginning to thin. "Especially Adam."

"Ready to order?" the waitress asked as she came back over. We placed our orders, and I let her know what we would need to take to go.

We sat in silence for a moment, and I watched as Alec played with his straw before finally speaking. "When do you think Adam will talk to us again?"

"Honestly?" I began, and his eyes met mine. "I don't know if he'll ever forgive your wife. You? I'm not sure about either."

"What about you, do you forgive us?"

I clenched my jaw as I stared back at him, a man, once a pillar of strength, aged beyond his years in months; one who seemed just as lost as Adam and me.

My body tingled. I hadn't even forgiven Mom. It seemed easier to hold onto that anger than deal with it—until that moment. Forgiving someone felt like the right thing to do. "Forgiveness has to be earned." His eyes dropped as he sucked in his cheeks, and I did something I never thought I would do. I reached across the table and put my hands over his. His eyes rose back up to mine, and I gave him a smile I reserved for Bobby. "I think you've earned it. I know coming here must've been hard, and I appreciate that you're trying. I forgive you."

Not Vickie, though.

His eyes pressed shut, the wrinkles around them deepening. They opened as he inhaled. "Thank you."

His thumb came up caressing my hand in a manner that reminded me of Dad. I didn't pull away. "There's something you should know..." he began, and his body tensed before he finished, "I left Vickie."

My hands withdrew slowly from the shock. "Why?"

"I reminded her too much of Bobby...she became bitter...mean—" he paused watching my expression. "Meaner."

I raised an eyebrow.

He pulled his hands back under the table as he continued. "Things have been hard. She was also livid with Bobby."

"Bobby?" I asked.

He nodded, reaching into his pocket and pulling out two folded checks. "He left you and Adam everything."

He passed the checks across the table, and I unfolded them. My vision blurred, darkening at the edges as I stared at the check drawn off of *The Estate of Robert Beckerson* with far more zeros than I could imagine. $250,000.00 payable to *River Ahlers*. I lifted the check, looking at the one below it for the same amount made out to Adam.

"He had a large life insurance policy—a certain amount set for funeral expenses and the rest to you and Adam."

A shiver passed through my body as I finally looked up at him. "He probably didn't think you and Vickie would be around when it came due."

Alec shrugged. "Doesn't matter, does it? We have enough money."

"This is a lot of money," I said as my eyes fell back down to it. My throat felt dry, and I reached for my drink, gulping it down.

"Exactly," he said, pausing to clear his throat. His eyes drifted across the restaurant before coming back to me. "So if Adam can't handle it, I'd appreciate it if you took care of it until he can."

My mouth opened and shut as I stared at the two pieces of paper and the huge amount of money they represented. I let my gaze rise to Alec. "Of course."

Half a million dollars.

Could *I* handle that?

~~~

When I got home, Adam's car was in its parking spot. I shifted my car into park, and breathed in, the scent of the paper bag and fries filling my senses. Maybe I overreacted by telling Dad about Adam having an issue with drinking, and maybe he was right. Maybe Adam just needed time. I made my way up the stairs, glancing over my shoulder at Bobby's apartment, suddenly reminded of the fact Alec agreed to let me handle Bobby's things. He didn't fight me on it and surprised me when he mentioned Vickie suggested I take care of it if I was willing. There was still so much to do, but Adam was good tonight, so it would have to wait. I unlocked the door and slipped my shoes off before looking up and noticing Adam wasn't in the living room. My throat thickened as I glanced over to the kitchen. He wasn't there either.

The bedroom door was closed.

I walked over to the counter and placed Adam's dinner on it before pressing my palms into the rounded edges of the concrete counter top. "No...No...No," I said as I shook my head.

He's not in there drunk.

My jaw locked as I tried, but failed, to swallow the bile coming up my throat. He seemed fine when he texted me.

I scoffed to myself. A text? Was I crazy? What could a text mean?

He could just be asleep after a long day at work. I fought the fatigue in my eyes. I was tired, so it was logical he would be too. I walked up to the door, my hand hovering over the handle as my pulse pounded in my ears. I pushed the door open slowly, and the pounding sped up as I looked at the empty bed. The rate of my breathing increased as my gaze left the bed and went to the chair by the window. My jaw slackened, trembling as I took in the figure sitting with the bottle of SoCo in his hands, drained to the bottom. His head lulled to the side as he glanced over at me, glazed eyes widening.

My eyes pricked as I stared at him. My vision clouded. I was so patient tonight with Alec, and because of that something inside of me snapped. My voice was too loud–too angry as I asked, "What the hell is wrong with you?"

Adam's lips twitched, the ball beneath his lip pushing tight against his flesh. "You know," he slurred; "It's the same thing that's wrong with you!"

He stood, his knees shaking as he made his way toward me, and I backed up against the door, shaking my head. My whole body trembled as I replied, "No...I'm not a drunk."

Adam's head jerked back, and he sat on the edge of the bed looking up at me. "Nah, you're just a raging bitch." My mouth dropped as the tears rushed down my cheeks. Last night he was perfect. He was Adam–tonight he was drunk, and I realized while I always *thought* he was drinking I hadn't interacted with him while he *was* drunk. Apparently it made him mean. I struggled to form any response, but I didn't have to because Adam continued to speak. His eyes locked on mine. "I still love you, though–do you still love me?"

My spine pressed hard against the door, and my voice came as a weak whisper when I replied, "Did you hear what you just called me? My Adam, the one who was my best friend, would never call me that."

Adam rubbed his fogging eyes, and his body rocked backward. "Don't give up on me."

I watched as he flopped back, passed out from too much booze, and I slid down to the sit on the floor. I put my head on my knees.

Level-headed, Dad's words echoed in my ears.

What I did was the exact opposite of level-headed.

Chapter 20

When I woke up the next morning, Adam was already up making coffee. He glanced over his back at me, and I looked away, biting my lip as my chest tightened. The night before was still fresh in my mind. I went into the bathroom to take a shower and when I got out Adam was already gone. No note. No text. He was just gone as if I was the one who said those horrible things and deserved to be ignored. I spent the day staring at my cell phone screen replaying the things we both said. I raised my voice at Adam when he was drunk, and he called me out about it–but he apparently thought he was in the right, or didn't remember. I shouldn't have been so hard on him, and when I realized he was loaded, I should've left. Instead, I took the verbal abuse and spat it right back at him. I closed my eyes as I put my head in my hands.

"A penny for your thoughts?" Jesse asked from behind me, and my head jerked back as I slid my cell phone off my desk. I didn't like the idea of Jesse thinking I was on it all day. I plastered a smile on as I spun around in the chair, my hands settling on my crossed legs.

"Sorry, just a bit distracted today," I replied.

Jesse nodded, putting his reading glasses into his suit pocket. "What's up?"

"I didn't realize there was therapist written on your name plate," I said as he moved to sit in front of my desk.

He chuckled as he took a seat. "There isn't, but for you, there is. What's going on?"

I looked at him for a moment and then sighed, giving in and explaining. "Bobby left Adam and I a bunch of money, and instead of talking to Adam about it...I kind of blew up on him."

"Why would you do that? You're usually so level-headed."

"Here I am," I replied, looking at the neatly organized files and my notebook with my pen resting on it. "With Adam, I never had to be before...I guess I don't know how to handle anything that's happened, or happening for that matter."

"It's good that you feel like you can be yourself at home," Jesse said as he tilted his head. "But some of your work skills are transferable, you know."

I smiled up at him. "It's complicated."

"And telling a vendor they're in breach of contract isn't? Especially when you've tried repeated times to get them to cooperate. You always seem to think that through and state facts in an efficient manner."

We locked eyes, and his gray brows rose into his forehead.

"You might be right," I replied.

"The good thing here is you can say sorry. It's kind of

hard to do that with a vendor if you tell them to screw them-selves," Jesse said as he stood, squeezing my shoulder as he walked passed me.

I bit my lip before turning as Jesse moved out the door. "Jesse?"

He peeked his head back in the door. "Yes?"

"Thank you for being more than a boss."

He winked at me before walking away.

Jesse was right, and I was determined to figure out a way to talk to Adam. I talked vendors into keeping their end of the bargain all the time. I didn't want to think about what happened when they didn't keep their end of the bargain because I was sure that wouldn't apply in this case. Adam and I could work this out, but I needed to put in the extra effort to hold Adam to his part of being in this relationship. So I left work early, arriving home before school even let out. I hoped Adam would come home on time so I could say sorry, and we could talk. I realized I might have left a little too early when I began to pace the apartment. As I did my eyes fell on my purse, thinking about the two checks in the side pocket. I walked forward, pulling them out and sitting on the couch to stare at them. Half a million dollars. I ran my fingers over the smooth paper, fighting to keep my eyes open against the sudden fatigue that washed over my body the moment I sat down. The door opened, and I jumped, sliding the checks into a notebook on the coffee table.

"Hey," Adam said, sliding his messenger bag off. "What you doing?"

Guilt balled in my stomach as he stared down at me. He

didn't seem mad. I shook my head, opening my mouth but no words came out. "N-Nothing." I finally stuttered as I sat back, pulling my knees to my chest. "Just waiting for you before cooking dinner."

"You look tired, why don't you relax and I'll throw something together."

I blinked at him a few times, and he gave me a smile before moving into the kitchen. "So you didn't tell me who the client you were with last night was?"

"Rep from the new clothing store I am working on a set of advertisements for." The words slipped from my lips so easily, and my hands balled into fists against my thighs.

"Sounds fun," Adam replied.

I rolled my shoulders as I stared at him over the top of the couch. "More photo shoots and staring at a computer screen for hours. How are the kids?"

Adam's neck reddened up to his ears, and I narrowed my eyes at him as he rubbed the back of it. "Good, good."

I didn't want to know what his embarrassment meant, and I wondered if I was the only one lying.

Adam pulled some lunch meat out of the refrigerator. "Sandwiches okay?" he asked, and I nodded. He pulled out a few more ingredients before going to the island to assemble them. "My mom called last night while you were at dinner."

My pulse quickened, and sweat beads formed on my forehead as I looked down at the threads of the couch. "Did you pick up?"

He shook his head as he cut the bread. "She left a message, though."

"You listened to it?"

He nodded, pausing to look up at me. "I usually do."

"I...didn't realize," I replied as he continued making our dinner.

Because we never talk anymore.

Just like we were doing now– a casual conversation that avoided the truth.

He nodded again. "She and Dad are getting a divorce."

"No shit," I replied, and I was surprised how well I faked shock.

His eyes met mine. "Something about not being able to look at him without seeing Bobby...and apparently me, though I'm not sure how the hell that's possible."

My chin trembled, and I looked away. I could understand perfectly now. It had been hard for me to look at Alec through dinner, and even harder to say goodbye. "Maybe he's changed."

Adam scoffed, his chin tucking into his neck as he did. His brown eyes flashed, and I realized it wasn't a battle I could fight without admitting the truth.

"How could all this make anyone better? I mean look at you and me," Adam replied.

My eyes dropped to the notebook harboring the checks, and my stomach rolled as I thought of the wall of lies I was constructing between us — the wall of lies that was already between us. I closed my eyes before standing and going to sit at the island across from him.

"Listen..." I began, and Adam shook his head, stopping mid squeeze of mayo.

"Don't worry about it, Riv. You were right to get upset with me."

My body rushed with tingles as I shook my head. "No–that's not it. I found the receipts," I said, my voice drifting as his eyes slowly came up to mine. He licked his lips. "And the hidden bottle."

He pressed his palms against the counter, his eyes locked on the sandwiches in front of him.

"I'm scared, Adam. I can't..." My voice cracked. "I can't lose you too."

His eyelashes fluttered against his cheeks, but his gaze remained on the food. Finally, he spoke, "I'm not an alcoholic."

My stomach sank as I stared at him. Level-headed. Facts–then feelings. What was next?

"You understand what it must look like to me then–you go to bed early every night. After finding all that–it just seems like you're having trouble dealing with the loss of..."

Adam's brows rose into his forehead, cutting me off with a single look. "And you're not? You work all the time, River. I had to have your boss lock down your computer so that you'd at least sleep–and you still don't."

"How do you know I don't sleep?" I asked, pacing the words, so it didn't sound like I was snapping. My heart raced in my chest, making it hard to breathe.

"Your makeup wears off by the time you get home. You look exhausted all the time, Riv."

Because I'm worrying about you. I'm dealing with organizing my dead best friend's things—oh, and my other best friend is struggling to learn how to walk and function in everyday life. I have to be strong for everyone.

I nodded, keeping my eyes on him as I answered, "I appreciate you tried to help me by locking down my computer. I'm trying to help you—what can I do to help?"

Adam's eyes finally rose to mine, and they were blank as he rubbed his hands against his slacks and turned to grab a bag of chips off the counter. He gave me a smile as he pulled it open and held the bag out to me with a smile saying, "I'm fine, Riv. Just stop worrying so much."

I stared at him before smiling back and taking a chip.

"You want mustard?" he asked as he gathered up the excess items to put back into the refrigerator.

"Sure," I replied, staring at the chip in my hand.

"You're worrying again," Adam said as he squeezed the mustard onto the meat before putting the bread on top and sliding the plate to me. He cocked his head at me, giving me a crooked smile, and I gave in, popping the chip in my mouth and smiling back.

My stomach twisted as I realized whatever relationship Adam and I had was fading.

And there was nothing I could do to fix it.

Chapter 21

I glanced at the clock as I pulled into the commuter lot Dad and I met at on a bi-weekly basis and for once I wasn't late. I looked around the lot and didn't see Dad's car. Surely, this was a first. Adam was the one who usually got my butt out of the house on time, but this time, I managed to do it myself. I tipped my head back to look at the fabric ceiling of the car. My body rushed with heat as I thought of why. All day I thought about Alec's words:

"So it's true...he's drinking."

My arms tingled, and I rubbed them as I clenched my jaw. There were only a few people who knew, and one of them may or may not have heard me admit it and couldn't remember anything new for more than a few minutes. The other was Dad. I watched his green Volvo pull in, parking next to me and waving for me to get in. I took a deep breath as I slid out of my car, locked it and then got into his.

"Hey, Duckie," he said, leaning over and kissing my cheek.

I stiffened, looking down at my hands. "Hi, Daddy."

Facts. Feelings. Be logical. It hadn't worked with Adam, but it would probably work with Dad.

He cocked his head, his hand on the shifter of the car. "That's a cold greeting."

I lifted my chin, and our eyes met as I replied, "You told Alec about Adam."

His body relaxed and his gaze dropped from mine as his hand slid to my knee and squeezed. "He had a right to know."

"Why?" I asked.

"River, don't be unreasonable."

Feelings–it was time for those, but they were bubbling, and I fought the urge to burst out about the fact Alec and Vickie didn't deserve to know that. But Alec seemed changed.

"Adam is struggling, and I told you because I thought I could trust you."

"Alec is going through a lot—"

"I know," I replied, inhaling. "But so am I."

"River—" his voice lowered to the lecturing tone, and I sunk into the seat, chewing on the inside of my lip. "Every single one of us is battling what this means. Alec has lost *both* of his sons because of this, and his marriage has disintegrated."

"I know," I replied, swallowing before continuing; "But I've lost both of them too, and Tara isn't really Tara...and..." I didn't finish the sentence. The words *neither am I* floundered, sputtered and disappeared as I looked down at my hands. It didn't seem relevant anymore. Dad was right. Alec did have the right to know.

Dad squeezed my leg. "I'm proud of you, Ducks."

I looked up shaking my head. "Why?"

"This means you agreed to meet with Alec, and you're being reasonable."

My shoulders raised up as I leaned against my hand and looked over at him. "I'm trying to be."

"I'm sure it was hard to meet with Alec, especially with everything you're dealing with too."

Alec's face flashed and then Bobby's—the eyes so similar, navy in their pain. *It was like staring at Bobby.*

I chose a subject less sensitive, but still just as crazy. "He gave me checks from Bobby's estate."

"It's a lot of money."

My jaw slackened as I looked over at him. "You know?"

Dad nodded before shifting his car into gear. "Where do you want to go?"

"I could use some fish and chips, and a walk on the beach," I replied as he merged onto the highway.

"Of course," he replied as he smiled over at me. His eyes raced over my face as if he was trying to determine if I was *actually* okay. Maybe it was because I was suddenly more rational, or maybe I just lost the will to fight. He didn't seem comfortable with either thought but didn't address it as we ordered our meal and ate at a picnic table in the chilly April night air. Instead, we talked about easy things like work and what research he was doing at Avery Point. I gathered something about green algae and micro-organisms, but pretty much just nodded to everything else as if I understood his job as a marine biologist. When we headed to the beach, the conversation tempered off. Dad sighed before glancing over at me, and I knew it was coming.

"So you've forgiven Alec?" he asked.

I looked out over the ocean and nodded. "Yeah."

"Doesn't that feel good?" He looked ahead now, but his eyes drifted to the corners where wrinkles deeper than Alec's resided– probably from being in the open salt air all day.

My shoulders rose up. "Better–but not exactly good."

"Ah," Dad said, and then he cleared his throat. "Have you thought about speaking to your mom?"

I stopped walking, and he turned to face me, eyes darting back and forth over mine. "Does she want to speak to me?"

"Of course — you're her daughter!"

I sucked on my bottom lip as I looked down at the sands sinking between my toes. I looked back up. "Then why hasn't she apologized? Alec apologized– he showed he was truly sorry for what he did. Mom hasn't done any of that."

"She was by your side at the funeral–" he began, but his words trailed off as he took in the look on my face.

"For show, Dad. That was for show, and you know it."

"River, you don't know that."

I bit my lip as I looked out to the ocean waves. "She's going to have to apologize for the things she said. When she's willing to do that, I'll be willing to consider forgiving her."

Dad's hands tapped at his sides.

I shook my head as I looked over at him. "I'm not being unreasonable. You have to admit that. All I'm asking for is her to consider the things she said and how hurtful they were."

Dad's eyes closed. "She thinks you should apologize to her."

My head jerked back as I stared at him, his eyelids slowly opening. "For what?"

He scratched the back of his neck. "For getting the tattoo." My mouth dropped open, and he shook his head. "I don't agree with her."

"Then you know I'm not going to apologize for that, right?"

He took a shaky breath. "Yeah."

At that moment, I felt bad for Dad. He was stuck in the middle of Mom and me–secretly visiting me and probably trying to make both of us be reasonable. Mom wasn't like me, though — she would never admit she was wrong, and she was a snob. It was a judgmental thought, but at that moment, I knew it was why she and Vickie got along so well.

I cocked my head at Dad, giving him a smile. "At least we know where I got my propensity to be unreasonable from."

He laughed at that, and we continued down the beach, where he began to talk about green algae yet again. I smiled, and this time, it was genuine. Just the sound of his voice made things better, even if I didn't understand a word he was saying.

Chapter 22

Sunday, April 24.

Four months, twenty-two days since Bobby left us. Fourteen weeks since Tara woke and began her recovery. Her post-traumatic amnesia was near its end according to the doctors. She was walking and aware of the fact she was in an accident. For the most part, she was ready to go home. There was just one thing keeping that back. She still didn't remember what happened to Bobby, and the doctors, along with her parents feared when the memory came back what would happen. She still needed twenty-four by seven watch just in case, and her parents worked full-time jobs. I stood next to the door, watching as Tara's mom talked to her. They sat next to the window, and I cocked my head as I looked at the way the sun slowly kissed Tara's skin slightly darker. She looked more alive now, her red-lipsticked lips curved into a soft smile as she laughed at something her mom said. I waved as Tara's mom saw me.

"I just need to talk to River for a second, okay?" she said to Tara, who winked at me before looking back out the window.

"How's she doing?" I asked as Becky shut the door behind us.

Becky's chest rose against her crossed arms as she took a deep breath. "I'd love to get her home, but she's started to have night terrors. She refused to tell the doctors what it's about."

I nodded as my mind drifted to the day she suddenly began sobbing in my arms. "Do you think it's because she's starting to remember what happened?"

She swallowed, reaching out and squeezing my arm. "Yes, and I need your help."

My body tensed as my eyes met hers, soft lines drifting from the edges of them. "I need you to tell her."

I held my chin up. "How?"

"When she asks, tell her. She's been getting better about it when we tell her, but we all need to be on the same page on this. I know it hurts for you to talk about it, but she needs to have things repeated."

I swallowed looking through the glass pane to Tara.

"I'll be with you–just in case anything happens," Becky said, and my eyes came back to hers. I nodded. If Tara needed me to do this for her, I would. A part of me wondered if I needed to do it for myself too.

I took a deep breath before going in the door. "Hey girl."

"River!" Tara said, standing and pulling me into her arms. "What was my mom telling you?"

I looked over my shoulder as Becky sat down on the bed, giving me a soft nod.

I shrugged. "Telling me how feisty you're getting being stuck in here."

Tara wiggled her eyebrows. "Let's go for a walk outside in the garden?"

Tara looked over at Becky, who nodded and stood to lead the way. Tara linked her arm into mine, and we walked slightly behind Becky.

"So how's Adam?" Tara asked. "He seemed a little bit out of it the last time he called."

Now was the time for truth. "He's struggling with everything. He's been drinking a lot–but he won't admit he has a problem."

Tara stopped, and her eyes searched my face. "Why is he drinking? And what does Bobby think about all this?"

I looked down at her arm linked in mine and put my hand over it. "Tara..." I began, swallowing as the tears pricked in my eyes. I let my gaze drift up to hers. Her jaw dropped slightly, her tongue running over her lips as she waited for my answer. "Bobby's dead."

I watched her eyes widened, fading into the depths of her memory as her arm tightened on me. My skin rushed with uncomfortable tingles, making my skin unbearable in its tightness as I added, "He died in the accident."

Her body began to tremble, and I turned to face her fully, placing my hands on her shoulders. Becky stepped forward, and I shot her a look, hoping it said I had this under control, before speaking to Tara again, "Tara–are you okay?"

She blinked fast as she rocked on her feet. Her head

began to shake back and forth before her eyes snapped back up to mine. "I remember."

I breathed in, cocking my head at her. "That's why Adam won't come to see you."

She nodded, putting her hands on my wrists. "How long has Adam been drinking?"

"Since the day it happened...I called him on it, and he's been trying to stay up with me, but I can see him shaking. Yesterday was my day with my dad and Adam didn't get home until after I was asleep. When I woke up this morning he smelled like booze," I replied, and Tara began to walk towards the gardens again. We walked out into the sunlight without saying anything else. The snow was gone, reminding me Bobby's birthday was only a few weeks away.

It was one he'd never see. I glanced back at Tara.

"I don't know how I'm going to go back to the apartment," she finally said, sitting down on a bench by the walkway.

"I've been cleaning it out for you. I hope you don't mind– Bobby's parents asked me to," I explained, watching her face and body carefully.

Her jaw tightened as she nodded. "Bobby's–?"

"Gone."

Tara nodded. "I keep having these dreams–and they're so real."

I pulled my lower lip into my mouth as I leaned forward. "Me too."

"What does he say to you?" she asked, and her eyes locked on mine.

My stomach rolled as I thought about the perverted, very Bobby-like comment about my shorts. I figured it was best to leave that out. "He only came once...told me everything would work itself out." I felt my jaw tightening and loosening in my subconscious unease. I looked down at my sneakers. "I wish he'd come back again..." I lowered my voice. "I know it's crazy, Tara, but it felt like it *really* was him."

She blinked hard, and I knew the memory of what we were talking about was gone. "I'm pissed at Bobby. I mean why the hell hasn't he come to see me in a week. It's bullshit."

I put my head in my hands, looking at Becky sitting in the chair across from us. She nodded for me to start again.

I turned to face her, taking her hands in mine. This time, I didn't look at her as I answered, "Tara, Bobby would if he could–but it's just not possible–"

"Why not?" she said, yanking her hands away.

I looked at mine, now empty and blew out a few short breaths as my head spun. "Because he's dead."

Tara made a whining sound, pulling her legs into her chest as she rocked. How many times would I have to say it? Dead. DEAD. *Dead.*

I couldn't do it. I stood, trembling as the tears raced down my face. Becky stood too, looking between her daughter and me. Both of us were sobbing, and she looked torn. I bit my lip before I wiped the tears away.

"River, please," Becky began, but I shook my head.

"I'm sorry I can't do this."

"No one should have to fight this alone," Becky replied, reaching for me.

I shook my head and then ran back to the door. When I reached it, I looked over my shoulder. Becky was sitting where I had been, and Tara was in her lap, like a small child, wrapped in her arms.

Tara wasn't alone.

My jaw clenched, but I sure as hell was.

Chapter 23

I looked up the length of the stairs and breathed in through my nose before tripping on the first step as I made my way up. *One step at a time* I repeated over and over again in my head. Eventually, I would make it up. I wasn't sure if my mind was referring to the stairs that I kept tripping on or my life. I knew I shouldn't have run out on Tara and Becky like that, but I couldn't take watching my best friend go through the phases of grief again and again when I could barely do it myself. Halfway up the stairs felt like it took an inordinate amount of time, and I found myself wondering why I didn't just take the elevator. I sighed as I pushed forward. *One step at a time.* When I reached the top of the steps Adam was leaning against the door frame, his foot perched at an angle with his hair tussled into a faux hawk. His eyes met mine, and they were clear– for once I saw Adam staring back at me, not the hollow shell he'd become. My stomach jumped as I blinked at him.

He stepped forward with a smile and pulled me into his arms. His words were muffled by my hair as he said, "I know I haven't been the best boyfriend lately..."

"I know I haven't been the best girlfriend either," I replied, and my voice cracked.

He held me out at arm's length, eyes searching my face as he cupped my cheek with his hand. "No...it's not the same, no matter what I say." His eyes shut as his chest rose with a shaky breath. "I feel like I've lost every part of me...there's nothing left but the parts I've given to you," he said, and his eyes opened. "I need you to hold those pieces together. Please don't forget who I was...otherwise there really will be nothing left."

I nodded but didn't speak. I wanted to tell him it was the same for me, but if neither of us could hold the other together, what was left?

The smile returned to his face, and he cracked open the apartment door. It was dark, and I narrowed my eyes at him as my heart began to race. His eyes teased me as he nodded over his shoulder for me to go in. I bit my lower lip before following him, and he slipped his hand into mine to lead me to the bedroom. When he opened the door, my mouth dropped. I stepped into our bedroom silhouetted in a beautiful glow from Mason jars scattered along the shelves, floor, and dressers.

"Fireflies are fairies that grant wishes," I said as my eyes raced across the room and my body began to tremble.

Adam wrapped his arms around me, steadying my body against his. "Glow sticks and glitter," he replied, his breath washing over the bare skin of my neck.

I squeezed my eyes shut, kissing his forearm before turning to face him. Adam's hands went to my face, and his thumbs collected my tears as I stared up at him with my pulse pounding in my ears. "You're still in there...why do you keep hiding it with booze?"

Adam's thumbs froze, and I watched as his eyes went from soft to hard. I had no clue what he was thinking, and as the seconds ticked by it became apparent he wasn't going to tell me.

"I'm trying, River. Can't you see that?" he finally replied, and his eyes slipped from mine as if he were ashamed.

I took a trembling breath. "I know."

His thumbs traced circles on my cheeks, but he didn't look back up at me.

"Say something," I said as I placed my hands on either side of his neck.

His gaze slowly rose to mine, and his eyes flashed over my face. "I know it's not the same, Riv–but *you're* not dealing with your pain either."

I couldn't breathe as I looked at his eyes, his words cutting into me. I pulled away to sit on the bed, and the glowing room spun with his honesty. He knew I was struggling, yet he kept drowning himself in booze and leaving me alone. I closed my eyes as I fought the wave of nausea that came over me. That wasn't it, and I knew it.

Adam's hands wrapped around mine, and I opened my eyes to see him kneeling in front of me. "I'm sorry, River. This was supposed to be romantic."

I licked my lips as I looked around the room–at the effort, he made to try to make things better.

"It's beautiful," I said as I let my forehead fall to his. "Thank you."

"I wish they could grant your wishes," he replied, and his hands ran up my arms, across my shoulders, up my neck and cupped my face, leaving a trail of goosebumps at the softness of his touch.

"Tonight they granted at least one wish." I lowered my head, so our lips drifted over one another. "I love you, Adam, no matter how lost you are...or I am...I will only ever love you."

Adam's body slide over mine, his fingers tangling with my own over my head as his lips drifted from my lips down my neck and to my collarbone. My body shivered as his fingertips moved over the sensitive skin of my arms and then up my sides as he slipped my shirt over my head. I wrapped my legs around his waist as I pulled his shirt over his head and then pushed our bodies together. Our lips locked again as his hands went up my spine to the back of my bra, and it slipped down my arms to the floor with the rest of our discarded clothing.

Talking didn't work for Adam and me, but this did.

Chapter 24

The next day kicked my ass. I couldn't concentrate. I screwed up during a meeting, and I felt like an idiot when Jesse corrected me. He assured me afterwards that it was fine, but I still couldn't shake the feeling of being incompetent. I parked my car, yanking out the key with a bit too much force and sent it skittering across the passenger seat as I stared at the empty spot where Adam's car should've been. I finally looked away when my eyes stung with dryness. I needed him home to talk to– to really talk to. It seemed when he was sober we never actually had a conversation. Instead, our emotional instability led us right into the physical. While it was a way for us to share our emotions, it just wasn't enough. I needed to voice what was going on aside from having to repeat *he's dead* over and over again. I swallowed as I grabbed my keys and finally got out of the car. I wondered where Adam was as I made my way up the steps with my wedge heels scuffing against the ground as I went. I opened the door slowly, stepping inside and sliding my shoes off before going to the refrigerator to grab a water. There, held up by a heart shaped magnet, was a note from Adam.

Riv,

Went to play a game of pool with the boys and do a little rehearsing. Don't wait up.

Love you,

Adam

I pulled the letter from the surface, sending the heart magnet across the room where it hit the side of the concrete counter and split in two before falling to the kitchen floor. Part of me wanted to go to every place with a pool table in the city to hunt him down, and the other part wanted to curl up in a ball in the bedroom and never come out. I would never find him, even if I tried.

I turned, looking around the empty apartment as I crumpled the letter in my hand before tossing it into the trash.

I had nothing better to do, so I grabbed the yellow pages from the door side table along with my keys and headed out to track my drunkard boyfriend down—to do what, I didn't know. I didn't know why the city still paid to send the yellow pages out, but I was grateful for it as I crossed off the seventh bar. I wasn't sure I would be able to sift through each of the locations on my cell phone. My stomach growled as I looked down at the next bar on my list and then at the clock on the dash.

6:oo PM

I already spent two hours looking for him. There were just too many bars in the city, but it was keeping me occupied as my emotions shifted somewhere between burning pain and fiery rage. I breathed in through my nose; maybe I was going about this all wrong.

Who were the guys in his band again?

There were only two, Mark and Joe.

I grit my teeth. Why hadn't I thought of them first?

Joe lived in an apartment, somewhere were a band rehearsing just wasn't possible. Mark, on the other hand, had a house outside the city in Ashland. It was a long shot. After all, I had no clue if Adam was *actually* doing what he said he was, but it was better than searching through the many bars left in Boston, even with a forty-five-minute drive. As I merged onto the Mass Pike, my mind went into cruise control. Since my days at Boston College, I drove this way too many times to count to go to my parent's house in Holliston before they moved to Connecticut. When I exited the highway, I lost myself in observing my surroundings. The houses were close together, but it wasn't nearly as bad as the city. I sighed as each house passed by, too expensive for me, even with a quarter million dollars sitting in my bank account. To get anywhere within my price range I would need to be at least an hour outside of Boston, and I wasn't willing to drive that far to work every day. I felt my palms beginning to sweat as the miles drifted by, and I headed deeper into suburbia. What if Adam wasn't there? I could keep driving, but where to? My parents house as a surprise visit?

I squeezed the steering wheel and my slippery palms squeaked against it. I didn't want to see Mom. My heart pounded in my chest in tune with my turning signal as I waited for the traffic to clear to turn onto Mark's road.

Shit. Shit. Shit.

Maybe I should've kept searching bars. My stomach growled again, suddenly reminding me I was hungry—at least if I was at a bar, I could eat. My heart stopped as I looked up at the grey-blue cape and the white GLI parked in front of it.

I swallowed as I slowed to a stop. I hadn't thought about what I was going to do if he was actually *here*. A lump rose in my throat as panic dotted the edge of my vision with sparks of stars.

What the fuck was I doing here?

Was I going to go in and yell at him? Tell him to grow up? Tell him I was lonely and he was selfish for leaving?

A car's lights flashed behind me, turning onto the road. I needed to either go home or park. Seconds. Seconds to make a decision. I turned my blinker on and pulled in. I wiped my upper lip as I put the car in park. I was pretty sure it wasn't *that* hot out, yet my insides were boiling. I stepped out of the car, and the cool breeze hit me, sinking into my skin and instantly cooling the sweat now accumulating on my forehead. I put one foot in front of the other, stopping at the front door, but my hand froze just as I was about to knock. I could hear laughter.

Adam's laughter.

He was happy, and I was here. I squeezed my eyes shut before shoving my hands in my pockets and turning. Who was I to take that away? Halfway down the walkway I heard the door open behind me, and I froze.

"River?" Mark asked, quiet enough only those outside could hear.

I blinked as I stared at my car, ten feet away. I had been so close to escaping my stupidity, but Mark must have heard the car pull in. I turned on my heel, my shoulders reaching for my ears as I gave a forced smile.

"Hi?" I managed to say, and my voice squeaked from nerves.

Mark looked over his shoulder before closing the door behind him and sitting on the step. He looked up at me and nodded for me to sit down. I made my way back up the steps and sat next to him.

"So," I began. "This is awkward."

Mark chuckled to himself as he rubbed his overgrown beard. "More for you than me."

"I'm not stalking Adam—"

"I wouldn't blame you if you were."

My head jerked as I looked over at him. "Do you know something I don't know?"

Mark shook his head. "Adam wouldn't cheat on you. I just don't blame you for wondering where he is."

"Is he drunk?" I asked, my voice barely a whisper.

Mark's lips protruded as he replied, "Nah, he's straight right now. He's not stupid enough to drink and drive, and he knows I won't drive his ass back to the city. I already drive there enough as it is for work. When we're in the city, I can't say the same. The kid never drank, until...well, you know."

"How much does he drink with you guys?" I asked as I stared down at my hands in my lap.

Mark coughed, and I saw him scratch his chin from the corner of my eyes. "More than he used to."

I swallowed, stretching my legs out and looking at the holes in my skinny jeans as my stomach rode the wave of his lack of information. It was a vague answer that couldn't be veiled by his stiffened posture beside me.

"Oh," I said, nodding. "Same at home."

"So, how are you doing?" Mark asked, tilting his head at me with a soft smile. "Because I can imagine this shit is just eating you up alive...especially if you drove all the way here."

"I don't know," I replied, tipping back and looking at the stars beginning to show in the darkening sky. It was the first time someone came out and actually asked how *I* was doing. The words came out in a slow, honest string. "Sometimes I'm just barely functioning...other times I'm just functioning on pain or anger."

"Which one is tonight?"

"Started with pain, melted to anger and now...I'm right back to barely functioning," I replied, propping my chin on my shoulder as I looked over at him. "You remember Tara?"

Mark's brown eyes twinkled, and I watched as his pupils dilated. "Kind of hard to forget. Feisty and–" His voice drifted as he looked over at me raising an eyebrow. He coughed. "Uh...very attractive."

"Yeah...well, she's coming out of her amnesia state–and the doctors think it's time to start telling her about Bobby. It's the only way she's going to get better," I replied, chewing the inside of my lip as I looked down at my hands. "It's killing me. I tried really hard to stay with her–to keep telling her. I just couldn't." I shook my head as my chest rose. "I shouldn't be loading this off on you."

Mark gave me a sad smile. "It's fine. I get it. I've been watching Adam fight this internally the whole time."

"He doesn't talk about it?"

Mark looked ahead. "No, but I can tell when he's thinking about it. Then I know he's not too far away from a bottle."

I knew exactly what Mark was talking about. I saw that look in his eyes as I left the apartment this morning, and a part of me was shocked he wasn't somewhere drunk like I thought he would be. The other part of me wondered why he came here instead of talking to me. But then again, I didn't understand much of what Adam was doing anymore.

"Why does he drink?" I asked. Maybe a guy would understand when I couldn't.

Mark rubbed the back of his neck. "I suppose it numbs him."

I pulled my knees to my chest. "I don't have to drink to feel numb. I just look at him."

"Don't give up on him, River. Do what you have to," his eyes locked on mine, and my breathing stopped; "but whatever happens; don't *really* give up on him."

"Do you think there's anything that would snap him back?" I asked, looking over my shoulder at him.

He cringed, his eyes looking into the distance before they locked on mine. "I'm sure there's at least one thing."

I blinked at him as my stomach rolled. A part of me knew what he was inferring, but I shut it off as soon as the thought began to spool inside my brain.

"Right," I replied.

Mark stood, holding out his hand. "It's getting chilly out here. Why don't you come in?"

"That's fine; I'll just head back," I said as I let him help me up.

My stomach growled.

Mark cocked his head at me as he pushed, "I was just about to order us a few pizzas. I can get you a salad?"

I shook my head. "Pizza sounds perfect."

"So you do eat!" Mark replied, eyebrows rising to his forehead as he opened the door and I followed him in. "Look who I found lurking in my driveway!"

Adam's eyes rose from the pool table where he was leaning over and eyeing the corner pocket. His arm jerked involuntarily and sent the cue ball bouncing off the eight ball. In turn, it skittered across the green before bouncing back off the edge of the table and away from the pocket.

"River," Adam said.

"Hey, I was bored, and..." I sucked in a breath of air, letting it stale in my lungs before I let it out with a weak laugh; "ended up here."

He came around the table, and I stood frozen as I waited for him to whisper something harshly at me or ask me into the other room, but instead he pulled me into his arms and kissed my hair.

"I would've waited up if I'd known you'd want to come," he said.

I squeezed my eyes shut as I hugged him, all of the numb parts of me melting into warm bliss.

"Sorry," I whispered into his shoulder.

"Well, you're here now." My stomach growled, and he smirked down at me. "And Mark was supposed to be ordering pizza."

"Should probably get some hot wings, too," Joe said as Mark walked by rolling his eyes and punched a number into his phone.

"And bread sticks!" Adam called to his back.

"You paying?" Mark asked as he turned on his heel to stare at Adam.

"Why the hell not?" Adam replied with a smirk.

The guys laughed, and I found myself laughing too. We spent the rest of the night laughing just like that, and a part of me felt like maybe things could work themselves out if only Adam could find the will to be like this more of the time. When we finally got home it was past 11:00 PM, and I didn't know how I typically stayed awake most of the night. I was exhausted.

"You going to make it?" Adam asked as he dropped his keys on the side table and turned to lock the door.

I shook my head as my shoulders slumped and I dragged my feet as I walked across the living room to the bedroom.

"You're normally still up at this time," Adam said as I stripped down and pulled on a baggy t-shirt before crawling into bed. He smirked as he watched me." Not even going to brush your teeth?"

I shook my head, groaning as I pulled the sheets up to my chin and sighed.

Adam's nose wrinkled as he stripped down to his boxers

and then pointed at me as I looked at him with one eye open. "I'm not kissing you in the morning."

I huffed, closing my other eye as he climbed into bed beside me.

"Not even going to brush your teeth?" I mumbled as he wrapped his arm around me.

His laughter sent his warm breath washing over my skin, and my chest rose with a happy sigh.

"So," Adam whispered into my ear; "what did you and Mark talk about outside?"

My eyes shot open, far less asleep than a moment ago and I felt Adam's breathing stop as he waited for my answer.

"Nothing," I replied, and my throat felt raw with the lie.

"Nothing?" he repeated, his lips hovering over my bare arm.

I shook my head, squeezing my eyes shut. "He just wanted to know how Tara was doing."

"Ah, yes. He's always had a thing for her," Adam said as he kissed my shoulder.

"I could tell," I replied, trying to ignore the stabbing in my chest that said she *has a boyfriend*, because she didn't.

"Thank you," Adam's soft whisper broke my train of thought, and I found myself turning into his arms to face him.

"For what?" I asked, my eyes racing over his face.

His hand reached up, and his fingers traced the shape of my chin as he looked at me. "For coming and checking on me."

I looked down at our chests rising into one another with

each breath we took. "I'm sorry I felt the need to find you. I know it was craz—"

His thumb stopped me from continuing as it pressed into my lips, and he tilted my chin back up to look at him. "I know I'm pretty fucked up, Riv. You don't need to lie. You thought I was getting cocked."

I clenched my jaw and squeezed my eyes shut. "I'm sorry."

"River," his voice was soft, and I slowly opened my eyes to see his face. His brown eyes reflected the sadness in his tone. "You don't have to be sorry for my actions. *I'm* the one doing them."

"The past few days have been so nice–you staying up with me," I said, biting my lip. "When you weren't home...I figured you slipped back into the drinking. I'm just scared."

He shook his head, his eyes racing back and forth over mine. "Of what?"

My chest heaved as I tried to bring the words to my lips.

Of what Mark insinuated–that you're drinking more than I know...that I'll lose you. That I've lost myself.

Finally, I shook my head, forcing a smile to my lips. "Nothing."

Adam's eyes closed as he leaned forward and pressed his lips to my forehead, his thumbs tracing circles on my cheek. "I love you, River."

I pressed my lips together as I felt the tears forming in my eyes. My chest tightened as his lips drifted down to mine, brushing against them as my hands tangled in his hair. His lips parted mine, and his tongue danced over my mouth in a way that made me fully awake again. He pulled away and brushed my hair out of my face as he gave me a sad smile.

"We should get some sleep," he said, and I shook my head, moving up to kiss him.

Adam put a finger to my lips. "You don't sleep enough as it is."

I could feel my eyes getting heavy again, and I sighed as he moved so I could put my head on his chest. I didn't get a chance to reply before the corners of sleep sunk in.

Chapter 25

I started my day on a high from the night before– from finding Adam not loaded when I thought he would be and from real laughter I missed so much. Those moments gave me some level of hope, but in a matter of seconds, that hope was leveled. The photo shoot planned for the next day brought me right past Adam's work, so I left early to grab us both Starbucks. When I arrived at the school the kids were out for recess, but his car was nowhere to be seen, and neither was he. I got out of the car and flagged down the girl standing outside with the kids.

"River?" she said, giving me a smile as she cocked her head. "I'm Adam's substitute, Regina. I recognize you from the pictures on his desk."

I swallowed before forcing a smile on my lips. "I didn't realize Adam needed a substitute."

She bit her lower lip before her shoulders rose up. "He's been sick on a pretty regular basis, so I've been coming up once or twice a week. It's a shame the doctors can't figure out what's wrong, you know? It must be so stressful for you two. Especially with everything you've already been through this year."

I opened and closed my mouth as I searched for the words, but I didn't know how to respond to something she obviously thought I knew was going on. Instead, I ended up nodding before realizing it made no sense I was here if Adam wasn't. Especially seeing I should know he wasn't.

Somehow I made my brain work.

"Yeah, it's been a rough year. Adam feels bad that you've been covering so much, so he asked me to get you Starbucks since this was on my way to a work meeting. I hope you like flat white lattes?"

Regina's eyes widened. "That is so sweet of you. Right around now is the time when I could use one of those. These kids will run you ragged!"

"Great," I said giving her a huge, fake smile. "I'll just get it."

I walked back to the car, and with each step, the pressure in my head grew. Adam was out of work at least once or twice a week? Doing what?

My body froze as I reached the car. I knew exactly what. I managed to get away from Regina without much more small talk, but by the time I got to the photo shoot my headache was making me nauseous. I managed to muddle my way through the next two hours and then texted Jesse I was going home.

I wanted to see if Adam was home.

He was.

I slipped my shoes off and tossed my keys into the bowl on the table by the door. The metal clinked against the bowl, only a faint sound against the TV show Adam was watching.

"Hey, what are you doing home so early?" he asked, looking around the couch as I walked wordlessly passed him into the bedroom.

I ignored him as I tried to decide whether or not accusing him of skipping out on work was worth it, or if it would make it worse. I slipped my blouse off before pulling on a baggy sweatshirt and yoga pants and climbed out the window onto the balcony. I stood there watching the sunset as my mind raced. I didn't dare go back inside. I couldn't face Adam when I was so pissed at him.

"Hey," Adam said, sticking his head out the window.

I kept my eyes straight ahead and didn't respond. I had nothing nice to say.

"Not talking to me anymore?" he asked.

I shook my head, gritting my teeth before replying with a half truth, "I drove passed the school today."

"Yeah?" he asked, his voice not changing in pitch like I thought it would.

Had he become *that* good at lying?

"So?" I asked, giving him a chance to tell the truth.

"So?" he repeated as he climbed through the window and came to lean against the rails next to me. His arm muscles bunched beneath the sleeves of his t-shirt.

"Where were you?" I asked, and my voice cracked.

"Out."

"Out?"

He turned, leaning backward, and his hands clasped

over his chest. "Yeah. I had to go out and purchase some instruments for the kids. We received a grant, so I went out to pick some stuff up."

Lie. It was all a lie, and a part of me knew I shouldn't do what I was about to do, but I had to know. I moved to the front of him and leaned in, kissing his liquor-tainted lips. Proof.

I buried my head in his shoulder as I bit my lip to hold back the tears.

"Are you feeling okay?" he asked as he rubbed his hands over my back.

"Migraine," I whispered, and I hoped Adam took the pained shaking of my voice to be for that reason.

He held me out at arm's length, red eyes searching my face. "Why don't you lay down? I'll get you an ice pack and order us some Chinese."

I nodded and followed him inside. I vaguely remembered him handing me the ice pack, but I didn't wake up until the next morning. I rolled over to find the space in the bed next to me was empty and cold. There was another letter underneath the now broken heart magnet on the fridge. Adam hadn't wanted to wake me once I fell asleep and he was going to be out the rest of the day. My pork fried rice and chicken fingers were in the fridge if I wanted them for lunch. I grabbed a fork and ate them cold for breakfast. I wouldn't enjoy their taste anymore if they were warm. I glanced around the empty apartment, swallowing the last of the day old Chinese food. I'd normally just take a shower and hit the road to see Dad, but today Mom had him otherwise occupied. I didn't trust myself alone with my thoughts so instead I decided to visit Tara a day early. Maybe I could talk to her about Adam, if only in a roundabout way.

"On a Saturday?" Tara asked when I came into the room.

"Yeah, my mom has my dad opening the pool up this weekend," I explained as I held out a Starbucks cup to her.

"Spoiling me?" she asked, taking it with a smile. She held it up to her face with both hands, and her eyes rolled back as she took a deep sip.

I smirked as she opened her eyes. "Not fully. It's decaf." Her jaw dropped as I sat down on the bed next to a pile of neatly folded clothes. "Can't tell, huh?"

She narrowed her eyes and took another sip before shrugging and placing it on the window sill next to the dried rose, now more beige than white. She moved to the dresser and continued putting clothes next to me.

"What's going on?" I asked as I watched her pull luggage out from under the bed.

Tara smiled as she looked up at me. "I get to go home tomorrow– well, not home, home, but to my parent's house. Maybe I can go swimming at your parent's house!"

I swallowed, nodding and looking down at the top of my coffee cup as I wondered if she remembered the fight with Mom about my tattoo.

"You're still not talking to her then?" Tara asked as she began putting the clothes into the luggage. When I didn't answer she came to sit in the now cleared spot and put her hands over mine, looking through her long lashes in expectation of my response.

I blinked hard. "No."

"It's been a long time, River. You should talk to her. You never know..." her eyes faded as she chewed on the inside of her lip. They came back to, and she replied in a firm tone, "You never know when something bad is going to happen." My mouth dropped, and she squeezed my hands. "Bobby would've wanted us to pick ourselves up and go on with life. Don't you think so?"

She knew. Why hadn't Becky warned me? She wasn't here right now; that was why–but why hadn't she called? I looked down at my cell phone.

MISSED CALL: Becky.

I rubbed my forehead with the palm of my hand. "It's not that easy."

"I know it's not easy, Riv. How can it be? I finally realized the nightmares I was having weren't nightmares, but memories," she said, moving her hands into a hard knot on her lap as she stared at them. "Once we hit that patch of ice and the truck started spinning..." her voice broke, and she squeezed her eyes shut; "The last thing I remember is the fear in his eyes and his lips whispering he loved me. That was it. I didn't even get a chance to respond."

I licked my lips as air rattled in my lungs. "I'm sure he knew how you felt."

Her head rocked back as she breathed in through her nose, and then her eyes opened slowly. "So it's hard. I know–but we have to move on from all the shit that's happened."

"This is my way of moving on," I replied, and she narrowed her eyes at me.

"Running away from the situation?" she asked.

My cheeks burned as I stared at her, my mouth going dry. "Some things can't be fixed, and sometimes they aren't meant to be. This was a long time coming with my mom. I'm not going back to dealing with being abused on a regular basis."

Tara's head jerked back at my response, and she stood shaking her head. "That's not what I meant, but if something were to happen tomorrow to either of you, would you be okay? Would you regret any of it?"

I locked eyes with her as she turned to face me. "No. I can't control her actions."

"You can control yours, though—"

"But I can't be the only one controlling things," I looked down at my hands as I shook my head. Anger heated my body as I looked up at her and continued. "I'm constantly thinking of everyone else. I do it every day with Adam — even with you. It's tiring. It's eating me up alive. I'm barely living because I'm always so worried about everyone else."

Tara's eyes ran over my face as her voice lowered. "I get why you're worried about me...but Adam seems better."

"He's not, Tara. He blames himself for Bobby's death. But really, Tara– it's because of me. Everything's because of me. I'm the reason that they were at war with each other–with their parents," I replied, the agonizing words I kept in so long rushing out in a pained whisper as I stood and went to the door. "And I'm not strong enough to keep Adam from drinking."

"River– you can't blame yourself for that," Tara said to my back.

I stopped, my eyelashes weighted down with water before I turned back to face her. "Why am I not enough for him to stop?"

Tara stepped forward and pulled me into her thin arms. "You're the only one who *can* make him stop."

"How?" I asked as I wrapped my arms around her, giving into the warmth of her arms.

"I don't know."

The problem was, I did, and I knew I couldn't tell her.

Chapter 26

When I went to bed that night, Adam still wasn't home, and when I woke up the next morning and asked if he wanted to go grocery shopping with me, he shook his head and continued drinking his coffee. When I got home, he was gone. I didn't bother texting him to ask where he was. I didn't want to know. The hope from Thursday was completely gone, and I replaced it with denial or just ignorance to the truth. Adam was just out with the boys or something. He'd gotten bored and decided to go out. Maybe he was at the gym. There could be any number of good reasons why he wasn't home on a Sunday afternoon.

I sought a distraction from my mind and found myself packing up the final remnants of Bobby's life up. I looked at the boxes that surrounded me; each neatly labeled with the names of who they needed to go to. I focused on Tara's stuff, knowing she would probably want it now that she was going to be going home–well, to her parent's house. I wondered if she wanted to move back here, but as I looked around the apartment, I realized it was just too big for one person. Bobby's parents were continuing to pay the rent until I was done boxing everything up, and Alec told me to take my time. I sank into the couch, melting into the leather, warmed from the breeze coming through the open kitchen window. It was an unseasonably hot day for May, exactly the way Bobby would like it to be for his birthday. I laid back on the couch, looking up at the ceiling as I fought the wave of tears.

The truth was after Tara's stuff was done, there was nothing left. All that remained where the labeled boxes and the furniture, ready to be divided up to who needed to take them. I closed my eyes as I thought of what would come next. Each piece would be removed from the apartment until it was bare, and then someone else would move in.

The tears came thick as the memories of the apartment and our lives in it rushed forward. It was just an apartment, but it was being vacated too soon.

"River..." the voice knocked into me, causing me to suck in a deep breath. Bobby repeated my name, causing my heart to patter. "River..." I sat up, and there he was, sitting with one arm thrown over the top of the couch and his ankle propped against his knee. "Hey, sleepy head. You always fell asleep so easily on this couch."

I swallowed as I leaned forward, moving a blond curl out of his blue eyes and touching the warmth of his cheek. He closed his eyes, inhaling as my hand dropped to his still chest. There was no heartbeat beneath my hands.

Being dead will do that to you.

Bobby shook his head, putting his hand over mine and moving it over my heart. "Part of my heart is here," he whispered as if he could read my thoughts. "Another is in

Adam's chest, and yet more in Tara's. As long as those hearts beat, mine is too."

"Why haven't you come back until now?" I asked as I tangled my fingers into his.

His brows pulled in as he cocked his head at me. "I was trying to help Tara...but then I realized it was keeping her from remembering. She..." he shook his head. "She had this me confused for the living version. I needed to say goodbye for her to remember fully."

"Now you're here to help me?" I asked, and he chuckled.

"Riv, you're too stubborn for me to help you," he said.

"Then try to help Adam– go to him–"

Bobby cut me off with a shake of his head, his lips pulling into his mouth. "I can't help him when he's lost in that fog. He's unreachable."

"He's unreachable for me too. What if the only thing to pull him out is if *I'm* gone. This is all my fault–"

"Don't blame yourself, River," he said as he leaned his forehead to mine. "The only wars we fight are the ones *we* choose. Adam's fought wars with me, with our parents...and now he's fighting one with himself. You were always there for us, but sometimes that's not what *we* needed. Sometimes that's not what *you* needed."

Bobby's eyes drifted to our hands as a sad smile pulled at the edge of his lips. It was the same look Mark had.

"Are you saying–?" I asked as he began to waver in and out. "Wait — I don't understand, Bobby!"

He leaned forward, his lips kissing my cheek and spreading tingles through my body. "Do what you know will pull him out, just know this battle is just beginning, and you'll have to fight, too."

Chapter 27

Go to sleep alone.

Wake up alone.

It was starting to become a pattern, and I had nothing better to do than to work away my thoughts. Even though sometimes at work I couldn't arrange my thoughts coherently because my brain was so fogged with worry. Being alone so much also meant I had no idea where Adam was– if he was working or when he was working, and I didn't have the strength to go passed the school and see. The photo shoot I did in the morning should've brought me right passed there, but instead, I took the long way around– to the tune of twenty extra minutes just to avoid knowing.

Not knowing was so much better. Back at work, I flicked through the photographs, happy my mental state wasn't showing through in my job– if anything I'd gotten better. I smiled at that thought. I was awful at relationships, but I knew how to do branding. Probably because when I avoided relationships I was working. I felt Jesse's presence behind me before he announced he was there.

"Hey you," Jesse greeted me from my door.

I looked over my shoulder and smiled at him. "Hey, come on in."

"So how was Tara?" Jesse asked as he sat down in front of me, putting his ankle on top of his knee and tapping his leg with his fingers as he waited for my answer.

I looked down at the notes in front of me, narrowing my eyes at them as the words presented themselves in incoherent swirls of ink across the page. Jesse coughed, and my head shot up.

"Good–Good, better than most of us would be after realizing someone you loved died months ago," I replied. "She's determined to move on."

Jesse's hands smoothed the slacks beneath them as he nodded, keeping his eyes on me. "Does that upset you?"

I ran my hands over the bare skin of my collarbone as my body became too hot for the light sweater I was wearing. "It's good for her."

"She has something to distract her. I'm sure she misses him just as much as Adam and you," Jesse replied, cocking his head at me. "Speaking of distractions– I have a proposition for you."

I raised an eyebrow at him, glad for a change in subject. "The last time you said that I ended up with a credit card and a new job title," I said with a smile. "Keep talking."

"You're a stellar branding expert...*and* an amazing photographer. The quality we get from you is fabulous."

"Thank you?" I replied, questioning the silent *but* at the end of the sentence.

"So I have a friend getting married...and they need a photographer. I thought you might be interested?"

I stared at him without blinking for a moment before I realized my mouth was hanging open. "Really? I mean, I have no experience with like live action shots."

Jesse rubbed his chin as he looked at me. "I've seen your style of shooting — you try to make it live action. I think you'll be just fine. So are you in?"

My eyes fell back down to the pad of paper, and I found myself rubbing my temples. A wedding wasn't something I ever thought about doing, and Adam and I didn't need any extra money. My chest tightened as I thought about Adam. It was something I should discuss with him, but what would it matter anyway? It would probably be on a Saturday when he was busy getting wasted with his friends, or playing music.

I inhaled, looking up at Jesse and smiled. "Yeah, that would be amazing. When is it?"

Jesse scratched his sideburns, pulling his lips into his mouth before replying, "Three Saturdays from now."

My eyes widened. "A little last minute?"

"Some people just get ideas into their heads and run with it," he said as he leaned forward and reached for my pad of paper. "May I?"

I pushed it in his direction with a pen. He wrote down a name and a number.

"Give Anna a call. You guys can discuss details."

I nodded as he handed the paper back. "Aren't you worried?"

Jesse cocked his head at me. "That you'll love wedding photography so much you'll leave me?"

It might have been written all over my face, and I felt my cheeks burn as he laughed. "Oh, I have ulterior motives."

With that he stood and left the room, leaving me staring at the chair swaying slowly from the absence of his presence. I looked down at the number before picking up my phone and dialing.

"Hello," the unfamiliar feminine voice at the other end answered.

"Hi, Anna?"

"This is she."

"My name is River; Jesse gave me your number. He said you were looking for a photographer for your wedding?"

"Oh my gosh! Thank goodness— then you're interested?" the woman's voice was high pitched in her excitement, and for a moment, I was caught off guard by the warm feeling building in my stomach. I almost forgot what it felt like.

"Yes, I'd love the opportunity."

"You're a God send, can you meet for coffee around two?"

We made arrangements, and I hung up the phone wondering what the hell I was doing. I looked across the room at the empty vase that used to contain flowers from months before. That feeling in my belly returned, and I realized I was filling that void with work...and more work.

Maybe this kind of photography wouldn't feel like work?

Maybe I could find the part of me I'd lost in it– if only I could figure out exactly what that piece was.

Chapter 28

I tried not to act shocked when I got home that night, and Adam was already cooking dinner. He even stayed up to watch television with me after. I stared up at him as we lay on the couch, and my chest tightened. I knew I should tell him about the wedding in just a few weeks, but I wasn't sure how he was going to react to it. I snuggled tighter into him, fighting the nagging feeling in my stomach. He would be okay with it–why wouldn't he? I didn't question when his music gigs were. Plus, it was an extra $2,000 in our pocket. My eyes moved to the locked drawer in the door side table. There was another $250,000 sitting in there with his name on it. I rolled over, turning my eyes to the Boston Red Sox game. I tried to concentrate on what was going on, but baseball never really seemed to have anything going on. It was more like a requirement to watch it and know what happened when you lived in Boston.

Tell him. The thought fluttered in my mind before my eyes closed.

I fell asleep that night, which was an excuse for not having mentioned it–but the following day I didn't either. I just couldn't bring myself to do it when Adam was acting normally– not that I could've if he weren't. Saturday came, and for once Adam let me know what he was doing. Fade Burn was playing at a local spot downtown, and Adam wanted me to go.

Two weeks, River. I forced a smile on my face as I handed Adam his bass guitar, and he slid it across the back seat.

I took a deep breath and closed my eyes as I buckled my seat belt. "So I've been meaning to tell you something."

"Oh, yeah?" Adam asked, putting the car into gear and backing up. "And what's that?"

I wove my fingers together and moved them back and forth. "Jesse referred me to one of his friends who's having a wedding..."

"To do what?"

"Do their photographs."

I watched Adam out of the corner of my eyes. His face paled, and his eyes set hard on the road.

"Adam?"

"And you said you would?" he asked, and his dark tone slammed into me.

My chest tightened. "Yes."

He nodded as he looked in his rear view mirror and then back at the road in front of him. We sat in silence for a moment before he finally spoke, "So, any reason you didn't ask me about it?"

I sunk in the seat, crossing my arms over my stomach. "I didn't realize I needed to get your permission?"

"You don't need my permission," Adam replied. "It just

would've been nice if you'd at least asked what I thought about the whole thing."

I put my hands up, my palms facing the ceiling as my chin stuck out. "Extra money?"

"Are we hurting for money and I don't know about it?" Adam asked, and the leather steering wheel squeaked as his hands grasped it.

I sunk deeper into the seat, swallowing the lump forming in my throat as I wished I could vanish into the black leather. "No."

"Then why do you need to work *more* than you already do? Fifty hours a week isn't enough? Let's throw wedding photography on top of it!"

"Adam," I began.

He cut me off, shaking his head. "Whatever."

I looked up at the ceiling before replying. "You're not usually home, and this is the first time you've asked me to one of your gigs."

I left out the fact I didn't judge him for not asking me before he went to one of his shows.

He glanced over at me, shaking his head. "I've always done the music gigs. That's nothing new; this is. I thought we were in this together. You already work too much."

I bit back the nasty words that said *at least I work* and exhaled slowly before answering, "I'm sorry — I was just excited when Jesse brought it up."

Adam heaved a sigh, and his hand went to my thigh. "Is it really important to you?"

I sat up at little bit, weaving my fingers into his as he

looked at me from the corner of his eyes. His lips were still drawn down, but his gaze searched mine as I nodded.

"Okay, then I'm sorry I reacted like that. It just seems like we're not on the same page all the time anymore–" my mouth opened, and he shook his head, dropping my hand to shift the car. "I'm not saying it's because of you, Riv. Just both of us. I'm glad you're with me tonight."

"I'm happy you invited me," I replied as my mind drifted to tomorrow and my regular trip to see Tara. Except this time she would be at home — *home*; not the apartment, but with her parents until she fully recovered. I wanted to ask Adam to come, but the idea made my temples pound.

My face must have shown my thoughts because Adam cocked his head at me. "You nervous about the wedding?"

My mind jolted as my body tensed. I could easily lie. It would make sense to be nervous about the wedding. I shook my head.

"Tomorrow is my day to visit Tara..." I began, watching as he shifted the car again, merging onto the highway. My eyes moved to the speedometer. He was hammering the car. "She's home now–well, at her parent's house."

The car's speedometer dipped down to a reasonable speed, and I felt the breath I didn't know I was holding release from my chest. He knew how to handle the car, but this highway was– I stopped the thought.

"Ah," Adam said but didn't offer anything else.

Ask him. He said you hadn't been on the same page.

I ran my fingers over the seams of the seat, sticking my

tongue into my cheek before looking up at him. "Would you come...with me?"

I watched his thumb drum against the steering wheel while the other down shifted as we exited the highway. The silence was drowned out by the sound of the tail pipe as the car moved through its gears. Adam merged onto the road and pain flitted through my chest as I stared straight ahead at the lights of the city.

"Sure," he replied.

My head shot up, turning to look at him. "Sure?"

He nodded, giving me a weak smile. "Sure."

Chapter 29

I felt the smile on my face as I woke wrapped in Adam's arms. I leaned up kissing his lips and for once he didn't taste like liquor. I slipped out of bed and walked out into the living room where my eyes moved to the door. The warmth of happiness was replaced with a cool recognition that I should bring Tara her boxes. I looked over my shoulder where Adam was still sleeping before heading across the way and pushing the door open. The boxes were stacked neatly, and although I was there for Tara's stuff, I headed towards my boxes. I opened the top one and pulled out the jersey, holding it to my chest as I breathed in Bobby's scent.

A cough at the door made my eyes shoot open as I jumped back, stuffing the jersey back in the box.

"Hey," I said, the word sounding strangled as I stared at Adam.

His fists were in tight balls as he stared at the jersey half poking out of the box. "Is this what you've been doing?"

I swallowed the lump in my throat. "Your dad asked me to."

"And you couldn't tell me?" he asked, and his eyes finally met mine. Their coldness sunk into me, making my chest tighten. His jaw clenched as he stood, nostrils flaring as he waited for my explanation.

"I'm sorry," I replied as I stepped forward. "I didn't think you were ready to pack everything up, so I did it on my own."

He stepped back from me shaking his head. "What else have you been lying about?"

My jaw dropped as I pulled my arms across my chest. "Nothing. I'm not lying to you–"

"Fine," he said, putting his hands up. "Then what else have you been *hiding* from me?"

I crossed my arms as I looked at his chest rising and falling in anger. Finally, I spoke, "I could ask you the same thing."

He scoffed, shaking his head as he rubbed the back of his neck. He held a finger up at me to make his point. "One bottle — one — in a guitar case doesn't mean *anything*, River."

Lies. More lies. I stepped towards him, and he ran his tongue over his teeth. I needed to talk to him. I needed to understand, and most of all I needed an explanation for everything I was seeing.

"One bottle, dozens of receipts, not being at your job–" My voice cracked just as Adam cut me off.

"I told you I was out buying supplies."

My chin began to tremble as I shook my head. I wanted the truth, but I was hardly able to tell him the truth of how I knew there were more lies between us than ever before.

"You tasted like alcohol when I kissed you that day," I said, and Adam's jaw tightened before he threw his hands up and turned out the door. I followed him, calling his name. "Adam!"

He kept heading towards the stairs as he held him his middle finger at me. The tears prickled at my eyes as he grabbed his keys out of his jeans. He never so much as swore at me, let alone do that.

"Adam, please!"

He cut me off with a shake of his head and continued down the stairs. I closed my eyes as I tilted my head back, letting them open to stare at the ceiling. Whiplash–that was what I had from Adam. One second he was fine, and the next second he was snapping. Something about the jersey set him off, and I found myself staring at it wondering what the hell that could be. I went back into the room and folded it before closing its box and turning to the ones for Tara. I chose the one with her makeup and other basics before grabbing a bag of clothing and heading back to the apartment. I showered and then sat waiting on the couch for Adam to return. My phone vibrated against the table, and I grabbed it as my heart hammered in my chest.

TEXT FROM Tara.

What happened with Adam? He just let me know he isn't coming.

I fought the urge to reply *I wish I knew*, and instead stood and grabbed my keys. The phone trembled in my hand as I stared down it when I got in the car. I wanted to type *fuck you* to Adam. To tell him I was done. I closed my eyes as the angry tears moved into my mouth.

My hands went into my hair.

I was so close to being done, and no matter how hard I tried to forget that thought as I drove to Tara's parents' I couldn't. By the time I got there, all my makeup was on the sleeve of my sweatshirt. I pulled it over my head and used it to sharpen the lines of my dripping mascara before getting out of the car and taking a deep breath. I grabbed the box and bag from the back seat before going to the front door.

"Hey!" Tara said as she let me in, her voice high and airy in its happiness. "You brought me stuff!"

I nodded as I tried to plaster a smile on my face. I didn't want her to know how close I was to cracking. I swallowed the rush of emotions and replied, "Yeah, some of your favorite outfits and makeup–not that any of your clothes will fit anymore."

Tara raised an eyebrow as I came into the house, the smell of fresh baked cookies hitting my nose and making my mouth water. "I have no plans on staying a bag of bones. I'm already working on fattening myself up. I need some curves back."

She was Tara again– at ease and beautiful in her bubbly personality. Her presence helped to force back my anger as I placed her box and clothes down where she signaled for me to.

"Cookies?" I asked. Her eyes narrowed, and I wondered how poorly I was hiding my feelings.

Her eyebrows wiggled as she put her arm into mine and guided me to the kitchen. "You look like you could use a sweet treat."

I didn't reply. Instead, I took a cookie off of the steaming plate and shoved it in my mouth. If we were eating, I wouldn't have to explain my dysfunctional boyfriend.

"So what happened with Adam?" Tara asked, sitting down on the other chair at the island and grabbing a cookie for herself.

"Milk?" I asked, and she pursed her lips at me. I looked down at my cookie as if it was the most exciting thing in the world. She grabbed two glasses from the cabinets before turning and facing me.

"You're not going to get away with changing the subject," she said before she turned to the fridge and got the milk.

"What was that? The refrigerator muffled you," I asked as I finished my first cookie and dove in for another.

She pushed the cup of milk towards me and crossed her arms. "Adam?"

I swallowed the remainder of the cookie and then took a few gulps of the milk.

Tara cocked her head at me. "River?"

I wiped my lip before replying, "He was just tired from the show last night."

"Then why did it take so long for you to come to that conclusion?" Tara asked, sitting back down next to me and putting her head in her hand as she smirked at me.

I could lie, or wiggle around the truth. I was obviously as good at that as Adam was. I closed my eyes, shaking my head before exhaling and looking up at her. "He didn't even tell me he wasn't coming."

Her lips drifted down at the corners, and she played with

the napkin in front of her. "That's weird, did you wake up and he wasn't there?"

"No–I went over to get your boxes, and I guess Adam followed me...I was looking through one of the boxes, and he freaked out. Maybe he was pissed I didn't tell him I was packing everything up. It just didn't seem like the right time to tell him."

And then he flicked me off. I decided leaving that part out was best. She didn't need to know what that made me think about because I knew she would ask and then I *would* lie. I didn't need another lie to eat me up alive.

"What else haven't you been telling him?" she asked, and I found myself blinking at her.

"What do you mean?" I asked, and my mouth felt parched even though I chugged my glass of milk.

Was she on his side?

She shrugged, looking at me from the corner of her eyes. "It just seems like you guys aren't communicating that well."

"You don't know the half of it," I replied, shaking my head as I tipped my head back to look at the ceiling.

"So tell me," she said, and her voice was flat as if she was already defensive.

I dropped my head back down and locked eyes with her. "He hasn't been going to work, Tara– he's drunk every night. I *wish* I could communicate with him, but he won't listen to anything I have to say."

"About his drinking."

My jaw dropped open as I shook my head."About anything! How can someone listen when they're bombed all the time?" I asked, and I felt my chest heaving as my hands tightened into fists at my side.

Was he talking to her and not me?

"Maybe you should listen to *him*," she said, and she quirked an eyebrow, her expression saying she didn't think I listened to anyone.

"I would if he would talk to me," I said, and my chin trembled as I looked back to my best friend, suddenly turned against me.

Her eyes dropped, and she traced the rim of her glass before replying, "You work a lot, Riv. You always have."

"Seriously?" I asked as I stood. Unreasonable River returned, and as much as I wanted to stay there with my friend, I couldn't take my finger flipping boyfriend and this— as if *I* truly was the cause of all of this. My chest ached as the thought crossed my mind and then the unreasonable words came flowing from my mouth in my shaking voice. "What bullshit is he feeding you? That's he's alright, and he's not *really* drinking that much?" Her face turned red. "I know, Tara. I *live* every day worrying about him. I can count on my hands how many times he's been sober or home in the last three months. I'm not enough to pull him out of this."

"What does that mean?"

I stared at her, and the trembling shifted from my chin to my whole body.

The battle is just beginning.

Bobby hadn't warned me I'd be completely alone. I didn't answer Tara. Instead, I turned on my heel and headed towards the door.

"Where are you going?" Tara asked as I yanked the front door open.

I stopped, looking over my shoulder at her. "Somewhere I don't have to think about this mess anymore."

Her eyes mirrored Adam's this morning as she asked, "Work?"

I closed my eyes, shaking my head. *I wish.* I closed the door behind me without answering. I found myself heading back home, parking next to Adam's empty spot and then heading upstairs without even looking at our door. I went to Bobby's apartment and sat on the balcony. The spring breeze, now strongly signaling summer, ruffled my cotton shirt over my skin. I leaned against the warm metal of the railing and memories flooded my brain.

Memories. That's all that there was left. I was in love with a ghost.

How do you raise the dead?

Make them realize there's something worth living for? I closed my eyes as my head dropped between my shoulders.

There's no way to raise the dead.

I swallowed as I looked over my shoulders at the boxes.

Either way, I was digging my own grave at the same time.

Chapter 30

I was vaguely aware of when Adam came home that night, and then vaguely aware when he got up and left without saying anything to me. I woke up and rolled over to look at his side of the bed. The silent tears came down my face as I got ready for work. I didn't bother putting makeup on, and when I got to work, I didn't leave my office all day, burying myself in editing files and writing proposals. My cell phone sat on my desk, but the screen never lit up. I left work on time, and my chest tightened when I pulled in next to Adam's car. I didn't know if he went to work or not, but he was home. Maybe we could talk.

As the door to the apartment building opened my body froze. The sound of singular guitar reverberated through the air.

It was one I knew all too well.

I tried to compose myself, my chest rising as I took a deep breath and crushed my eyelids down. The talent was unmistakable, but then again, so was the pain. It rippled with the sound of the pick striking the strings, vibrating throughout the building and into the air. Every note screamed out to me and pulled me in; just like it did every time he played. I could only imagine the state he was in as he strummed the guitar, and as I moved up the steps, the squealing of the guitar got heavier and heavier. When I reached the top of the stairwell, our landlord greeted me with a soft smile and sad eyes. He reached out and squeezed my shoulder as he passed me.

"It'll get easier," he said, and I wondered how often this happened.

I opened the apartment door and walked slowly across the hardwoods until I reached the bedroom door. Adam lay across the bed, looking at the ceiling with the guitar laying over him. My eyes drifted to the half empty bottle of liquor, and my nerves frayed with anger. I stared at him for a moment, expecting him to notice me and stop, but instead he continued the lonesome riff he was playing. It didn't feel like I was breathing as I made my way across the room and pulled the cord out of the amp before turning and staring at Adam. He didn't move, and his hands kept playing the guitar. The notes were tinny against the pick without the amplifier, but he didn't flinch against the harsh noise like I did.

"Adam," I said.

He didn't reply.

"Adam, please," I repeated.

His hands froze over the guitar, but he didn't move.

"Have you been skipping work?" I asked as I sat down on the edge of the bed.

He didn't reply.

"I'm sorry I've been so hard on you," I said, but I figured he wasn't listening. "I just want to help, but I feel like every time I try you just get further away. I don't know what's going on in your head — I don't...I don't understand, no matter how I try."

"It's okay," he said, and I glanced over my shoulder at him. "I know you work to get away from me."

I pressed my eyes shut as I shook my head. "I wish I could get away from myself."

Adam scoffed. "I try to get away from myself, but all I end up is more nauseous."

Shits like truth serum. Tears pricked at the edge of my eyes.

"Then why do you keep drinking?" I asked.

"Don't know," Adam replied. "I want to be strong for you, and then I...I don't know, Riv."

I thought of the day before, and Adam's reaction to my holding Bobby's shirt.

"Do I remind you of him?" I asked, sliding off the bed to sit on the floor and put my head in my hands. If that was it, there was only one thing that would solve his mess–space.

"I feel like I'm still fighting to win you from him...even though...he's not here anymore," Adam answered, and I felt the bed move behind me. He was surprisingly stable as he walked around it and then sat down next to me, putting his head between his knees. "I think he has more of a hold on us now that he's gone. Now it's like we can't let go."

My eyes widened as I looked at him, shaking my head. The words came easier than they ever had before. "He's dead, Adam. *Dead*. He doesn't have a hold on me now–and," I paused biting my lip as I stood and looked down at him. My voice cracked as I continued, "The only person who ever had a hold on me was you. There was never a war or game over who I loved. I love you, Adam, and I'm sorry that you can't see it any clearer now than you could then."

Adam shook his head at me, eyes red. "You were in love with the idea of me–but not me. Now the idea's gone."

My throat thickened as my jaw dropped. I couldn't stay there; too many hurtful things had been said already. I stood and headed to the door.

"River," Adam said as I reached the bedroom door.

I paused, holding onto the frame of the door as I glanced over my shoulder. Adam stared back at me, and my chest hitched as I shook my head and then left the apartment. I usually cranked up the radio to try to forget everything, but now I drove in silence. I needed to think, but my mind was just rolling around from one thing to another. My stomach shifted in unease as I pulled into the cemetery. It closed at dusk, but I was sure no one was going to say anything about me being here when it was dark.

Who would see me anyway?

I stopped at the walkway that led to Bobby's headstone and sat with the car in park before finally deciding to get out. I pulled the hood of my sweatshirt up before weaving my way through the dead until I stood in front of the headstone.

Son, brother, best friend.

Robert Beckerson.

I shoved my hands in my pockets as I tried desperately to feel something, but everything was so numb. I sat down and stared at the marble stone as if Bobby might magically appear. His face in my dreams, the feeling of his hand on my skin washed over to me, and I pressed my head against the cold rock. "I think I get what you were saying."

I wondered if he could hear me, or if I was simply going insane for believing it was him in my dreams. "I feel like I'm the one keeping Adam down–that I'm not strong enough to pull him out of this...I almost told Tara, but I think Adam's feeding her false information, so she believes he's fine. But he's not."

I leaned back, running my fingers over the etching on the stone. "I'm starting to wonder if I ever really knew Adam — if I knew myself. I don't even know what to think any-more..."

I stood, wiping my slacks before leaning down and kiss-ing the top of the stone. "If things end up...going the way you said they were going to, I need you to help Adam. I'll be fine. I'll figure it out, but he's going to need you– get through the fog. Please."

Chapter 31

When I got home later that night, Adam was in the same position I left him in. His head was on his knees as he slept, and I grit my teeth as I sat on the bed and pulled him slowly up onto it. He didn't wake up. I tucked a pillow under his head and covered his body with a blanket before slipping to my pajamas and going to sleep on the couch. Even in my deep, dreamless sleep I felt his lips against my forehead before he left, and I knew when I woke he wouldn't be there. Still, when I did, I glanced into the bedroom, only to find it as empty as my chest.

I went into auto mode. I exercised, made myself a coffee, poured it in a thermos and shoved a granola bar in my mouth as I opened the door to the apartment. When I turned, I swallowed and the oats sunk hard. Alec stood in front of Bobby's apartment talking to the landlord. I watched as Alec's eyebrows furrowed, causing deep creases in his forehead

"All times of the day," the landlord said. My muscles tensed as he looked over at me with a sad smile before making his way down the stairs.

"River," Alec said as he rubbed the back of his neck. "Is

Adam?" I shook my head, and he inhaled through his nose, nodding. "Can you and I talk then?"

"What's up?" I asked, and Alec's eyes drifted to my coffee and briefcase.

"I'm sorry I should've called last night–" I shook my head, and a shaky exhale rattled through his lips as if he knew what I meant without me saying it. "Let's go inside?"

I followed him into Bobby's apartment, and he ran his hands over the carefully labeled boxes. "Is this everything?"

"Yeah. I'm sorry I didn't tell you I finished packing everything. I guess I needed some more time," I replied as I opened my box and stared at the jersey I loved so much.

"No worries," Alec said, and his jaw tightened as his eyes washed over me.

"It's okay," I said as I closed the box back up. "I know it's time."

"How will Adam take it?" Alec asked, and his eyes raced over my face. The hope in his eyes disappeared, and his arm came to rest on the top of one of the boxes.

"As good as he's taken anything else," I finally replied. "I'm sorry."

Alec stepped forward and put his hand on my shoulder. "You have nothing to apologize for."

I bit the inside of my lip as I nodded. It was oddly comforting when Alec pulled me into his arms.

"Thank you for doing this," he said into my ear.

I hugged him back, and his warmth reminded me of Bobby. "Thank you for letting me."

He pulled away. "You know both of my boys best."

My lip trembled as tears welled in my eyes.

At least I used to.

"Would you mind putting our boxes in the apartment for me?" I asked.

I could only hope I was home first so I could figure out where to hide them.

"Of course. How is he?" Alec replied, and when our eyes met he swallowed. "I see."

He squeezed my shoulder, hugging me once more. "Try to have a good day at work?"

"I'll try," I replied, but by the time I got to work my head was killing me, and I couldn't get rid of the twisting feeling in my stomach. Adam left far before I did, and it seemed like Alec hadn't been there that long, so he wouldn't have seen him. I put my cold hand against the back of my neck as I leaned back in my chair. Something didn't feel right, and even though I convinced myself it was nothing more than the fact someone else would be living in Bobby's apartment, I knew it was more than that. My eyes kept darting down to my cell phone. A part of me felt like there was something very wrong with Adam. My fingertips tingled, and I couldn't help it– I dialed his classroom number.

"Hello," Regina answered.

"Uh..." Speech seemed to have failed me. "It's River — is Adam there?"

"I'm sorry, River — he's not," she replied, and her voice was soft. "You might want to call his cell phone."

"Yeah, I'll do that– thanks."

I hung up and stared down at my cell phone screen as my

headache intensified. Regina didn't sound surprised I didn't know where Adam was. This was all wrong. I dialed his cell phone. It rang, but no one picked up. I felt like vomiting. I needed to find Adam, but I didn't know how. I packed my work things and headed towards Jesse's office, thankful to have such an understanding boss.

"River, you don't look so well," Jesse said as I leaned in his doorway.

"Massive headache," I replied, squinting against the light of the fluorescents. "That's why I was coming to see you."

"No problem," Jesse said with a wave of his hand. "Take the day off. Feel better."

By the time I got home, I didn't feel better. My head felt tight, and I was starting to see vibrant flashes of color at the corners of my vision. Adam wasn't home. I dialed his number as I made my way up to the apartment. Once inside my eyes settled on the boxes, neatly stacked on the left side of the door. Adam wasn't picking up, and my stomach clenched. I made it to the kitchen sink just in time to lose my granola bar. I splashed water on my face and then went into the bathroom, popping open the cap of the headache medicine with shaking hands. I tossed the pill in my mouth before going into the bedroom and passing out. Every time I woke up, my head still splintered in pain, but I still tried calling Adam, and every time I did, no one answered. I fell back into the fitful sleep just to get away from the pain raging in my head and the rolling of my stomach.

God, that hurts.

A combination of buzzing and ringing woke me up, and when I realized it was my phone, I shot forward, grabbing it off the nightstand.

"Adam?" I whispered, my voice hoarse. "Where are you?" Panic threaded through me. "I've been calling for hours."

"They fired me," he replied, and his slurred words told me he was drunk.

My whole body tensed, and the pounding in my head subsided as I sank back into the bed. "Why?"

"Tardiness." The s' slurred out too long, and I felt my hands clench hard against the metal casing of the phone. At the end of the word, it became a sob. "I'm sorry, Riv...I tried. I swear I tried. Sometimes I couldn't take it, though."

My nerves seared, my throat burning with pain. Had I let this go too far? Guilt pricked at my eyes.

"River?" Adam asked.

I crushed my eyes shut, asking, "Where are you?"

"With Bobby."

I swallowed before inhaling until stars popped in my eyes. "Okay."

"I love you, River. I swear it."

"I know," I said as I stood. My head was still pounding, but I needed Adam home–safe with me.

"Do you still love me?" he asked.

"Yes, Adam," I replied, and the tears ran into my mouth. "No matter what I will always love you."

There was silence on the other end, and I wondered if he believed me.

"I'm coming to get you," I said, breaking the silence. He didn't respond. "Please don't go anywhere, and stop drinking."

As I drove towards the cemetery the pounding in my head cleared, and I wondered if it was somehow connected directly to Adam. If my headache was what drinking made him feel like I had no idea why he would want to do it. My hands squeaked against the steering wheel as I gripped it too tight. During the blackout pain, I had barely thought of anything. It was when I was awake that I remembered.

That's why.

One pain for another. I swallowed hard as I shifted the car into park behind the GLI, hidden among the headstones and grass. When I came around Bobby's marker Adam was hunched there, his back pressing against the hard rock with an empty bottle at his feet. His head hung between his knees and behind him, I could see where he'd been sick.

"SoCo, Adam? Really? Please don't tell me you drank that whole bottle?" I asked as I knelt down on the damp ground in front of him. He rocked forward before mumbling a response I didn't understand. His head tipped back, and I could see his bloodshot eyes were empty. I bit my cheek against the tears that formed in my eyes.

"Please Adam, this has got to stop. I can't take much more," I said, and my head dropped so I no longer had to gaze at those broken eyes.

"I need you to fix me, River," he replied a shaky hand touching my elbow.

"I can't..." I choked on the words, and the tears came in a

rush. I looked up at him, and his eyes locked on me. "I can't fix you, Adam. I can barely pick up the broken pieces of me."

His eyes closed, and his head bobbed backward. My whole body trembled as I grabbed the bottle at his feet and stood, chucking it into the ditch that split the cemetery in two. I heard it shatter against something before I put my hand on my chest, calming my breathing.

Mark said there was one thing that could knock him out of this stupor, and while I had spent so much time denying it, I knew it was true.

Only one thing could fix this.

My chest began to stagger breathes irrationally as my mind settled on the thought.

I had to leave.

Chapter 32

I opened my eyes slowly as the aroma of coffee brewing wafted over me. My eyes felt dry and scratchy and taking a moment to adjust to the light of the room and the figure sitting on the love seat across from me. Adam had the laptop in front of him and was tapping it furiously. I sat up and stretched my arms, reaching for my cell phone on the table. Adam was pale, but he didn't look anywhere near as shitty as he did the night before. I tapped the screen of my cell phone and the time showed 6:30 AM. I glanced over at Adam, and it took a moment before he stopped typing and looked up at me.

"Hey, I'll get you a cup of coffee," he said, putting the laptop aside and going into the kitchen.

My eyes followed him, watching as he poured two cups of coffee. My mouth opened, but nothing came out as he came around and handed me a cup before settling back down in his previous position. The coffee cup balanced precariously in his lap between the computer and his torso. Finally, my mouth figured out how to work.

"What are you doing?" I asked, and the words sounded harsher than I wanted them to. I stuck my mouth over the cup and took a sip, hoping it would look like I was tired and not pissed. I honestly wasn't sure which I was.

"Promoting," he replied, not looking up from the computer.

"Promoting?" I asked before taking another sip of coffee. At least, this time, I sounded curious and not bitchy.

"Fade Burn," Adam said before taking a sip of his coffee. My jaw must have slackened, because he continued, "Plan B."

I blinked at him. Plan B? *As in be a rock star?* My body stiffened. At least he fit the stereotype– alcoholic. I squeezed my eyes shut at the thought. I needed to try to be positive — maybe this would help him straighten out. I stared down at my coffee before inhaling and standing

"Sounds fun," I replied as I leaned down. He turned his face up and kissed me.

"I might be asking your advice," he said as his eyes went back to the computer screen. My gaze moved down to the screen– Twitter.

I shook my head. "I'm not a fan of social media."

He chuckled to himself. "Aren't you a marketer?"

"Sure am," I replied as I raised an eyebrow at him. He smirked up at me. "But I'm high enough up that I can delegate that particular task to someone else."

"Ah, like someone who has a social life?" Adam asked, and his tone showed it was a playful dig, but I found myself swallowing. The truth was somewhere along those lines, and the fact I completely gave up social media after Bobby died. It was sickening to have people always sending sympathetic messages that meant nothing.

"That's more Tara's playground than mine," I replied as I headed to the bathroom to get ready for work. "You should ask her about it when you call her today."

I glanced over my shoulder, wondering what reaction the pointed sentence would garner. It wasn't much more than him looking at me from the corner of his eyes with his head still facing the computer.

"I just might," he replied.

I stopped mid-stride as the lack of boxes near the door caught my eye.

"I put them in the closet," Adam replied, his voice flat. "Yours are on your side while mine is on mine."

I swallowed the lump in my throat before asking, "Did you..."

"Look in them?" Adam finished my sentence. His lips pursed, but he didn't stop typing or look up from the computer. "No."

"Adam–"

"I'm fine, Riv. You're going to be late for work if you don't get going," Adam said, and his head moved to nod over my shoulder to the bathroom.

My body went cold as I stared at him. He raised his eyebrows, and my stomach twisted. I might as well tell him the rest of the news.

"Your parents gave the apartment up."

"Good, it was a waste of their money to be paying for it when no one was living in it," Adam replied, and his eyes were empty as they turned back to the computer screen. My mouth opened and closed, but no words came out. This colder, matter of fact Adam was a surprising apparition, and it made me feel as sick as the drunk one.

"Okay," I managed to say before going into the bathroom. If this was the way Adam was going to be, at least he wasn't drinking, but when I came home that night, he was out cold with a bottle of SoCo dangling from his hand as he lay on the couch belly down. He wasn't even hiding his drinking, and I still didn't know what to do. I pulled the bottle from his fingers and drained the remaining contents in the sink before going out on the balcony and dialing Dad.

"Hey Ducks," he said, and his voice softened the hard edges of my heart.

"Hi Daddy," I replied, and my voice cracked as I slid down to sit on the grated metal

"What's wrong?" he asked.

I put my head on my knees. "Adam."

"What happened with Adam?"

"The drinking...he lost his job yesterday, and he was loaded when I finally found him...and then this morning he seemed fine but.."

"When you got home he was drunk?"

I looked through the window, where I had a clear view into the living room where he lay on the couch. "Out cold. I just don't know how much more I can take, Dad."

"What are you saying, Ducks? Are you thinking about leaving him?" he asked, and his voice strained as if the idea physically pained him.

I crushed my eyes shut, looking across the city, lit by the setting sun. "I don't know...I don't think we're any good for each other anymore...I feel like if I leave, he'll figure his shit out."

Dad's response was unexpected. "What about you, River?"

"Me?" I repeated, and my voice was weak. "This isn't good for me either. I don't know who I am anymore–or if I ever really knew who I was or wanted to be outside the Beckerson boys.

"There's nothing else you think will help? What about counseling?"

I hated to scoff at the idea, but I did.

"He won't even talk to me, Dad. I've tried being reasonable. I've been unreasonable– neither works." My voice cracked. "Nothing works. — I can't watch this anymore."

Dad sighed before replying, "I'm concerned about Adam, too, River–I just worry what this is going to do to you."

"I'll figure it out," I replied looking over my shoulder. Hopefully, Adam would too.

"Just think about it River," Dad replied.

I looked out across the city. "I'll give it a little more time...but Dad, I know Adam and my leaving is the only way to pull him out of this."

"I get that, River, but who's going to pull you out once you push him away?"

My breath caught in my throat, and I looked down at my hands. Leaving meant I was leaving a huge chunk of myself behind, and I wondered how many pieces of myself I could lose without being completely lost to the agony of not knowing who I was. Who was I without Bobby? I felt the tears forming in the corner of my eyes as I stared at Adam. My chest tightened as my vision blackened at the edges. Who was I without Adam?

I needed to find out. I just hoped Adam would find me after...whatever was left of me.

Chapter 33

Adam's drinking the day before must have been pretty decent, because when I woke up, he was still passed out. I watched him for a second, my heart hammering in my chest, which only ceased when he inhaled deeply. I ran my hand over my face before going to take a shower and heading into work early. There was no point in me working out and waking up Adam. He'd probably have a migraine anyway, and I didn't want to make things worse than they already were.

"Earlier and earlier," Jesse said as I tried to sneak passed his office. I stopped in my tracks and took a deep breath before turning to face him. He stood and came to lean against the front of his desk with arms crossed. "Pretty soon you'll be sleeping here."

I swallowed hard at the thought because I honestly wasn't sure where to go if Adam and I broke it off. I couldn't very well go to my parent's house when I wasn't talking to Mom. Their house was also an hour away, but I couldn't afford anything in Boston on my own, could I? My hands tightened around my Starbucks.

"A little distracted, or a little overtired?" Jesse asked, pulling me out of my thoughts.

I ran my hand through my hair before leaning against the door frame. "A little of both, to be honest with you."

"Mhmm," Jesse replied as he took his reading glasses off and tucked them in his suit pocket.

"So what are *you* doing here so early?" I asked, and my eyes narrowed as I watched his eyes widen. "Secret project?"

Jesse chuckled to himself, signaling for me to come in the room as he went back to sit in his chair. "You kind of nailed it."

"Secret project?" I asked, tilting my head to look at the paperwork he was twisting around for me to see.

"Something like that," he replied as my eyes ran over the lease agreement.

My eyes stopped on the location. "This is a building in Framingham. Are we moving?"

Jesse sat back in his chair, and his hands formed a triangle as he shook his head slowly. "We're expanding."

"To Framingham?"

His head changed directions, this time bobbing up and down slowly. "Indeed. The business is expanding rapidly, and we need a new division to keep up with the demand."

"Two locations? That's going to be a lot for one person to manage–plus, a lot of driving," I said as I stared at the dates on the page. It looked like the building was already in existence, but would need some renovations based on Jesse's various sticky notes. When he didn't answer, my eyes rose to meet his and a wicked smile on his lips. I wasn't sure what it meant, or if I wanted to know what it meant.

"It would be, wouldn't it?" he finally replied. "How do you like Framingham?"

I shrugged as I told myself not to think too deeply into what he was asking. This was Jesse– he bounced ideas off me all the time. He probably just wondered if I felt it was a good idea.

"It's another city, I suppose," I replied. "It would be good for business."

Jesse nodded, forehead creasing as he cocked his head. "Aside from a business perspective?"

My pulse pounded in my ears. I didn't need to jump to conclusions, especially when something like this could help.

"Some nice towns surround the area. If I ever got out of the city, I'd probably go for somewhere like Ashland or Bellingham. Those areas are a little bit more reasonable than the city, so I could probably get a nice condo."

"So you've been thinking about moving?" Jesse asked, and his reading glasses came out to perch on his nose as he took the paperwork back and pretended to look it over. His eyes weren't moving, so I knew he wasn't reading.

The air in my lungs staled as I stared at the top of his grey hair, and then his eyes rose back up to mine over the black rims framing his face.

"I guess I've been toying with the idea," I finally replied, my voice squeaking with nerves.

"How does Adam feel about it? Isn't the school he works for close to here?"

Tingles rushed up my spine as I forced a smile on my face. "Yeah, it is. We haven't talked about it yet."

And we probably never will.

"Mhmm," Jesse replied, and then his eyes actually started moving over the paperwork. I figured it was time to make my escape before I asked if he wanted me to go to Framingham. My mind flicked back to Adam on the couch passed out. If he asked right now, the answer would be yes, and I wasn't sure if I was in a state to make a decision like that.

"Well, you have fun figuring out how you're going to be driving back and forth," I said as I stood.

Jesse's head moved up, and his eyes locked on mine. "Believe me; I already have that all figured out."

My jaw went slack before I managed to smile at him.

"That's exciting," I said as I turned and headed to the door.

"You have no idea how much," he said, and I only briefly looked over my shoulder to see the smile on his face.

When I got to my office, I opened my various project folders and began running analyses but within an hour, my eyes were going funky from the lighting. I paused, looking down at my phone. There were no text messages. I heaved a sigh as I opened the Internet browser and my fingers typed without me consciously knowing it.

Condos near Framingham, MA.

I bit my lip. I had enough of a down payment thanks to Bobby, but I was definitely jumping to conclusions. My eyes squeezed shut as a wave of cold rushed over me, and I shoved the phone across my desk. Adam might be all right, and then I wouldn't have to leave. When I packed up to leave at the end of the day and peeked my head into Jesse's office, he looked up with a smirk.

"Signed the lease," he said with a wink.

"That's great — exciting news. I'm heading out," I replied as I nodded over my shoulder towards the door.

Jesse looked at his watch and then stood. "I'll walk out with you. I'm glad to see you're getting out at a reasonable time. You working when you get home?"

I rolled my eyes as he held the door open for me. "I've been getting into reading, and I have one of those adult coloring books."

Jesse chuckled, looking at me from the corner of his eyes. "*Adult* coloring book?"

I pursed my lips. "It's supposed to be relaxing."

"Is it?" Jesse asked as he pulled his keys out of his pocket. I shook my head and he laughed as he hit a button and the convertible top of his BMW came down. "Well, you have fun with that tonight."

When I got home that night, Adam wasn't there, but for once there was a letter under the broken heart magnet.

Don't wait up. Gig with the band. – Adam

Obviously, I wasn't invited– not that night, or the night after that.

Chapter 34

Every day passed the same. I went to work and made sure to get home on time. Every time I pulled into the parking lot I prayed Adam was home, but he never was. If or when he came home he smelled like the booze he consumed God only knew where. Adam didn't tell me where he was going, and he didn't text when he wasn't coming home, probably because he was too wasted. When I tried to talk to him — or text him to ask him to come home so we could talk, he didn't respond.

I told Dad I'd give it some time, but two weeks of this new pattern and I knew Adam was pushing me away. He was fading further into the bottom of a bottle while I faded into my silence–deeper into the knowledge that this wasn't working anymore.

I put my head against the steering wheel, my insides twisting like they did every day when I got home to find his parking spot empty. If I went inside, there might be some vague note from Adam, but it wouldn't say he loved me. I bit my lip– he didn't even bother saying it anymore. I wondered if that was because he didn't, or maybe he never did. Maybe *he* was the one in love with being in love with me.

Either way, I didn't want to see the note. I shoved my finger into the power button for the radio, turning it off, so I engulfed myself in silence as I drove away from the apartment. Blasting music didn't rid me of my emotions, and I was sick of it. Music only reminded me of Adam and the inevitable fate drawing in on me faster and faster. I drove without direction as tears began to stream down my cheeks. I wasn't strong enough for this anymore, and Adam wouldn't listen. He didn't need me. My throat thickened as I turned down Tara's parent's street. I parked in the driveway and looked up at the brick house. What was I going to say to her, and could she handle the truth?

I moved up the walkway slowly, letting the summer air warm me. I knocked on the door once before turning and looking at the sun setting behind the trees.

"River?" Tara asked as she opened the door. I turned back around, and her eyebrows hung over her eyes. "Is everything okay?"

I nodded, but no words came out of my mouth even when though it was open. Her eyebrows moved up her forehead questioning me without her needing to speak. My chest rose as I inhaled and finally answered, "I just needed someone to talk to. I've had a lot on my mind lately."

"Come on in," she said, stepping aside. "My parents went out to dinner, but lucky you, I don't like being the broken third-wheel."

I laughed because that was exactly how I felt whenever I was with Adam. Him and his bottle...and me the third wheel. Tara sat down on the couch, turning off the television and pulling her legs up, so she was sitting cross legged facing me.

"So what's up?" she asked as she propped her elbow against the top of the couch and rested her chin on it. She filled out over the past few weeks, and while she was still small like me, her soft curves and round cheeks had returned. She looked good, and that made me smile. At least one of us was happy.

I looked down at my hands and picked my nails. "It's Adam."

Tara sighed. "Yeah, he told me he lost his job."

My eyes rose up to hers. "What else does he tell you?"

"I don't know," she said, her shoulders rising as a blush spread from her cheeks. "He asked me some stuff about social media and told me he's helping to push the band. I guess he's hoping for a record deal."

My breath caught, and I looked away as my body rushed with a chill. Record deal? He hadn't told me that. I never thought he would pursue being a full-time musician. Performing always seemed to drain him– like the crowds energy was being taken directly from him.

Tara's body tensed when I didn't reply.

"He didn't tell you?" she asked.

I let my gaze return to her. "He doesn't say much of anything anymore. When I'm home, he's either gone out, or too far gone."

"He's still in there," she said, reaching forward and squeezing my hands.

The tears returned, and when our eyes met, I shook my head unable to say the words.

"What's going on with you, River?" she asked, and her voice was a harsh whisper. "Have you given up on him?"

I put my head in my hands. "I've given up on believing we're supposed to be together."

"You're thinking about leaving him?" she asked, her voice pitching higher. My head rose to take in her expression. Her face was red, and her mouth hung open as she shook her head. "The three of us are the only pieces of Bobby left. We're all struggling..." Her voice drifted, and so did her eyes. She licked her lips before locking eyes on me. "If you give up on Adam, then I'll have to give up on you."

"What does that mean?" I asked as my chest tightened. I knew what was coming. Everything would shatter with this one decision.

Her chest rose and fell as her eyes flashed over my face. "You're more messed up than the both of us."

I blinked at her as my face flushed and the rest of my body burst with heat. The sensation of warmth made it hard to focus.

"What do you mean?" I managed to ask as my vision tunneled.

Tara sucked her cheeks into her mouth before she answered, her eyes locked on me. She wanted me to hear this, and she wanted to know I was paying attention. "You've forgotten how to feel."

My sight blurred at her words and the sudden heat dissipated into an aching cold. I opened my mouth as I tried to form a response, but I found myself closing it.

She couldn't know.

Every breath seared into my heart. The numbing pain was constant. I felt everything– the hole in my chest where Bobby used to be; the part of my soul that died with him.

A part of me slowly died as I struggled to remain above the water of my grief while I was blasted by Adam's. She was right; I was too weak. I was too selfish. I couldn't watch him self-destruct, and I was going to lose everything because of that. I stood, stopping at the door frame and bracing my body against it.

"I'm sorry I didn't wake up soon enough to save you, River. I really am," she said to my back.

My fingernails grated against the wooden door frame before I walked out without responding.

I'd already self-destructed.

Chapter 35

I didn't know where Adam was, and he didn't have any idea where I was. At week three he stopped leaving notes under the magnet. Maybe he figured I'd ask if I needed to know, or I should be aware by now since he put the same thing on it every time.

"Are you sure about this?" Dad asked as we pulled up to the condo complex. We were thirty minutes outside the city and only an hour away from my parent's house.

I leaned my head against the glass of the passenger seat window, shaking my head as I looked up at the end unit exactly in my price range and perfect from the pictures. My response came in the form of a whisper, "No."

Dad squeezed my knee. "It's an excellent location."

I chewed my lip as I looked over at him. "Thank you for supporting me even though you think this is a shitty idea."

"No," Dad said as he turned off the car and faced me. "I didn't say it was a shitty idea, or that you were wrong. I just said that you'll be lost without him."

I closed my eyes as I exhaled. "I'm already so lost...and alone."

Dad reached up and rubbed my cheek. "I know, Ducks,

but look on the bright side, this is a great location and it's still close to the city– and closer to me."

I opened my eyes and looked up at the pale blue townhouse with white trim and the perfect little pathway leading up to the door. "It is cute from the outside at least."

Dad nodded forward. "Ready to see if the rest of it is as cute as the pictures?"

My eyes moved to the bay window– the perfect place for me to read a book with a little puppy in my lap. The weight I always felt on my chest lifted, and I felt my pulse rising. "Yeah, I think I am."

The inside of the home was just as cute as the outside, and it felt like home. It was open, much like the apartment and had clean, crisp white trim and dark cherry floors, or at least something that looked like it. The kitchen was open to the living area, and there was a little deck off the back. Off the kitchen was a bedroom I could make into an office while the master bedroom and bath were upstairs next to what I'd make into a guest room– not that I'd have any. The smile grew on my face as I passed from room to room and thoughts of what I could put in each room ran through my mind, along with the tantalizing idea of having a puppy. I glanced up at Dad, and he nodded. His smile was as sad as it was happy; like he was caught in between both feelings. I looked out to the backyard, where a tree house rested in the large oak at the end of the fenced in area, and my stomach sank with memories.

The realtor peeked her head back in the front door. "So what do you think?"

My gaze met Dad's again as I replied, "I love it."

The woman came the rest of the way in the door with paperwork in her hands. "That's what I thought you might say."

My breath caught in my throat as I realized what the paperwork must be. I felt my stomach tense as my eyes darted from her hands to Dad and then outside to that tree house. Adam and I used to escape to a tree house, and now I was escaping *without* him.

"Are you thinking about an offer?" she asked as she placed the paperwork on the island separating the kitchen and the living area. My face paled, and she titled her head. "How about this–you take the night to think about it, and I'll give you instructions on how to fill how the paperwork if you want to move forward. You'll just need to sign and scan it into me. I can handle the rest from there. You said you were pre-approved, right?"

I swallowed as Dad's body stiffened next to me. I hadn't mentioned that to him. The banker that deposited my huge check asked me if I had any plans for the money, and when I mentioned buying a home, she convinced me it wouldn't hurt to figure out what I could afford. It didn't help she managed to show me I'd be paying almost the same amount owning a home as when I was renting.

"Yeah," I replied.

Dad squeezed my shoulder. "That's my girl, always being prepared for anything."

I smiled up at him before turning to the realtor. "So how do I fill this stuff out?"

She explained each section and then Dad, and I drove back the commuter lot in silence. Only when he parked did he speak. "Probably a good idea to look at a few different places."

I nodded, looking down at the paperwork in my lap. It was exactly what I wanted and the right price.

"It felt like home," I replied, and my voice cracked. "Except for one thing."

Dad pulled me into a hug, kissing the top of my head. "Does your apartment feel like home?"

I glanced up at him, and my pulse quickened at the question. Did it?

When I arrived at my empty apartment and found no note or text messages indicating when Adam would be home, I realized the answer.

I didn't have a home. I cried myself to sleep after scanning in the paperwork.

Chapter 36

The days following my offer on the condo passed in the same fashion they always did, except I stopped coming home on time. It didn't matter when I got home because Adam was never there, but I still couldn't work past seven. I figured if I pressed it too much Jesse would restrict my hours further, so I made sure to leave by six. By six thirty I had nothing to do. I dropped onto the couch and my eyes settled on the bookshelf now overflowing with books. I stared at the titles until I made up my mind on which one would be next. I picked up the pretty purple book with a young girl in period dress holding a pair of scissors like a weapon and smiled to myself as I flipped it over to read the description. It looked like it would be amusing, and right now, I needed that–something to make me smile. I went into the kitchen to brew myself a cup of tea, one hand with the book open and the other doing the tasks it took to make the warm liquid. As I put the pot on the stove, I heard a faint buzzing noise coming from my purse on the entryway table. My heart beat sped up as I put the book down and rushed over to my purse.

What if something was wrong with Adam? My stomach twisted as I fumbled with the purse and pulled out my cell phone to look at the screen. It wasn't Adam, but the name made it hard to breathe.

I almost forgot.

"Hello?" I answered, and my fingernail found the side of my mouth as I looked up at the ceiling.

"Hi River, it's Suzie. I have some great news — they accepted your offer."

My jaw slackened as I took in a mouthful of air. My vision darkened at the edges, and I leaned back against the wall, tipping my head back again to look at the tiles on the ceiling.

"Really?" I asked, and my voice was faint.

Suzie took my lack-luster response as shock, and her voice was overly cheerful as she answered, "Yes, isn't it great? I have your lender's information, so I'll reach out to them to schedule your appraisal and home inspection. Once those are complete you'll need to work with the bank and get your home owner's insurance in place."

I stuttered as I replied, "Okay."

"Talk soon!" Suzie ended the call, and I found myself staring vacantly down at the screen.

I walked back to the stove in what felt like slow motion, turning off the burner and pulling the pot off it before walking back over to my purse. My brain was on autopilot. I needed to know where Adam was. I needed something to tell me this wasn't the right thing to do. My body rushed cold as I put my hand on the doorknob and pulled the door open. Our new neighbor was just going into her apartment with her boyfriend. She gave me a soft smile as she closed the door behind them. I stared at the closed door for a moment before making my way down the stairs and to my car. When I got there, I realized I didn't know where the hell to go. I ran my hand through my hair as I stared down at my phone. I doubted Adam would pick up if I called. He was either getting loaded, with the guys, playing a set or all three. I bit my lip as I typed in the words *Fade Burn* into the search bar. All sorts of social media pages came up, and I realized Adam must have done all of it. I clicked on the last tweet. It said they were playing at Friday Night Fever, a popular concert venue in the city. I wasn't sure how they lined it up, but the show didn't start for another forty-five minutes. It was just enough time to get there to watch the show—if that was what I was doing. I kept the radio off as I drove without thinking. The wind whipped my hair around my face, warm with the fresh summer air. It was summer, and a part of me couldn't believe the length of time that passed since Bobby died, or since Tara woke from her coma. We hadn't spoken for weeks, even though she was now back to work part time. She avoided me better than I thought possible, and she wouldn't respond to my text messages or voice mails. A thin layer of sweat built on my neck.

What if she was here? Did she know where he was when I didn't?

My stomach rolled with nausea as I drove up to the venue. It was slammed, and I realized I might not get a ticket. As I stood in line, I bounced on my feet, ringing my hands in front of me.

"River?" Mark's voice broke through my scattered

thoughts, and I jumped as I looked up. He tilted his head at me. "I didn't realize you'd be here."

I glanced over his shoulder, and he shook his head before nodding to the entrance. "He's already inside. I was just grabbing my cell phone. I left it in the van by accident."

I nodded as a shaky breath rattled over my lips. "Can you not mention that I'm here?"

Mark's thick eyebrows drew over his eyes. "He's going to notice you're here."

I glanced at the line in front of me, and then the one already twice as long behind me. "I doubt it."

Mark's tongue pushed into the corner of his cheek before he replied, "He'll feel you."

The idea made me scoff–as if Adam felt anything about me anymore. If he did, he would know I was thinking about leaving.

"We'll see," I replied, trying to give him a smile instead of standing looking like a total bitch. "It's good to see you."

Mark started to walk away, but stopped mid-stride and turned back to look at me. His eyes locked on my own. "He's always straight for the show...but after...I can't promise anything."

I bit my lip as I nodded, tears threatening the edges of my vision. He sighed before turning and heading to the entrance. He stopped at the ticket stand and pointed at me in the crowd. The guy nodded and Mark tossed me a weak smile before going inside. When I came up to the booth, he slid me a ticket. "You're all set."

I seemed to have lost the power of words and nodded

without thanking the guy and headed inside. The ticket wasn't for a seat. It was just admittance in and re-admittance if you left for any reason. When I got inside a hostess asked me if I wanted to be on the floor or a table.

"Table," I replied, and she led the way to one.

"Are you waiting for anyone else?" she asked, giving me a smile as I took a seat at the table she stopped at. I shook my head, and her smile faded a bit. "They'll be waitresses taking orders for the bar wandering around. If you're interested, just flag one down or go over to the bar. You won't lose your seat since we mark it as filled. You can also go on the floor if you'd like, but I wouldn't recommend it with this band. They'll be moshing."

I blinked in response, and she turned back around as I tried to mold myself into the wall. When Adam came onto the stage, I felt myself swallow. He wasn't paying attention to the crowd but instead went to tune his bass. I breathed out a bit, leaning forward on my arms as the rest of the band took the stage. Mark's eyes drifted over to me, and I looked down at my hands. When my eyes came back up, he tugged on his beard before twirling the drumsticks in his hands. My eyes moved to Joe, also tuning his guitar and then out to the growing crowd. Even if I wanted to be on the floor, I wouldn't have much of a shot. There was barely any room for the waitresses who navigated through the crowd with red cups. For a moment I thought of flagging one of them down, but before I could Adam's voice rang through the room and any thought of alcohol vanished with the twisting of my stomach.

"Welcome everyone. We hope you enjoy the show! This first song is new. It's called Fading," Adam said, and I found myself pushing back against the wall as the heavy rift began. Adam's hand settle on the top of the microphone, and his voice came through smooth as he started singing.

I tried

I tried to hang on tight

But you're fading

He pulled away from the microphone and then came back screaming.

Fading from my sight

His voice faded into singing again.

I just want to feel you again

Your skin against mine

But there's nothing I can do

You're fading

The scream returned and this time, it held longer than the last.

Fading from my sight

No matter how I try

I can't hang on tight

I swallowed as the guitar riff in the background deepened, and something inside Adam clicked with me. His eyes rose to mine, and his fingers tightened until his knuckles went white against the microphone. His voice was faint as he continued singing, closing his eyes.

I close my eyes

Try to bring you back into the light

But you're not by my side

The beat softened, and he pulled away, slapping at the bass before his lips pressed against the microphone once more.

This is the hardest part
You're a part of me
I'm fading
I'm fading inside

He shook his head, and the beat pulled back in, strong and as angry as the scream that came out of his lips.

I try to hang on tight
But there's nothing left
When you're fading from sight

My whole body trembled, becoming numb from the words. He knew. He knew I was thinking about leaving, and he wasn't trying to stop me. I didn't know what was worse—thinking he didn't know or knowing he did. Tears blurred my vision as his voice turned soft again.

I just want to feel you again
Your skin against mine
But there's nothing I can do
You're fading
Fading from my sight
No matter how I try
I can't hang on tight
Everything is fading

The crowd tightened, moving closer to the stage and surging as Adam's voice roughened into a growl.

Fading into the darkness of this night
No matter how I try

I can't hang on tight

When the song ended, I wanted to flag down the waitress more than before, but I wasn't sure how I was going to drive home in the state I was already in. I leaned forward, putting my head in my hands as the next song played. This time, my brain didn't comprehend the meaning or the words.

I was numb– so numb to everything as the words played over and over in my mind despite the noise and craziness around me. *You're fading from my sight. No matter how I try.*

He wasn't trying. He was giving up. My stomach rolled and my hands sunk further, clasping chunks of my hair. That's what I'd done, wasn't it? But only because he wasn't trying. A familiar cough brought me out of my thoughts, and as my eyes adjusted I realized the crowd in the room was thinning, and Adam wasn't on stage anymore. He stood in front of me with his hands in his pockets and his tongue ran over his lips as he inhaled, chest rising to his chin.

"What are you doing here, Riv?" he asked, and his voice was soft like his singing.

"I don't know. I never know where you are, so I decided it was a good time for me to figure that out," I replied, and he looked down at the ground nodding.

His lips pursed out before he rubbed the back of his neck. "You think that's it?"

"What?"

His eyes locked on mine. "The reason you came."

Tears blurred my vision again, and I swallowed hard against the thickening of my throat. "No."

"Then why?" he asked, his voice hard.

"I wanted a reason to stay, but you've already given up," I said, my voice faint against the crowd behind us. I looked passed him and then let my eyes concentrate on his. His lips were in a thin line and when he didn't reply I continued, "Please give me a reason to stay, Adam."

"Why? You're not happy," Adam replied, and I felt my chin tremble as it tucked back into my neck in surprise. My body flushed hot and cold as I blinked at him.

"You're not going to change are you?" I whispered.

"Change what? This? I need to do something, River. I can't just sit at home."

I bit the inside of my lip, feeling my nostrils flare as I stared back at him. "You want me to leave?"

He stepped forward, shaking his head. "No...but I can't give you a reason to stay."

"Why don't you come home some nights?" I asked, and I watched as his neck went red up to his ears. "Because you're too drunk?"

His lips twitched, along with his body. "Kind of comes with the territory."

The bitter laugh passed over my lips before I could stop it, along with the harsh words that followed. "Yeah, of course, you'd have to be a fucking drunk– you're a rock star now."

Adam's eyes turned hard. "I'm not going to change, River. If you want to hear me say I'm going to– I'm not. I can't."

My eyes moved passed him to the stage, and my whole

body trembled as I stepped forward to look up into his face. The tears streamed down my face. "You say you're trying. You keep saying you're trying. But I think you've given up."

He licked his lips, closing his eyes as he lowered his face to mine. "Haven't you, River?"

His hand reached up to catch a tear, and my face moved into the feeling of his callused hands.

"Not on you," I whispered. "I'll never give up on you...I love you, Adam...always. But I don't think we're good for each other anymore. I feel like I'm the one breaking you because I'm not strong enough."

His eyes faded as he swallowed. "I'll stay with Mark for a few days."

"That's it?" I asked, my voice cracking.

Adam shrugged before pulling me into this arms. "I get it, River."

He kissed my head before turning and going back onto the stage and disappearing into the back. My eyes went to the ceiling as waves of emotion rolled over me. It shouldn't have been that easy. I headed towards the exit, turning as I reached it. Adam looked at me as he stood with the band, guitar case in hand. Our eyes locked, and my lips moved without any words coming out, *find me.*

I was too hopeless in my grief to save him from his. We'd broken one another when we should've held each other together– but wasn't that what we always did?

Chapter 37

My stomach rolled as I tried to concentrate on the computer screen, but instead of seeing the creatives I needed to get done, all I could think about was Adam. Six months ago he picked me up from this office, swept me off my feet–and for a moment I thought he was going to propose.

Everything felt like it was coming together. Now everything had fallen apart.

I packed my things over the weekend, leaving Adam pretty much everything except my clothes, jewelry, makeup, guitar and my box of Bobby's things. My eyes glossed over as I thought of the one picture I took off our dresser. It was of Bobby and Adam looking up at me on their shoulders laughing. They were both smiling– exactly the way I wanted to remember the three of us. Not faded or broken– completely whole as three best friends. It seemed like that was the way things always should've stayed, but nothing ever stays the same. My jaw clenched as my mind drifted to the check and note sitting on the counter. I hadn't written much, and I wasn't even sure if he'd read it. I pushed my fingers into my eyes as I fought back the emotions. Nothing seemed right anymore. I moved my hands to look at the computer screen–not even this. Lately, I was being pulled in so many different directions I barely had time for the part of my job I loved so much — branding. Not only that, what I was putting out felt rushed. I pushed my hands underneath my desk, rubbing them across the soft cotton of my slacks. Maybe it was all in my head. My hands formed fists. I felt like a complete failure at everything.

"Hey, you," Jesse's voice came from behind me, and I found myself looking at the ceiling as I bit my lip.

I plastered a fake smile on as I turned to see him standing at the door. "Hi."

"May I?" he asked, and he pointed to the chair in front of my desk. I nodded, and he moved around me to sit. It was the only awkward part about having my back facing the door. People needed to walk around me to get to their seat. The window view usually made up for that, but today it was thundering and lightening out. I could barely see outside with the pounding rain against the glass. My eyes moved from the window back to Jesse as he cocked his head at me, his hands forming a steeple in front of his face as his elbows rested on the arms of the chair. "You look tired, Riv."

I ran my hand through my hair, shaking my head. "Sleep alludes me, and I can't work at night."

Jesse smirked. "Thanks to your awesome boyfriend."

My face caved, paling as my eyes went to my desk and my body tensed.

"Oh," Jesse's response was barely audible, but I could feel the sadness in the realization.

He liked Adam. I loved Adam. That hadn't changed, but it just hadn't been enough.

Jesse cleared his throat before continuing, "I was wondering how that wedding you did went?"

My eyes widened as I leaned back in my chair. It seemed so long ago now, blurred between tears, books and wondering where the hell Adam was. I rubbed my bare arms as I shrugged. "It was alright."

I enjoyed capturing the moment, and it did distract me from life between the actual day and the several nights it took to go through and select which pictures to keep, toss or edit. It was stressful, though.

I watched as Jesse's eyes raced over my face. "I have, to be honest with you...I was curious to see if that would fulfill your bug for photography. You're great at it..."

My forehead creased. "Why would you want to," I made air quotes; "fulfill my need for photography?"

He leaned forward. "I think we've gotten to the point where we need to pull you as a pinch hitter for photography and give you something specific to your marketing talents. I thought maybe if you did photography on the side, that would appease you."

"You're worried about my hobbies?" I asked, finding a smile creeping to my lips. Either way, I had a feeling, I'd like where this was going, especially if it was going to Framingham.

"I don't want you to see this as losing something–you'll be gaining a lot–but also a lot of work," Jesse began, and my eyes locked on his as the air in my throat caught. "I want you to be our Framingham Division Director."

He wanted *me* to start up a new division.

"I know it's a drive..." His voice drifted as his eyes narrowed on me.

I bit my lip. "Not really... I just bought a condo in that general area...twenty minutes, give or take."

Jesse's head tilted as he blinked a few times before leaning back. "We're offering you $75,000 a year."

My jaw dropped, and I stared back at him as a smile spread across his face.

"No photography, though?" I asked.

Jesse scratched his chin. "No, but I'd like you to pick a few photographers for the two divisions—that way if one goes AWOL we always have another one to mix things up."

I laughed as I stared at him with my head shaking in shock. "So I'll be doing what you do here—there?"

"Exactly, and you'll get an officer title too. Vice President—it's mostly a title, but you'll get an extra week of vacation."

I blinked at him. He knew very well I could hardly use the three weeks I already had.

"Okay, I know that's not *that* much of a benefit to you, but it's an excellent opportunity."

I would be doing what Jesse did. I felt my chest tighten and my face heat. I picked up the pen in front of me and tapped the desk. Finally, I let my eyes meet his. I watched as his gray eyebrows rose at me in question.

I opened my mouth before closing it and chewing on my

lip. I needed to ask; no matter how bad it sounded. I swallowed. "What do you do anyway?"

"Excellent question," Jesse replied. "I run the business — review contracts, invoices, make *our* marketing plan and budget, watch our brand equity and provide oversight on projects. I also oversee Media Designers and Media Managers. I let HR handle hiring them, though. Can you imagine me hiring people?" I bit my lower lip to keep from laughing. "Exactly. Anyway, I basically do everything for this business that we do for other people's businesses."

"Sounds good," I said, giving him a smile that didn't reach my eyes.

"Do you want to think about it overnight?"

"No, I'm good," I replied as my body rushed with heat.

"Great, I'll shoot you over the paperwork. We'll take a road trip tomorrow," Jesse said as he stood, straightening out his suit jacket as he did.

I watched him leave before letting my eyes drop to the notebook filled with four pages of to-dos. I felt like I was drowning now, what would those extra responsibilities mean?

I bit my lip.

I kind of wanted to drown.

Chapter 38

"This is it?" Jesse asked as he leaned against the door frame with arms and ankles crossed. I smiled, looking up as I put the remaining of my closed project folders into one of the two boxes that contained my entire office.

"Paperless is the way of the future," I replied, making air quotes as I cocked my head at him. "I think some old guy told me that."

Jesse rolled his eyes before letting them settle on me. His lips tugged up in the corners, creasing his dimples into his cheeks. "I think some young person prompted the research into our document management system."

"Seems like she's pretty smart," I said with a smirk.

"Don't let this go to your head," Jesse replied, and he straightened up, running his fingers over his suit before letting his eyes rise to mine. His lips dropped into a serious line. "I mean it. This kind of power can go to a person's head. There's a hierarchy, but no one will ever want to admit that, let alone hear it."

The smile dipped from my lips, and I swallowed. "Of course."

Jesse reached forward and squeezed my shoulder.

"You're going to do great. I'll be with you for the first week, so no worries."

The first week and then I was on my own.

"You're going to have a nice relaxing weekend, right? It may be the last one you have in a while," Jesse said as he leaned down and lifted one of the boxes. I almost stopped him, thinking about his expensive suit, but his eyes narrowed on me, and I got the idea that he wouldn't listen anyway.

"Yeah, relaxing, that sounds like me," I replied as I lifted the other one and grabbed my purse from the back of the door.

"I'm serious, River," Jesse said as we headed down the hall.

When we passed Tara's desk, I caught her staring, and I felt my whole body go hot. The farewell cake at lunch with all the team members of the building, some of which were also coming with me, was the epitome of awkward. Tara was finally back full-time, but she continued to avoid me, and if she couldn't avoid me, she shot me cold looks that earned me even odder looks from the others who saw it. We had been best friends, and I was pretty sure no one thought I had it in me to piss someone off that badly– especially not Tara. Apparently, I did, though–even when what I was doing was better for everyone.

"So what are you doing?" Jesse asked, bringing me back to the present. I realized I was staring at Tara as if I could find the words to fix things between us before I left, but I couldn't. Her eyes rose up, and her lips formed a severe red frown.

I looked away as I replied, "Dinner with my dad at the condo tonight and then wine and a good book the other days, I suppose."

"Not celebrating with any friends?" he asked as he held the door for me, and we were still close enough to Tara's cube that she heard. She gave a bitter laugh, stopping me in my tracks as my muscles tensed. She knew just as well as I did I had no friends.

Jesse's brows furrowed as he looked over my shoulder at her and back to me. My face felt hot as I finally made my feet continue moving.

"What was that about?" he asked as we entered the vestibule and then went out the front door.

I figured he wouldn't drop it, and it couldn't be that much of a secret anyway. "I don't have any friends."

I kept my eyes straight ahead, but I could still sense the tensing of his muscles.

"Not even from college?" he asked, and I shook my head. "Oh...well, I'm still not unlocking your hours."

I finally looked over at him. "I wasn't going to ask."

"Maybe you should go to the beach?" Jesse suggested as I used one hand to open my trunk.

I dropped my box into it and then turned to look at Jesse. "By myself?"

"You have to have *some* friends," he said, and his eyes raced across mine as he shut the trunk and I leaned back shaking my head. "None? How's that possible? It's not like you're a nasty person."

My shoulders lifted to my ears as my stomach twisted. "Drive will sometimes drive away people. Or other things..."

"Other things? Is that why Tara is speaking to you?" Jesse put his hands up. "No, I shouldn't pry. It's none of my business."

"She's still friends with Adam," I replied, and his eyes locked on mine.

His forehead wrinkled. "I'm sorry, River."

"So am I, but I couldn't change him, and he didn't try to stop me."

I felt my hands curl into fists.

Jesse heaved a sigh, looking passed me to the city skyline. He rubbed his neck as he bounced on his heels and his gaze finally came back to me. "I have another friend getting married..." I blinked at him unsure why he was mentioning it. "They asked about you, but I said with your new position it was probably a bit much."

My blinking increased over my widened eyes. "Did you now?"

"I'll give them your information if you promise me you'll try to meet some friends there," Jesse said, and his eyes narrowed at me as I laughed.

"You're trying to set me up with friends?"

Jesse lowered his chin. "Just friends."

It was my turn to look at him with suspicion. "What does that mean?"

"There may be a famous cousin...known to be a woman-izer..."

"Who is it?" I asked, and he sucked his lower lip in so I knew he wasn't going to tell me. I burst out laughing as I shook my head. "I'll do it so that I can see who this famous toolbox is."

"Remember to stay away from him," Jesse replied, and his eyes didn't move as they focused on mine.

"Do I have newly single across my forehead?"

Jesse scratched the back of his head. "Not exactly." My brows rose, and he looked up at the sky. "It's more like you have *I'm a challenge,* which is far more alluring than *I'm single.*"

I blinked hard at him. "I'll keep that in mind."

Chapter 39

My cell phone vibrated its way towards me across my desk, which faced out into the open floor plan office. Jesse made sure I wasn't going to put my back to my employees. He'd been fine with it before, but things were different now. I was the leader here, and I needed to create a welcoming feeling for my employees. The fact I had employees felt a bit strange. I picked my cell phone up, cradling it against my shoulder as I clicked through the invoices on the screen.

"Hello, this is River," I said as I hit the approve button and moved to the next one.

"Hi River, this is Maggie. Jesse gave me your number to call about doing photography for my wedding," the woman replied, her voice bright. "I was wondering if you could meet up?"

My eyes flicked to the corner of my monitor screen, and I found myself leaning back in my seat as I looked up at the ceiling. I lost track of time again. The days just ran into each other now, and I hardly left before six at night. That explained why it was six-thirty on a Friday, and I was still reviewing the week's invoices. Pretty soon my screen would shut down and say *Contact System Administrator.* "Sure, when were you thinking?"

"The sooner, the better," she replied, and I imagined her grimacing as she waited for me to answer.

"Uh, sure." My stomach growled. "Were you thinking tonight? Or tomorrow morning?"

"I can do tonight — I was just looking through take out menus since Jared is at a conference and won't be home until late. What do you like?" she asked, and I could hear the sound of paper ruffling.

"I'm not very familiar with the area, to be honest with you. I just moved from the city about a month ago. I grew up in the area, but everything changes so quickly," I replied as I began to gather up the pieces of paper that made up my to-do tasks.

"I hear you— I just realized like half of the places I have menus for are gone already. What's your favorite place in Boston, maybe then I can figure out where we should try?"

I laughed, and I felt my muscles relaxing after a day of being tense. "Vanek's."

"Oh! They have the best milkshakes. We should meet at Central's then— it's probably about fifteen minutes from your office. They have these amazing fries. I'm a freak. I like to dip my fries in my shake."

"That's my favorite thing to do," I replied as I stood and tucked my MacBook into my oversized purse. I put my to-do file into a drawer, knowing it would be useless to bring it home for the weekend since I didn't have login rights.

"And I thought I was the only person who enjoyed that!

I'm about thirty minutes out if you want to finish up whatever you're doing," Maggie said.

"Dangerous proposition for me—you'd likely be waiting for me until tomorrow. I'll get there a little early. I'm sure they'll be slammed, and it'll be that much less time for you to wait," I replied as I stood and shut the light off to my office. The rest of the desk lights laid out in front of me were off, and only the overhead lights remained. This whole setup was novel to me—there were no cubicles, just open desks. Luckily, although my door was glass, like the wall next to it, I at least had some way to tune people out.

"Sounds good! I'll see you in a bit, do you need directions?" Maggie asked.

I laughed genuinely at the idea. "Even if you gave them to me I'd get lost. I'll just pop it into the GPS."

"Alright! See you soon."

I drove the short distance in silence, only interrupted by the GPS signal to turn left or right. I somehow managed to find a parking spot and then went inside to find there was a forty-five-minute wait. I sat down and began going through an application with a collection of idea boards for photography among other things. I was so invested in looking for new wedding inspiration I didn't notice the woman coming towards me until she said my name.

"River?" A pretty blonde stopped a few feet away, and she bit the inside of her cheek as if she wasn't 100% sure who I was. I wasn't sure how she had some clue who I was in the first place.

I stood and held out my hand. "That's me, so you must be Maggie."

She let out a sigh of relief. "That's me. Jesse described you to me via text message, so I wasn't sure if I had it right. Especially when 'always has her nose in her phone' describes nearly every person on the planet."

I looked around us and realized she was right. Everyone was on their phone. I needed to get that little habit in check a bit.

"So what gave me away?" I asked just as the device the hostess gave me began to buzz.

"I just had a feeling," she said, and her cheeks burned red. "It would've been mortifying if it hadn't been you!"

I laughed as we walked up to the hostess station. Maggie was a little taller than me, and her curves weren't hidden despite her flowing blouse and black trouser jeans. Her round cheeks were accentuated by the red of her lips and her bright blue eyes popped against the pink of her top. She was gorgeous– the way I imagined country singers might look.

"You're braver than me. I would've searched Facebook until I found you," I replied as we followed our hostess.

Maggie's cheeks flamed red, and I realized she did just that–except I didn't have one. "Can't say I'm not guilty of trying."

"Sorry about that," I said as I smiled up at our hostess and thanked her for my menu. "I don't do the photography thing enough to have a website or anything."

"I saw Anna's pictures. They were amazing, but it must

be a lot with your day job," Maggie replied as she began looking through the menu. Her eyes drifted up to mine. "So how do you do it– photography and being a Marketing Director?"

I laughed a little as I ran my finger around the rim of ice water the hostess poured. "Newly single."

And friendless.

"Ah," she replied, and her full lips dipped down. "Long-term relationship?"

"Something like that," I replied. I supposed knowing someone your whole life and being in love with them just as long must qualify as long term. My eyes blurred as I stared down at the menu with my muscles tensing. It was July. It was a year in June, and I hadn't even realized it.

"You look like whatever you're thinking of just caught you off guard," Maggie said, and her voice was soft as I shook my head, coming back to reality.

I gave her a small smile. "Pretty much that's my life right now. Nothing goes as planned."

She reached across the table and squeezed my hand. "Plans are for suckers. My wedding is in three weeks, and I don't have a photographer."

I squeezed back, my smile growing. "Well, now you do if you'll have me."

Maggie tilted her head back to laugh, and the noise warmed me. "I think we're going to be good friends."

"I think that was Jesse's plan," I replied as our waiter came up.

"Jesse always has a plan," she replied before giving the waiter a smile.

He looked between the two of us as he pulled out a pad of paper. "What can I get you two lovely ladies to drink?"

Despite the fact our heads were still pointed in his direction, Maggie and I's eyes met, and we both smiled. Maggie wiggled her eyebrows at me. "You first, *single* lady."

My eyes widened at her before I looked back up at him. His hands were behind his back now, flexing his chest against the buttons of his shirt as he smirked down at me, light brown eyes locked on me.

Single sure seemed to be working for this guy, and for some reason, the idea of talking about him the second he walked away made me blurt out the first thing my eyes fell to on the menu.

"Excellent choice," he replied. "That pairs nicely with our house brew."

"I'm not much of a beer person," I replied, leaning forward, so my head was in my hands. "What else do you recommend?"

He looked up at the ceiling, the corner of his eyes wrinkling with thought. His gaze fell back to mine, and the thoughtful contour of his lips tilted up, causing dimples to appear on his cheeks. "We have an amazing pineapple margarita."

"That sounds good," I said as I glanced over at Maggie from the corner of my eyes.

He wrote it on his pad of paper and then pointed his pen at me. "Frozen with sugar on the rim?"

"Nailed it," I said, and his tongue darted over his lips before he turned to Maggie.

"I'll take the same — margarita and all."

"Great," he said, taking our menus, his hand brushing over mine as he did. "I'll get you some guacamole and chips on the house."

I watched him walk away, my eyes drifting lower than I meant them to.

"You totally just checked out his ass!" Maggie said, laughing. "And he looked like he wanted to nail something other than your food request."

My face burned bright red, and I realized exactly why Jesse referred Maggie to me. She was a lot like Tara; the complete opposite of me–someone who could bring me out of my recluse shell.

"He's cute," I replied, glancing to the table he was now taking orders at. He caught my gaze and winked at me, causing my stomach to do little flips. I forgot how amazing that felt.

"And you were flirting!"

My jaw went slack as I realized I still knew how to do that. I shook my head, but Maggie's widened eyes made me laugh. "Maybe a little bit."

"Wait until Beck sees you," Maggie said as she twirled her straw in her glass of water. Her eyes came up to mine. "He's going to make a beeline at you."

"Is Beckham the famous cousin?" I asked, and Maggie's cheeks flushed as she shook her head. "And why don't I believe you?"

She made a zipping motion with her hand. "Jesse told me not to mention it...and to tell you to stay away from him."

I put my palms up. "How am I supposed to prepare myself for meeting him?"

Maggie chuckled to herself. "It's probably better you didn't anyway. I don't think anyone can ever be prepared for him. He's both attractive and friendly– but he's a challenge."

"And why do you think he'll like me?" I asked, pursing my lips at her.

"You're a lot alike," she replied, and I shook my head. She signaled for me to lean forward and then ran her finger over my forehead. "Challenge."

"I was just openly flirting with our waiter," I said, my voice high pitched in my rebuttal.

She leaned back, and her brows rose up into her side swept bangs. "He knows he doesn't have a shot in Hell. Beck likes not having a chance in Hell–but for different reasons than most people think."

I sighed, sitting back in my chair. "You're talking in circles."

Maggie shrugged. "He's who is he. That's pretty much all I'm willing to say."

"Now you have me intrigued. I'm going to have to look up every famous person named Beck on Google."

"It won't get you far, seeing that's just his nickname," Maggie said, and my lips moved down. She pointed at me with narrowed eyes. "Oh, you hate surprises. Even better. This way you'll be super excited for my wedding."

"I already am," I said. "And that has more to do with you than the famous mysterious cousin."

Maggie laughed, and I joined her. I was going to have to thank Jesse on Monday. I hadn't laughed like this in a long time, and I hadn't realized how good it felt.

Chapter 40

Another Friday; another night alone. I tapped my hands against the steering as I stared up at the stop light. Last Friday Maggie saved me from myself, but there wasn't anyone there to save me this time. Well, except for my automatic lockout screen which meant I couldn't work straight through the weekend. My eyes dropped down from the stop light to the tattoo parlor up ahead. The walk-ins welcome sign blinked a bright pink against the dimming evening like it did every single night. Most nights I went to a spin or Zumba class–anything to keep me away from home or away from that steadily blinking sign, but tonight the person who usually held the class had something special going on– an anniversary or birthday — I hadn't paid enough attention to know.

And that light was drawing me in as if I were a moth without enough of a brain to resist. The light must have turned green because the car behind me laid on its horn.

"Okay! Okay!" I said to myself as I threw my hands up and headed forward. My fingers seemed to gain a life of their own, flicking the turning signal on and then pulling the steering wheel to the left and into the parking lot of the tattoo parlor.

I could do this. Last time it didn't even hurt.

But you had Bobby then.

I shook the thought from my head, putting the car into park and getting out before I could change my mind. When I walked in two guys around my age looked up and smiled at me, but kept talking as I turned to look at the wall covered in typical designs.

The butterfly Bobby wanted me to get stuck out without having to look. It was obviously something every tattoo parlor must have with its lacey wings, swept by invisible wind in pale pastel pinks and purples. I wondered how many teenage girls had the thing on their lower back. I smiled at the thought, knowing for them it was just an unfortunate decision. For me, it would be a permanent reminder of Bobby. Now I just needed to figure out which one of the hunky tattooed guys was going to give it to me. My face flushed hot as I thought of where I was thinking of getting it, on the middle of the back of my ribs. I'd have to either pull my shirt off or hike it pretty far up. At that moment, I became aware of the guys and their conversation.

"What appointments do you have?"

"You'll have to take the girl. I have Beckerson in fifteen minutes."

My jaw went slack, and the room was suddenly too hot. "Again?"

"Yeah, he got that one a few months ago for his brother

and now, with the record signing, he's getting something else. Lyrics to a song, I guess."

Fucking Christ. Adam would be here any minute. I turned too quickly, and my stiletto popped from under me, causing me to lose my footing with an almost inaudible squeal. I didn't know how he did it, but before I could fall on my face, a tattooed arm wrapped itself around my waist.

"You alright?" the guy asked, and I looked up from the rippling muscles of his arm into a bright green set of eyes.

My mouth was still perched open, and my eyes fell in embarrassment, only to be greeted by his pec muscles showing nicely beneath his cotton t-shirt. I blinked hard, his arms still around me.

Stop checking him out!

I shut my mouth as discreetly as I could before standing up straight. His arm lingered around my waist as a smile curled up the edges of his lips and he waited for a response. I was having trouble breathing, let alone forming a thought other than *holy hot hell*. I'd just been caught by a younger, taller, even more gorgeous version of David Beckham.

"Yeah," I finally managed to squeak out. I breathed in, calming the erratic beat of my heart. It picked up again when he smiled, lip ring pulling tight against his thin mouth. Now there were two people in the world I thought could pull off that facial hardware. I swallowed, pulling away as he cocked his head, brows deepening over those speech-removing eyes. "You'd think I'd be used to these things from wearing them seventy hours a week."

The guy's eyes dropped to my legs, and the lip ring

tugged against his lips as his gaze made its way back to my face.

Oh.My.God. He was checking me out.

And Adam was five minutes closer to walking in the door behind me.

"I don't know how chicks manage to walk around in those things ten minutes, let alone that many hours," he said as he walked around the reception table. "So what can I help you with? First tattoo?"

"Second actually," I replied, and his eyes quickly ran over my arms, looking for it. "Hip bone."

His lips already pulled up in a smile, twitched slightly as if he liked that idea. I was going to have to take my shirt off for him. My eyes went back to his chest, and my mind went to *him* without a shirt. I flicked my gaze back up to his smiling face. Being single was apparently reeking havoc on my hormones.

The guy looked down at the watch on his wrist. "I have an appointment in a little under ten minutes," he said before nodding over his shoulder. "Paul can help you if you want, or I can book you an appointment with me?"

"An appointment would be great," I replied, and the response was a little to quick and airy. I'm sure he took it for me wanting *him* to do the tattoo, but it had more to do with the panic that Adam was going to be here any minute. Plus, if Adam trusted this guy to give him ink, then I did.

He pulled a red appointment book from under a pile and a pencil. My heart hammered against my chest as he opened it up to this month. He tapped on it with his finger before looking up. "I have Sunday at 2?"

"Great, I'll take it," I replied, glancing over my shoulder as a bead of sweat dripped down my spine.

"Cool. I just need your name and number."

"River Ahlers — 508-555-2222," I replied watching as he wrote the details down in neat scrawl with his left hand.

"Great, I'll see you soon. My name's Westley, by the way– but everyone just calls me West," he said, holding out his hand.

I laughed, reaching forward and shaking it. "See you Sunday."

He nodded, and I took a deep breath as I fought the urge to run to the door. Once I was in my car I tipped my head back, exhaling slowly through my nose as I pressed my hand to my forehead. I froze as an SUV pulled up next to me.

Mark's SUV.

My stomach rolled as I caught the movement of the doors opening. I reached up flicking my visor down to cover half my face as four guys walked around the front of my car. Adam lead the way, followed by Mark, Joey and some guy I didn't know. I bit my lip as Adam's laughter filtered in through my half rolled down window. Somehow they didn't notice who I was. I closed my eyes, my head now dropping to my steering wheel. Thank God for my popular black Honda Civic. There was nothing unique about it, and nothing that made Adam think of me, obviously. Guilt flushed white hot in my veins as I thought of the fact I'd just been drooling and flirting with the guy about to affix ink permanently to his skin. I shouldn't feel guilty, but a part of me couldn't shake it, even after I drove away–even after a glass of wine and a book. As I stared across my backyard to the tree house, I realized it wasn't guilt. It was something heavier– the fear that maybe Adam was better off without me. His laughter triggered the emotion. His band was signed, and he was happy, because if I knew anything about Adam still, it was that the laugh I heard was real.

Kind of like mine when West shook my hand.

When arrived at the shop on Sunday afternoon West was waiting, the playful smile he first gave me coming to his lips as he looked up. He stood, coming to greet me and his eyes fell to my feet.

"Too bad," he said, nodding to my Converses. "I was hoping you'd fall into my arms again."

Our eyes locked, and I couldn't help the smile that came to my lips. "You'll get to see me with my shirt off, though."

His jaw went slack as he flushed from his exposed tattooed collarbone up to his cheeks. I hadn't thought someone so bold could be flustered. He reached up, rubbing the back of his neck. "So it's another hidden one?"

"Those are the best kind, aren't they?" I asked, cocking my head at him.

His eyes widened. "I like tattoos anywhere on a woman, especially one who wears a suit and stilettos to work."

"I'm secretly a bad ass," I replied wiggling my brows at him.

He laughed, and it was a deep rumble that raced through me, causing tingles to go down to my toes. "The Cons were a dead giveaway that you have a secret rebel inside you...aside from the fact I already know you have a tattoo. So what am I going to be able to grace that body of yours with?"

The flirting was so obvious, but I had to admit it made me feel good. I nodded over my shoulder. "A butterfly– and I know it's one from the wall, and it's cliche, but it's not to me."

His bold smile softened as he glanced over my shoulder and then back at me. "I don't judge. We all have reasons for everything we get– some better than others, of course."

His green eyes were so sincere that I lost my train of thought; that is if I'd had one other than *you're so pretty*.

"So which one?" he asked.

"Oh, yeah," I said, turning and then placing my finger on the butterfly. "This one."

West stepped next to me, crossing his arms as he looked at it and then my face. "Someone died."

My eyes remained on the butterfly, clouding at the edges. "Yeah."

"Boyfriend?" he asked as I followed him to his chair.

"Best friend. He came with me when I got my first one. He wanted me to get that one...but we were never really on the same page, so I didn't," I replied as I watched him sit.

He chuckled to himself as he began selecting the bottles of color and filling the tiny caps. "So where do you want it–other than the vagueness that you're going to take your shirt off."

I turned, pointing to the area. "Here."

I faced him again, and he nodded for me to take a seat as

he pulled a pen from out of a drawer. "Do you mind if I free-hand it? This way you get something that's a little bit unique but still faithful to the design."

"Sure," I replied as I pulled my shirt over my head to reveal a black string bikini. When our eyes met again, his were locked on my own, and not on my body, but his face was red again.

He coughed as he wheeled his chair around me, pulling his movable cart with his gun to be within arm's reach. He rinsed off the area, which caused a rash of goosebumps to race over my skin and just when they were about to go away he rested his arm against my bare skin. I inhaled, not because of the sharp pen but because of the warmth of his touch.

"So I get the reason you're getting this one off the wall...but how about we give you another one where people can see it, *not* off of the wall," West said, and I could tell he was concentrating from how low his voice was.

I glanced over my shoulder at him, and his face rose to look at me, pen hovering over my side. "And how much are you going to charge me for one of your original designs?"

He shook his head, nodding to the ink laid out. "As long as it's one of those colors, nothing. I already have the ink out."

"I have no idea what I would get or where," I replied, realizing I wasn't totally against the idea– or against it at all for that fact.

West placed his pen behind his ear before reaching into one of the drawers of the mobile station and pulling out a sketch book. He flicked through a few pages before turning it and showing me a picture of an arrow. It was made of fine little dots that varied in size leading to a detailed and soft looking feather on the opposite end of its opposing point. Soft swirls around the arrow seemed to symbolize its movement through the air. My fingers reached out to run over its shape before my gaze lifted to his.

"Why an arrow?" I asked, and my voice was as soft as his when he mentioned it.

"An arrow can only be shot after being drawn back– it symbolizes pushing through dark times to get to positive ones," he replied, and his hand reached forward, over the top of my palm to my wrist. His fingers gripped it lightly twisting my arm, so my forearm showed. He let his fingers run over my wrist, goosebumps trailing after his touch. He stopped halfway up my arm, and his eyes lifted from my skin to my face. "Here. Where everyone can see it."

Tingles shot up my spine yet again, and my breath caught in my throat. The feeling only intensified as his eyes flicked back and forth over my face, his lips slightly parted as he waited for my response.

"Okay," I managed to say. "It sounds perfect."

"I thought it might be."

He pulled the pen from behind his ear and started drawing on my skin again. This time, I was able to see the concentration as he did it. Lines creased his forehead as the pen moved in smooth, soft motions against my skin. As the arrow came to life, I wondered if I could do what it symbolized; if I could win this battle.

Chapter 41

Work too late. Go to some crazy workout class. Go home and read until I fell asleep.

Repeat. Until the weekend. Those started with a day with Dad, then grocery shopping on Sunday, and last weekend I took Jesse's advice and went to the beach. I took a book, and it wasn't too bad– no worse than reading the book alone at home. At least I got a good tan.

The next weekend was an entirely different story. Saturday meant more work, but of a different type. Instead of Marketing– paying invoices, signing off on designs, and fixing people's screw-ups I was on my own, entirely reliant on myself and my camera. The day started early because I wanted to get shots of Maggie getting dressed, framed with the perfect August sunlight as it streamed through the windows. As I stared down at my camera screen, looking at the last picture I took, I smiled to myself. This wedding was easier than the last, but then again, no one was loaded off their ass yet. Plus, Maggie and Tom were perfect for each other. I kept my camera over my face as their happiness sunk into me, and while I wanted to me happy, I couldn't help the sinking feeling in the pit of my stomach. Or the flash of Adam holding a box in his hand. My body rushed with tingles as I licked my lips and closed my eyes for a moment as I took a breath. I kept my finger pressed on the shutter, making sure it took pictures as I composed myself. When I opened my eyes, the two of them were walking back down the aisle. I changed angles taking shots as I walked backward. My heart raced as they left the room and I moved to the corner, out of the way of the exiting guests.

Please. Please say I got it.

I pressed the viewfinder button with shaking fingers, skimming through the pictures until I landed on the shot. Jared held Maggie's face in his hands, and her hands laid on his wrists as they kissed.

I looked up at the vaulted ceiling of the church, exhaling through my mouth before following the stragglers. The next hour passed in a well-planned blur. I gave instructions, and to my relief, people listened. The mother of the bride asked for some special photos and Maggie kept us on track by telling her I could get them at the reception. Her eyes brightened as she looked over at me, her words pointed. "Besides *Beck* is already there by now. You don't want to call him all the way back for a handful of photographs do you?"

I rolled my eyes, and we kept going, getting through a mind-numbing amount of pictures in a short period. Then it was time for the reception and as my stomach growled I was glad I caved and let Maggie make sure there was a place for me to eat. It just happened to be with Jesse and his wife— thank God, no hot forbidden cousin appeared to be at the table filled with middle-aged friends. Jesse's eyes narrowed as I reached for the basket of bread, and then his hand was around my wrist.

"What? I'm not allowed to have bread?" I asked, looking at him out the corner of my eye.

His lips pursed as his gaze ran over the arrow on my forearm. "I was wondering why you'd been wearing blazers every time we video-chatted."

He released my arm, and I put my bread on my plate, buttering it before looking up at him. "I've been wearing blazers or sweaters every day, all day."

Jesse glanced over at his wife, and his blue eyes were enhanced by the wrinkling next to them as he laughed. "You don't have to do that."

"What?"

He put his hands up as he shrugged. "We have a loose tattoo policy, as long as it's not huge, distracting or offensive, you can show it. Board meetings– wear a blazer, though."

"Well, that's a given," I said, shaking my head. "I guess I should've just asked in the first place."

He nodded as he leaned forward, placing his chin on his fist. "But you've been pretty busy. How are you doing?"

"Jesse," Janice, his wife, said. "This isn't work–well, it's not marketing firm work."

Jesse sat back, signaling to my plate. "Sorry, go ahead."

"So where's this bad boy I've been sworn away from without even meeting — the infamous cousin — I haven't seen anyone fitting a famous description yet," I asked as I lifted the piece of bread to my lips. It was warm and filled with little chunks of garlic and Parmesan cheese. The whole meal could be that bread, and I'd be happy.

Jesse picked up a roll for himself, looking up at me through his eyebrows as he buttered it. "You'll know him when you see him."

"Mhmm," I said, rolling my eyes before changing the subject because I knew I wasn't going to get anywhere. "I went to the beach like you suggested."

"You took my advice? How shocking!" Jesse replied, smirking at me as he took a sip of wine.

"Most of the time it's not bad advice, but no I didn't meet anyone fun. Well, besides this little beagle that kept licking my toes," I replied, and I felt a smile tugging at the edges of my lips as I thought of the too big ears practically tipping the little guy over, and then his owner apologizing profusely as she scooped him up.

"Are you a dog person?" Janice asked as a waiter came and began placing salads in front of us.

"Yeah, but I'm really fond of beagles. I've always wanted one since I was a kid, but my parents always said they'd howl too much."

"Why don't you get one now?" Jesse asked as he picked up his salad fork. "Does your condo complex allow for animals?"

"Yeah, there's even a little dog park, but I'm not home all that much–"

"They have a doggy daycare, and you'd have a cute, furry alarm system," Janice said.

Jesse pointed his fork at me, finishing chewing his bite. "She's right. There are benefits to having a howler."

I laughed at that, and then Jesse was dragged into a conversation with the person across from him about the very thing his wife chided him not to talk about– marketing. I tuned out then, looking around the room in between bites of food as I tried to determine who in the hell the famous person was but no one stuck out. I gave up when dessert came out — a crème brûlée with raspberry drizzle. When I finished the last bite I wished I didn't eat it so quickly because that meant it was time for me to start working again. Music filled the room, and I stood to begin taking pictures. After all the important dances I was able to blend in with the crowd, as much as that was possible with a Nikon glued to my face. My camera scanned the room, stopping at irregular intervals and snapping action shots of people dancing or talking. Just like during the ceremony I felt removed from the happiness around me, a casual observer with a camera covering my frown and sad eyes. I continued to capture the moments, catching the backside of a guy with gorgeous yet dangerously bad boy styled hair talking to Maggie. As my finger moved to snap the picture, it stopped, suddenly as limp as my jaw was. The guy turned, and my finger moved involuntarily, catching the corner of his lips lifting as he reached over the top of his casually pushed back length of blond hair and looked directly at me with stunning green eyes.

Beck as in looks like David Beckham, and that was exactly who West looked like. *Tattoo Artist* West.

And he was looking right at me with a golden eyebrow arching.

I twisted around so my back was to him, keeping my camera hovering over my heated face as I moved it without taking shots.

Famous? West, was famous? The burning in my face ignited throughout my body, just like when his fingers ran over the skin of my wrist up to the spot where he put my arrow tattoo. How was he famous? Maybe it was a different guy that just happened to also look like David Beckham that was the womanizing cousin. Although, the womanizing part did seem plausible. We openly flirted before, during and after he gave me my tattoos.

A cough came from behind me, and I turned back, the camera still covering my expression to find the very man staring down at me.

God, he's tall. I already knew that, but suddenly I was examining everything about him, more so than I did before. His nose was angular, fitting into the perfection that was his chiseled jaw line. Part of the length of his hair had come undone and was hanging over his eyes. He put his hand on the exterior of my camera lens and lowered it from my face.

"River," he said, and his voice sent heat rushing to my face again, but I managed to push an eyebrow up as my frown trained on him.

"West," I replied, and my voice was far more breathy than I wanted it to be. He looked even better in a button-up than his black cotton v-neck t-shirts. The hunter green shirt was unbuttoned to show the tattoo gracing his collarbone, and the pushed up sleeves to showed his tattooed forearms.

"I thought I'd never see you again," he said as he put one hand in his slacks, the other holding a whiskey glass. "Well, unless you wanted another tattoo."

"It's not like you don't have my phone number," I said, cocking my head at him. "So if you wanted to see me again, you could call."

West pursed his lips and shook his head. "That would violate client-artist privilege."

My heart beat quickened. "Not telling me you're famous kind of did that already."

"Shit. Who said that I'm famous?" His neck flushed up to his cheekbones as he pushed the stray hair back over his head.

"Maggie mentioned her cousin nicknamed *Beck* was famous. I would never put two together...I mean how *are* you famous?" I asked, and I felt my body leaning towards his.

"I wish she'd stop calling me that. As for why I'm famous..." He stepped forward and my eyes fell as his chest rose. I blinked hard before looking back up and waiting for a response. West took his hand out of his pocket and reached for my wrist, flipping it, so the tattoo faced up. His fingers traced the shape, and my body trembled before I could stop it. My eyes rose slowly as his finger reached the tip of the arrow. "It's because of these."

My mouth worked before my brain as I asked,"So you're like Kat Von Dee?"

He chuckled, brows rising. "Not really, but I guess so."

"I didn't see any cameras."

"They aren't there all the time," he replied. "I do get a break, and besides, we always ask if clients want to be on camera, and I get the idea you wouldn't have been receptive to that."

"You already know me too well," I replied, laughing a little as his fingers lifted and left my skin cold.

He stuck his hands into his slack pockets, tilting forward slightly as his lips pursed and he shook his head. "I know your name and your tattoos, but I don't really *know* you."

Jesse hadn't wanted me to talk to West, but I already had– not that he knew that. I scanned the room, wondering where he went. My eyes landed on Jesse at the bar where he was slowly shaking his gray head of hair at me. I rolled my eyes before returning my gaze to West.

He chewed the inside of his cheek, green eyes fixed on me. "I'd like to be your friend, River."

"Why?" I asked, tilting my head up as the air in my lungs hitched.

"You need a friend, and I could always use a real one," he replied, and his teeth raked over his lower lips as his eyes paced back and forth over mine.

"A real one?"

"One who wasn't nice to me because they knew I was a famous tattoo artist and they wanted something for free," he explained, and despite how tall he was, his face was inches away from mine. I realized why–he was leaning down, and I was on my tip toes.

Oh god.

I dropped back on the balls of my feet. "Friends?"

"That's it," he replied with a nod. "For now."

For now. The thought made my cheeks burn, and as I looked up at him, he was blushing too. It was adorable that someone so obviously brash could be embarrassed. I bit my lip, and his eyes dropped to them, his Adam's apple rising and falling.

"I'd like that," I finally replied.

"Great," he replied, and his eyes moved to the camera. He signaled with his hands for me to give it to him. "We'll start with relieving you from your photographer duties."

"But–" I began, and he nodded over my shoulder. My gaze followed where he was looking, right at Maggie whose smile confirmed it was okay. "Thanks," I mouthed. I turned back to West and pulled the camera over my head, handing it to him. "Someplace safe."

"Of course, and what can I get you to drink?"

"Moscato?"

His lips tipped up at the edges. "My pleasure, if I get a dance out of it."

"I think I owe you two."

"Even better," he replied with a wink before turning away.

I was really, truly smiling and the warmth spreading through my limbs felt amazing.

Chapter 42

Bobby smiled at me, and my heart lifted. He looked so happy—so put back together, as if nothing had happened—as if he wasn't...dead. My chest rose as I smiled at him sitting on the dock at the lake, his jeans pulled up over his muscular calves as he dunked his toes in the water. It had been months since we'd last spoken in my dreams– even longer since I really heard his voice. I swallowed– just over eight months; two since I left Adam.

"Hey, Riv," he said, and his voice sent a shock to my system. My whole body trembled with the joy of hearing it, and I stepped forward. I knew it was a dream, but it felt so real I wanted to stay in it forever. My heartbeat quickened because I knew I had minutes before it would all fade away.

"Hey, Bobby," I replied as I sat next to him, examining each of his features again. He looked like the angel he was as the sun cascaded over the contours of his face and reflected off of the blond highlights in his messy hair.

He put his arm around me and pulled us back, so our toes were still in the water, but we laid back in the sun. Bobby turned his head, opening one eye and then the other. "So..."

"So?"

"West Brighton," he said the name, wiggling his brows at the same time.

The smile on my lips faded as I thought of the way I flirted with him the night before and forgot about every shitty thing in my life. I even forgot about Adam.

"I'm trying to make friends," I managed to say, turning my face up to the sun, so I wasn't looking at him.

"Friends? Riv, we both know that hardly ever works between a guy and a girl...look at all the shit that put you, Adam and me through. He really likes you...but you don't know him," Bobby said, and I turned my body towards him, leaning up on my elbow.

"I don't even know myself anymore," I replied, locking my eyes on his blue ones. They were so similar to the sky behind him.

Bobby turned to rest on his elbow, reaching forward and tucking a piece of hair behind my ear. "That's why this is so dangerous for *both* your hearts. Not to mention Adam."

"I think he's doing fine."

Bobby's eyes narrowed as his jaw clenched. "He's doing as *fine* as you are. He's following a new dream because it's the only thing he sees in front of him. You changed him — you fixed him."

My throat made a choking noise as I shook my head. "I left him broken."

Bobby's eyes drifted down and then locked on mine, stoic as his brows crushed over them. "No, but you're going to leave Brighton broken."

"He's a womanizer."

"So was *I* — so was *Adam*. We each have our reasons for protecting our hearts that way and River; you don't *know* him. I know you need someone–just be careful. He can't help you find yourself again because you won't let him. And he's not going to listen even if you try to push him away, but you need to be honest with him."

"I know your right," I whispered, my voice breaking. "God, I miss you."

His forehead lowered to mine, and he held me there, his warmth and love encompassing me, so the anxiety in my soul disappeared. His eyes searched mine, and our noses met. "I miss you too, the real you—the you that you buried in the ground with me."

"What am I supposed to do?" I whispered, but his body was starting to shimmer in and out. "Bobby? Please, don't go!"

His lips rose to my forehead and pressed there. "You'll figure it out, Riv. You always do."

Then he was gone and every part of me that felt suddenly mended back together split at the seams. I woke up with a start, the morning sun streaming across the room and warming my body. I swallowed as I pulled my knees to my chest. *You're going to leave Brighton broken.*

I didn't want to leave anyone broken, and I knew at that moment that I could only let West in so much. I needed a friend, and he needed me to be only that because otherwise I could shatter him. I didn't know how, but a part of me knew Bobby was right. My phone buzzing against my nightstand pulled me out of the thought. For a moment my heartbeat raced, thinking I forgot to text Dad last night that I wasn't going to be up to hanging out. I grabbed the phone, glancing at the time above the text message– eight thirty. My whole body ached, but my mind raced. There was no way I could go back to sleep, especially when my eyes fell to the text message, not from Dad, but West.

West – Hey, I know it's early, and you're probably exhausted but if you're interested, today is my day off, and I volunteer at a local animal shelter.

Volunteering at an animal shelter wasn't date-like at all, and I didn't have enough brain power to read a book today. At least this way I wouldn't be watching television all day.

I can't sleep anyway. What time were you thinking? And is there coffee involved?

My phone buzzed in my hand as I stood and stretched my muscles, tight from being overworked.

West – Makes two of us. If you want, I can pick you up in thirty minutes. We can get burgers after– as friends, of course.

I smiled, my mouth watering at the idea of a burger and fries.

Of course. Is there going to be coffee waiting for me when I get in your Lambo?

I placed the phone on the sink as I turned on the shower and pulled off my pajamas. Just as I was about to get into the hot pulsating water, my phone buzzed, and I couldn't help but look down at it.

The coffee I can do. Afraid a Lambo is a bit out of my

reach. You'll have to deal with my Audi TT. It's orange, if that helps.

I laughed as I typed quickly. **Convertible?**

His reply was a wink face, and I felt my body flush as I realized I was *naked texting him*. My mind rushed forward, wondering if he might be doing the same thing– and what exactly that tattoo on his chest said...and was there more?

Friends, River!

My shower was hot, but I was tempted to turn it ice cold until the warmth hit my aching muscles. The relief momentarily cooled off the hormones in my brain; that is until my doorbell rang. I fumbled with the shower nob, grabbing a towel and drying quickly as I slid my finger across my phone's screen. I didn't know how I managed to stay in the shower that long, but the last text message from West said received thirty-three minutes ago.

The doorbell rang again. Naked texting and now this. I wrapped the towel around my body, and then headed down the stairs, my hair still dripping water down my neck as I opened the door. West's eyes locked on my face, green eyes twinkling as they stayed there.

"I'm not going to look down," he said as his lips pulled up, dimpling his cheeks.

God, those dimples.

"Thanks," I replied looking at the two Dunkin Donuts coffees in a tray and a paper bag that smelled like amazing pastry.

"I could've given you more time," West said as I stepped

aside so he could come in. His neck was red, and a vein in it pulsed quickly as he stared straight ahead.

I laughed, and my towel started to unravel, causing me to move quickly to catch it which also made West's locked glance come down. The red traveled up to his cheeks, and he closed his eyes.

"I'm sorry. I didn't mean to look," he said, and his voice was deep in a way that made my stomach flutter.

"Don't worry if you came to the door in a towel I wouldn't have your level of self-control," I replied, and I bit my cheek hard.

Why the hell did I just say that?

West's eyes opened, and an eyebrow arched over his eyes. "Is that so?"

It was my turn to blush, but I kept my eyes on his. "Maybe–I mean with all the tattoos teasing me through that v-neck, you can't blame me for being curious at what they say."

He chuckled to himself, nodding over his shoulder. "Mind if I take a seat while you get dressed?"

"Go ahead," I said as I headed up the stairs. I paused halfway up the stairs and glanced over my shoulder at him. His eyes were on me, just like I thought they would be.

He licked his lips, eyes traveling from my bare legs to my face. "My soul, forever, yours to keep."

My eyes widened as my jaw went slack. "What?"

"That's what it says," he replied, pulling at the v-neck so I could see the words *my soul* connecting to *forever*.

"That's beautiful," I said, and his eyes fell as he swallowed.

"Yeah." He gave me a soft smile, but it strained at the edges as if the reason behind the tattoo pained him. He signaled to the living room. "I'll wait to eat, but I can't promise I won't drink half my coffee."

"As long as you don't drink mine you'll be safe," I replied, and I heard his laughter as I made my way back up the stairs.

When I got back into the bedroom, I let the towel unravel, my eyes going to the ceiling.

Maybe Bobby was right. Friendship wasn't a possibility. I needed to be honest with him then– when and if this bordered on something more than friendship and an undeniable attraction.

Chapter 43

We spent the ride over to the shelter talking about crazy things that happened at work, and West's stories were far more insane than my own. When we arrived West slid across the hood and opened my door before I could, his eyebrows wiggling. I burst out laughing, shaking my head at him and he gave me one of those dimpled smiles that made my heart race. In the short periods we spent together all I seemed to do was smile and laugh—and that was a nice feeling.

"So let me introduce you to each of my friends," West said, walking backward through the row of pens. Each had a doggy door to the outside so they could easily run out and exercise, and a nice soft bed as well. It was a shelter, but the dogs all seemed so happy, especially when they heard West's voice. "This is Bella," he began, and he introduced me to each dog, explaining what he knew of their background. At the last cage, he stopped, crossing his arms over his chest and narrowing his eyes. "You have to promise not to fall in love with these ones."

I blinked at him. "What makes you think that I'll fall in love with *these* ones more than the others?"

A wide smile spread across his lips as he opened his arms and signaled for me to come forward. I peered into the cage to see three beagle puppies sleeping in various positions on the bed in the corner. Every single one was as adorable as the next. I couldn't help the sound of adoration that slipped through my lips, a bit high pitched and very girly. It woke up the puppies who stumbled over one another before tripping over their ears to get to me. I looked over my shoulder and West looked up at the ceiling shaking his head. "Go ahead. Go in."

I walked in and sat on the floor crossed legged so the puppies could crawl over me. I laughed as the littlest one attempted to climb up my chest to lick my chin. He slipped, and his paws went down my shirt.

"Watch out, they're feisty," West said as he stared down at me with that smile still plastered on his face.

I picked up the little pup and held him up, looking into his brown eyes, one circled by a black patch, the other a tan spot. I put my nose against the puppy's moving it back and forth.

"Wow, Jesse was not kidding." West's laughter filled the cage, echoing off the concrete surround.

I opened my eyes, lowering the puppy to my lap where I scratched behind his ear, and he thumped his back foot. "I didn't know you knew Jesse."

West ran his hands through the length of hair slicked back over his head, stopping at his neck. His muscles flexed beneath his tattoos, so it appeared the petals of the flowers were moving. "I've known Jesse for a few years."

Our eyes locked and his shoulders rose before he sat down across from me. He put his forearms over the top of his knees.

"A few years?" I asked. My stomach twisted as I wondered if the reason Jesse didn't want me to talk to West was the same reason Bobby warned me—maybe it wasn't about protecting me but protecting *West*.

West nodded as one of the puppies attempted to climb up the front of his legs. He put his hands around its waist and lifted it onto his chest where he rubbed its back. His lip ring pulled into his mouth before he continued, "Yeah." My mouth began to form the word *how*, but he cut me off. "Client confidentiality."

My mouth slacked. "Jesse has a tattoo?"

West rubbed his palm over the scruff of his chin. "Or two."

"Or two?"

He winked at me and then looked down at the puppy still in my lap, who apparently fell back asleep as I pet him. "I think you have a new friend."

"What's his name?" I asked as the puppy's little eyes fluttered with tiny black lashes.

"I've been calling him Cuddles for obvious reasons," West replied as I ran my fingers over the soft fur. "What would you call him?"

I let my eyes rise slowly. "Bagel."

"Bagel?" he repeated, his chest shaking with a chuckle. "That's interesting."

"Bagel the beagle." I narrowed my eyes at him before lifting the puppy up and looking in his sleepy eyes. "Wouldn't you like to be called Bagel?" The puppy's tail wagged, and his eyes perked up. I looked over him at West. "See, he likes it."

"I think he likes *you*," he said, and his eyes drifted back down to the other two puppies playing– one was pulling the other around by its ears. "Be nice you two!"

Bagel cuddled closer to me, his eyes seeming to narrow on his siblings.

"Beagles howl," I said with a sigh.

"Not all of them," West replied as he reached over and separated them. "Besides, you can work on training him."

My eyes widened. "You tricked me! You and Jesse together– you planned this!"

"No," West said before biting over his lip ring, so it was entirely in his mouth. "It's a coincidence that I happen to volunteer at a shelter, and these three came in last week...and that Jesse mentioned you love beagles."

"And you asked me here to?"

"Help me out...and maybe fall in love–" his eyes locked on mine and he coughed looking away; "with the puppies."

"Well, your plan worked," I said as I looked down at the dog. "What do you think Bagel? Do you want to come home with me and keep all my neighbors up at night?"

West leaned forward, scratching Bagel under the chin. "We'll get you trained so you *won't* wake up the whole complex."

"We'll?" I asked, raising an eyebrow.

"These two certainly need it," West replied looking at

the other two, now in reverse roles. The smaller of the two was now dragging the bigger one around on its back by its ears. "Especially if they're going to be coming to the shop on a regular basis."

"Maybe one of them should be Bagel, and the other CC—for cream cheese," I said as I stood, Bagel still in my arms.

West stood, then leaned down, so Bagel was within licking distance of him. "No, I think he likes that name, don't you little guy?"

Bagel licked West's chin, and he laughed as he stood, wiping off the slobber. "I was thinking Sadie and Walter."

"Those names aren't fun."

"They kind of are because they're awful," West said, wrinkling his nose. I nodded my agreement, and he gave me a soft nudge with his elbow, signaling with his chin out the door. "We need to get some chores done, fill out the adoption paperwork and then we can bring these three out shopping."

"What about lunch? And how are all five of us going to fit in your car?" I asked as I put Bagel down and he immediately tried to climb back up my leg, whining.

"Good point," West replied as he shut the door behind us. The three puppies came up to the gate and looked up at us; foreheads pulled back by the weight of their ears. "Clean, paperwork, lunch, pick up your mommy mobile and get the puppy crew."

I rolled my eyes. "A Honda Civic *SI* is *not* a mommy mobile."

"Soccer Mom car?" West suggested as he looked down at

me from the corner of his eyes. I stuck my tongue out, and his shoulders rose as he laughed. "No, that's right– puppy mobile."

"I guess so, especially if we're all going to be going to training classes on a regular basis," I replied, chewing the inside of my lip as I looked over at him. The smile on his lips made my heart beat stagger.

"At least two times a week, *friend,*" he said with a smirk as he grabbed bowls from a shelf. His shirt lifted in the back, showing that his face wasn't the only dimpled part of his body. As he turned my face flushed and my eyes shot back up to his.

Friends, I reminded myself. That didn't mean I couldn't stare, right?

He bit his lip, wiggling his eyebrows and I took the bowls he held out to me as he chuckled.

He didn't seem to mind my wandering eyes, and I certainly didn't mind his.

Chapter 44

"Are you sure it's okay that they do that?" I asked, nodding to the puppies three in a row dragging one another by their ears.

West laughed as he leaned back on the couch, tapping on my shoulder as he did. "Relax, Mommy. They'll be fine."

I bit my lip and sat back, sinking into the cushions to avoid the warmth of his arm behind me. My whole body was warm enough as it was from the five hours I spent laughing with him– I didn't need a reminder of the physical attraction too. We sat in silence for a moment, and it wasn't awkward. This was too easy. I glanced over at West to find him smirking at something on the wall. My eyes followed his to my Yamaha guitar. It was one of the only reminders I kept of Adam. I couldn't stand to leave it in the case, so the day I moved in I also bought a wall hook for it, but I hadn't touched it since.

"You play?" West asked as he nodded at it.

My chest tightened. "A bit."

West's eyebrows wiggled at me, and I rolled my eyes as I stood, stepping over the tumbling puppies and took it off the wall.

"What kind of music do you like?" I asked as I sat on the couch again, bringing my legs up under me and crossing them as I put the guitar in my lap. I stared at him with wide eyes. "Tool? Deftones?"

"Eagles."

I looked down at the guitar and took a deep breath before I began to strum. The lyrics flowed from my lips as my fingers moved over the strings. I hadn't played for so long that the pressing of the strings bit into my fingers, but I kept playing because it felt so good. The tightness in my chest from the thought of Adam eased away as I realized I enjoyed playing, and I enjoyed being around West. It was nice not have him expect me to be a certain way. He hadn't known me as I child, and I could do and say things that felt like me— the me I was now. When the song ended, I looked up to find West leaning forward, arms pressed against his knees and fingers entwined. He shook his head, jaw slightly slack.

"You're beautiful— I mean your voice— it's beautiful. I mean well, you are too." He sat back pushing his fingers into his temples. "I'm sorry if I crossed a friendship line there by saying that—" his eyes rose up to mine, and his cheeks flushed; "it's just...you are."

I bit my lip to keep from smiling. My face was as hot as his. "You're not too bad yourself."

Bobby's words echoed in my head–*Tell him.*

"It's good to have a friend," I finally said as our eyes locked on each other. It was kind of liking telling him — at least I was drawing a line with my words. My heart, on the other hand, was hammering in my chest. He wasn't hard on the eyes at all– especially with those eyes and tattoos–plus the smile and personality. A cry from Bagel broke my wandering gaze, and I shot up from the couch. West stopped me, putting a hand on my arm and sending tingles through my body.

"Easy," he said, and he nodded to Bagel now biting Walter's hind leg.

"I guess this is going to take some getting used to," I said as I sat back down and I meant more than just the dogs playing. I took a deep breath as I pulled the guitar back into my lap. I began to strum again to distract myself and then started singing more to myself than anything– Foreigner.

West chuckled to himself, and I glanced up to see him leaning back shaking his head, eyes locked on me. "I guess so."

I played two more songs, carefully watching my fingers as they glided over the strings before looking back up to see West with a pile of puppies sleeping on him. I laughed as I stood and placed the guitar back on its hook before carefully extracting Bagel from the sleeping pile. I laid back on the couch, putting him on my chest. His eyes blinked slowly at me before he gave me a single kiss on the chin and fell back to sleep. My own eyes began to get heavy as I pet him, and my gaze flickered over to West. His head rested on top of Sadie as she sat on his chest and over his shoulder. I grabbed my cell phone from the coffee table, careful not to move enough to wake Bagel and snapped the picture before closing my own eyes. I sank into a deep, dreamless sleep– but instead of being the damming darkness I knew for the past eight months it was warm and comforting–like West.

My mouth watered as the smell drifted over me– garlic, basil, and tomatoes as if I fell asleep in an Italian heaven. My eyes opened, and I leaned up, stretching to find all the puppies and West were gone. I glanced over the top of the couch to see West humming to himself as he leaned back against the counter next to the stove, a steaming pot next to him. His gaze lifted. "I know you're probably sick of me by now, but I figured I would cook us dinner and then leave you alone."

I was far from tired of his company, and I didn't mind at all. I stood and made my way into the kitchen, but as I came around the corner of the column between the two my foot slipped on something wet. I tried to grab for support, but the column was round and just as slippery as the wet hardwoods. I came down in a heap–sprawled out in a puddle of puppy pee. West walked forward, arms out as he tried to hide a smirk.

"It's not funny," I replied, my tone harsh but there was a smile forming on my lips as I glanced at the puppies looking anywhere but at me; as if they knew it was their fault.

West gave me a hand up. "It kind of is."

My mouth dropped open, and I huffed, crossing my arms as I narrowed my eyes at him. "You should've been paying attention to them."

He threw his hands up, still smiling. "Well, sorry! I was busy making dinner while you got some beauty sleep."

The word beauty reminded me he slipped up and went

utterly red when he called me beautiful. I bit my lip as he walked back into the kitchen, his jeans perfectly fitting over his ass.

You're covered in puppy pee!

I looked down at my soaked jeans and felt the warmth of it sinking through my thin cotton t-shirt. "Fine, well, how long until dinner's done?"

West leaned down, popping open the oven and my eyes went to his ass *again*. Followed by them drifting up to where his t-shirt wasn't covering his back dimples anymore.

I needed a shower. A cold one.

"Ten minutes," he replied, glancing over at me. "Not sure if that's enough time for a chick to take a shower."

I rolled my eyes. "You don't know me that well."

As I walked away, I heard him say, "Yet."

I inhaled through my nose and out my mouth before continuing up the stairs. When I came down less than ten minutes later, West was on the back porch, where he set out our food and was pouring glasses of wine.

"I hope you don't mind I popped this open," West said as I came outside. His gaze wandered over me quickly before he coughed and sat down. It wasn't like there was much for him to look at with me in yoga pants and a baggy t-shirt that hung off one shoulder, but he still seemed unnerved by it.

"Not at all," I replied, sitting down across from him. I lifted my glass, and he followed suit. "To this."

I didn't say to friendship. I wasn't sure what *this* was, or what this was going to be, but I did know I didn't feel like I was in that hole with Bobby. West's chuckle warmed me.

"To this," he repeated.

We ate in silence for a moment, and then my gaze drifted up to him. He gave me a light smile before taking a sip of the wine. I grabbed a piece of bread, debating what I was going to say.

"It's nice not being alone for once," I finally said.

West tipped his head. "Are you alone a lot?"

"Single, determined woman– alone is kind of what I do well– besides working," I replied as I took another sip of wine. "Did Jesse mention why he set me up with Maggie as a photographer?"

West's lips slipped downward as he shook his head. "I figured it was just because you're good. I did think it was odd because it seems like you already work a lot and he'd know that, being your boss and all."

"He's also kind of my friend," I replied, pushing my ravioli around my plate before looking up again. West leaned forward, eyes intent on me. It was time to tell him. I needed to be honest because I was obviously attracted to him and it seemed like he was attracted to me. I bit the inside of my cheek before finding the words. "He watches out for me. A few months ago I broke up with my boyfriend, and I kind of lost everything because of it and things that happened before that. I guess Jesse thought I needed some friends and meeting Maggie would help with that."

West's lips parted, but he seemed at a loss for words. "You can't not have friends– you're so–"

"Nice, but driven and being driven tends to *drive* people away. In college I drove away all my friends by the end...except..." My voice faded, and I swallowed, glancing out at the dimly lit yard.

West reached across the table and put his hand over mine. "The tattoo?"

I bit my lip nodding.

He squeezed my hand and leaned back, his thumb drawing soft circles over my skin. "What about family? In my experience, they're kind of hard to drive away."

I scoffed, shaking my head as I looked down at our hands. "I see my dad once a week– he comes up on Saturdays, and we spend the day watching TV, having dinner and talking."

"That sounds nice–so why do you seem so angry about it?" West's voice was soft, his words said slowly, as if he was afraid to insult me.

I fought the urge to stand up and sit in his lap–to be in the warmth his smile sent me– to be wrapped in his natural happiness.

"My dad comes secretly. My mom and I... I'm not on good terms with her. I guess we were never on good terms but last year on Thanksgiving she crossed a line and I haven't been able to get passed it," I said, and my eyes moved up his hand to his arm spiraling with color –waves, koi fish, lotus and cherry blossoms. Mom would die if she saw him. If I was skanky, he was an absolute man-slut.

Jesse did say he's a womanizer. And you're a man-eater.

"Doesn't agree with your choices?" West asked as he lifted his wine up to his thin, very kissable lips.

My chest rose as I nodded.

"Well, let's say you'd probably go into shock if you met my family– blue collar, nose in the air, house on the vineyard people. Very un-tattooed."

"And how do they take to–" I signaled to his arm and collarbone, my pulse hitching as he winked at me.

"You haven't even seen them all," he replied, and his eyes locked on mine, devious in their twinkle as if he knew I wanted to know where the others were. As if to say it's only a matter of time.

I swallowed hard, looking down at my pasta.

"Let's just say they got used to it...and my mom tries to think of it as art–my dad tries to think of it as proving I have a high pain tolerance and a talent with my hands."

My eyes shot up at that, and he leaned back laughing. My face burned, and my mind raced to places it should definitely not be.

"Do you now?" I managed to stutter.

Flirt. You're such a damn flirt.

I wasn't sure if I was chastising him or myself in my head–or worse, neither.

He reached across the table and flipped my arm, running his fingertips up to the tattoo he gave me and traced its outline. The tingling started from somewhere other than my arm, and I bit hard on my cheek as he sat back, wiggling his eyebrows.

"Yeah," I said as I leaned forward and grabbed my glass of wine. "You're talented alright."

Chapter 45

I heaved a sigh, pulling the covers down from my face and looked at the foot of my bed to the crate. Bagel sat pressing his nose against the bars, a whimper coming from his lips as his sad puppy eyes stared back at me. I couldn't resist him, and ended up getting him and cuddling him into my arms. When my phone rang that it was time to wake up I opened my eyes to see Bagel on his back, paws draped over my arms and ears splayed over against the pillow.

He thinks he's a human.

I laughed to myself as I reached over him, careful not to disturb him and grabbed my phone. I swiped my finger across the screen, silencing the alarm and then looked down at the still sleeping puppy. He could probably sleep through anything. I laid back next to him and lifted my phone over us to take a picture. Bagel was adorable. I was a hot mess, but the puppy made the picture. I typed in West's name and then looked down at Bagel, now awake. "Is it weird for me to send this?"

Bagel blinked at me before licking my face.

I laughed, pushing his face away as I replied,"You're right, we're just friends so it isn't."

My phone buzzed as I slipped out of bed. I glanced down at the preview to see a picture of West, shirtless, with one puppy on his chest; its head tucked into his shoulder and one laying out frog style against his side. His green eyes were soft with sleep, enhanced by a crooked smile. I bit my lip as I opened the text and the picture enlarged so I could see the whole of his tattooed body beneath the puppies. The full sleeves capped at his shoulders, connected only by the words Sadie's head obscured, but she didn't entirely hide his chiseled chest. I rolled my eyes, cheeks flushing before flipping back to the text portion. If he were my boyfriend, that would be my screen saver. The text above the picture read:

No fair.

But didn't allude to what wasn't fair. Him looking so good certainly wasn't fair to me or the friendship zone I was attempting to set up. My phone buzzed again.

I see being convincingly cute and sad is a trait that runs in the family.

That made sense. I typed back a response:

Yeah, not fair at all. I had no chance.

I placed the phone on the bathroom sink as I pulled my shirt over my head, and it buzzed across the surface.

I don't have one either.

I slid my pajama bottoms off before turning on the water and glancing back at my phone. My stomach fluttered, and I grabbed it, naked texting yet again. I wondered what West would think of that, but shook the thought from my head.

Whatever will we do?

The response came before I could put my phone down.

I guess we'll just have to wait and see. But if things keep going like this I'm a total goner. Not that I'm complaining.

My heart hammered in my chest. I had a distinct feeling we somehow veered into talking about us. My breath caught in my throat as I replied:

Same here. So what days work best for your schedule for doggy training classes? I'll have to move around my Zumba and spin classes ?

I wanted to see him again. I wanted to hear his laugh; to feel the warmth it embraced me with and to forget what I was running from. My eyes lifted to my silhouette in the mirror. Maybe I wasn't running from anything anymore, though. I took a shaky breath as my eyes fell back to my phone. That idea was scarier than running.

Tuesday and Thursday at six?

Ready or not.

Sounds perfect.

I inhaled, letting the air in my lungs out slowly before putting the phone down. As I got into the shower, it buzzed, and I saw his response on the screen.

I'll meet you at your place at 530. Take your car? I make dinner?

We texted like that the whole morning, in between me getting dressed and driving to work. My eyes drifted to the tattoo parlor as I drove by and I saw the unmistakable orange Audi already in the lot. My mind kept going to him throughout the day. I hadn't texted anyone like this since...my throat thickened. Since Bobby. Adam and I never really texted that much, but Bobby and I were non-stop. My phone buzzed again, and I stopped typing to look down at it.

You're wrong. Luke Holland does not beat Rian Dawson. Besides have you seen the guy?

I bit my lip. He did have a point there.

"And who exactly are you texting, smiling like that?" Jesse's voice interrupted my thoughts, and I jumped, barely saving my phone from flying out of my hands and through the glass wall next to me.

I put my hand over my chest, opening a drawer and dropping the phone into it. "No one."

Jesse moved from the door frame and sat down in the chair across from me, leaning back with his hands forming a steeple. "Doesn't seem like no one."

"We're friends."

Jesse's eyebrows rose. "So did he convince you to get a puppy?"

My shoulders lifted up to my ears as I pressed my palms against my desk. "Maybe..."

He leaned forward signaling to my desk drawer. "I expect some pictures right about now."

I grabbed my phone out of the drawer and flipped passed the saved one of a shirtless West, moving to a few more appropriate ones and handed it to Jesse. He ran his finger across the screen, and his smile grew. His finger flicked one more time, and I felt my jaw tighten. One eyebrow rose and then his eyes came up to my face.

Of course, he found it.

"So you saved this one for what, eye candy?" Jesse asked,

and his tone was as playful as the smile on his lips. I narrowed my eyes at him before grabbing my phone back and putting it away. Jesse chuckled to himself.

"We're just friends," I said as he crossed his arms and nodded, his eyes showing he wasn't convinced. I needed a change of subject, maybe something embarrassing enough to get him to drop the fact I was very attracted to my *friend*. "And where are your secret tattoos?"

Jesse's head jerked back as he looked at the ceiling before standing and placing a foot on the chair. He lifted the back of his slacks to reveal a tattoo of pine trees on the back of his calf. The forest's shadows seemed to leak down, taking the beautiful trees into someplace haunting. "By the way, this isn't the only reason I know him."

He sat back down, and his eyes became serious. "Maggie's husband is my best friend — we grew up together– and Maggie's best friend is West. So we've hung out more than just for my tattoo. He's a good guy."

"Then why didn't you want me talking to him?" I asked, leaning forward. His eyes paced over mine and my muscles tightened.

"He *is* a womanizer...it's just not the way you took it. He's not cocky. He's guarded."

"And you think I'll break him?" I asked, and I felt my throat thickening. Bobby said I would, or the Bobby in my mind did.

"I don't know what's going to happen between you two. I'm not going to pretend I do. If you say you're just friends, I trust you, and I know you both need that." Jesse's eyes dropped to his hands now propped on his knees. "You'd be good for each other, though, if you two can get passed your pasts."

"*Our* pasts?" I asked as Jesse stood.

He looked over his shoulder at me and gave a firm nod. I knew he wouldn't say any more; he was West's friend, and it was West's choice to tell me, just like I expected Jesse not to tell West about my past. He nodded towards my door. "Ready for the monthly team meeting, Directorress?"

The team was already gathered around the coffee and donuts I brought in.

"Sure, and they better have left me a Boston Creme donut."

"Their lives depend on it," Jesse said with a wink.

As I followed Jesse out of the room, my eyes drifted back over my shoulder to the drawer where I knew my phone was. I felt my body heat as I wondered just what West had hidden in his past. He seemed secure and confident like there was nothing for him to hide. But I didn't know him.

And he didn't really know me.

Chapter 46

I glanced over my shoulder at the three puppies in the backseat, harnessed and sleeping on top of each other and then back over at West. I let him drive now since I didn't particularly like to, and I hadn't gotten my bearings outside of the city yet. He caught me staring and smiled over at me, his hand on his thigh clenching and I wondered if he was thinking about putting it over mine. My palm tingled, and I my hand formed a fist as my eyes moved out the window to the suburb we were passing through. Since the day I started my new job I hadn't returned to the city, and I felt tears prick a the corner of my eyes as I thought of the things I left behind. I wondered how Tara was doing. Every once in a while I'd pull her name up on IM at work and think about saying something–at least over IM it'd be somewhat safe. She couldn't say anything nasty about me leaving Adam, but then again she could just ignore me. I pressed my eyes shut, tipping my head back against the seat. I missed her and even though Maggie filled part of that hole, she wasn't quite Tara. Their personalities were close, but no one *was* Tara–just like no one was Bobby or Adam.

Adam.

My mind hadn't drifted to him in over three weeks–the weeks since I last saw him, striding up to get a tattoo from the man who sat next to me. I swallowed, and somehow a sigh slipped passed my lips. West's hand fell over mine and squeezed.

I opened my eyes and glanced over at him as he put the car into park in front of my condo. His eyes raced over mine. "Are you okay, River?"

I looked down at his hand over mine. "Yeah, just thinking."

"About?" he asked, and my gaze flicked back up to his. He leaned forward, and I felt the warmth of his body lingering near me–the caring and worry in his eyes.

Could I tell him? Should I tell him?

"I burned a lot of bridges when I moved here...I just wonder if I could've done things differently. If I could've..."

Saved Adam from himself.

West knew Adam. He knew what kind of state he was in– he knew Adam signed to a label. He was probably friends with him for all I knew.

"It's good to reflect on the past, but only to learn from it in the future," West said, and his pupils dilated as he stared back at me.

He had a past too. Maybe I could tell him.

"I just...I don't know...It's like I can't fully escape it."

West shrugged, cocking his head at me. "Maybe you shouldn't try to escape it. If you keep running, you'll lose yourself."

"I think I already have."

I'd wanted Adam to find me, but he was too busy finding himself, and I was...my eyes lifted to West. I was here with this man who obviously cared about me.

I watched as his Adam's apple rose and fell. "The only person who can find you–the real you–is yourself. Maybe you ran from who you were because you weren't that person anymore. Now you just have to find out who you are *now* and learn to love that person." His eyes dropped, and he flipped my arm so I could see the tattoo he gave me. "I think you have that strength, River. You just need to realize it."

"Everyone kept saying I was so strong when everything was happening," I replied, and I could feel the tears forming in my eyes. I was dancing around telling him the truth, but I was finally saying the things I held in. West's hand lifted to my face, cupping my cheek and I closed my eyes. "And I was so weak." I let my eyes open to find West's bearing into mine. "No one ever saw it– no one tried to help. They just kept saying you're strong. While I was completely fading."

"Maybe what they saw was that you were strong for everyone else–but you needed to be strong for yourself. If you're not strong for yourself, eventually everything else falls away." West's thumb stroked my cheek, and the aching hollow that had returned seem to move away. "I don't know what happened before, but I don't think you're weak for moving here–away from what was dragging you down. I think it took a lot of strength to make the decisions you did."

The breath I'd been holding kept out in a whoosh as I shook my head. "He's always right."

West's eyes narrowed, and I took his hand to press it to my lips before letting it fall. His jaw slackened, and I blushed as I realized what I just did — kissed him– well, his hand.

Crossed the friend line much?

He withdrew his hand slowly, letting it fall into his lap, and I put my hand over my mouth as I glanced down at the floor of the car. West coughed, and my eyes lifted. He was blushing too.

"Who's always right?" he asked.

"Oh," I replied, shaking my head. "Jesse."

"Why, what did he say?"

"That we needed each other," I began and when his eyes widened I quickly added; "as friends."

"Ah," West said, looking ahead and tapping his hands against my steering wheel. "Yeah, he's usually right." His gaze moved to the corner of his eyes, and he asked, "What else did he say about us?"

We'd be good together.

I pursed my lips, and it was my turn to avoid his gaze. "Nothing really."

West chuckled to himself. "I hope he's right about that too."

My body shot with tingles as I looked back at him, a crooked grin on his lips. Had Jesse had the same conversation with West?

"Well, I owe you dinner for tonight," West said as he glanced into the back seat.

"No, you drove, so it's my turn to cook," I replied as I got out of the car and went to unbuckle Bagel.

"Can you cook?" West asked as he leaned in to unbuckle his puppies. His eyes twinkled.

"Yes, and very well, I'll have you know."

"Alright — I'm excited to see this," he said as we made our way up the walk. "And what are we having?"

"Thai chicken salad," I replied, and he blinked at me as I opened the door.

"Salad?"

I nodded as I placed Bagel on the ground and headed into the kitchen.

"The best damn salad you'll ever eat," I said, smirking at him.

"You do realize it's just grass smothered in dressing, right?" West asked, crossing his arms against the kitchen island.

"You'll see," I replied as I began taking the ingredients out of the fridge.

"I'm not a bunny," he said as he came around the island and took the cutting board out of the cabinet. He already knew where everything was. "But I'll be a man and help you put together the salad–which by the way is hardly cooking."

I rolled my eyes. "You're testing your luck, boy."

"*Boy?*" West repeated, raising his eyebrows. "Hardly."

Our eyes locked and the insinuation in his tone made my pulse rush until my whole body was unbearably hot–kind of like him. I looked down at the chicken– slimy and cold. That put my hormones back in check.

"So," West began, interrupting the awkward silence that fell over us. "How do you like your new job?"

"Honestly?" I asked as I put the chicken in the pan to cook along with some garlic. "Sometimes I feel like I'm doing it all alone–like I'm drowning. Before I never really felt like that."

"What do you think is different?" West looked up quickly before concentrating on the cabbage I had him shredding.

"I don't know–maybe it's that Jesse isn't there all the time–or that I have less reliable people around me– or that I feel like I'm starting from scratch. In my old job I was well respected and even though I'm working with the same people, I feel like I've hit the reset button. It was hard enough proving myself then, and now I'm doing it all over in a brand new job with a lot more responsibility."

West stopped what he was doing and put the cabbage into the bowl I placed next to him. "Maybe you just need to ask for help?"

"I would if I could trust the people I'm working with–but when I ask for things to get done, they don't."

"I know this is going to sound unrelated– but when I was having trouble getting people to accept accountability at the shop I found ways to put processes in place that would physically hold them accountable. Some people don't have that natural drive to do things, and you have to give them a process that holds them to it. How you'd do that, I don't know, but it's just a thought," West said as he came up next to me and took the spatula to stir the chicken.

I leaned back against the counter and looked up at him. "I think you're right, and I just might have an idea."

"I'm not just some dumb tattoo artist," West replied, winking at me and I leaned up to kiss him on the cheek.

I didn't care if I was crossing a line. I didn't want there to be lines. I wanted us just to be us–and if he were Bobby, I would've done the same thing.

"You'll never just be some dumb tattoo artist to me," I said before falling back onto the balls of my bare feet and going to the refrigerator to get the ingredients for the dressing. "Have people said that–that you're just a dumb tattoo artist?"

West glanced over at me from the corner of his eyes, his neck fading from red to pink. "I said my parents are open-minded, but not all of my family is."

"That sucks, but you love what you do right?" He nodded. "Then that's what matters."

"Do you still love what you do?"

I stopped whisking the soy sauce, oil, and honey for a moment and looked up. I swallowed as my stomach tightened and my shoulders lifted. "I don't know...but I think someday I will."

"Speaking of love, from the smell of that dressing and this chicken...you might be right," West said as he pulled the chicken off the stove and added it to the salad. I came over and poured some of the dressing over it, tossing it and then taking a piece of chicken out and holding it up to his lips. His eyes locked on mine as he took it, his lips gliding over my fingers in a way that made me swallow. "I guess Jesse isn't the only one who's always right."

Think of something else, River. Something else. Not those lips.

Not that laugh. Not the warmth spreading through your entire body. Not his body.

"Are you volunteering at the shelter this weekend?" I asked, and the words came out so fast I wondered if he could understand them.

He covered the smile on his lips by scratching his cheek. "Why, you interested in joining me? It's bath day for all the dogs."

"Does that mean you'll be shirtless?" Again, the words came out without my mind catching up.

West winked as he grabbed the plate I served him. "That's really the only way to give ten dogs a bath."

"Should I wear a bathing suit?" I asked as I followed him out to the deck. "The only one I have is the one I got my tattoo in."

West's fork stopped halfway to his lips. "That works just fine."

It was my turn to wink, but I looked down at my salad before I could see his reaction. The slight rumble in his chest let me know he liked the idea as much as I did.

Chapter 47

I rubbed my temples as I continued to review my staff's creatives on the computer screen. I put West's idea into place on Monday, and the first due date was today, which apparently meant everyone completed everything exactly a half an hour before it was time for them to leave. I opened the notation button, irritated that I still couldn't get it through Joyce's head that you didn't begin a sentence with a coordinating conjunction. It was meant to *coordinate*. It was going to be a long night. I heaved a sigh as I plugged my headphones into my cell phone and opened my favorite streaming music station. The music relaxed me, and I fell into a rhythm, rejecting more than I approved. It wasn't a swimming start, but at least I had a tracking mechanism for workflow. A knock at my door made me jump, and Charlie stuck her head in, chewing on the inside of her lip.

"Bad time?" she asked as she stepped inside.

I shook my head, pulling the earphones out and nodding for her to take a seat. "Just listening to some music and going through the creatives." I looked down at the time. "Shouldn't you be getting ready to go home?"

Her shoulders lifted. "I wanted to ask you something

about the new system for the creatives. Are we allowed to ask for extensions?"

I raised an eyebrow. "I try to set reasonable time frames."

"I know, and I appreciate it–it's just sometimes other things get in the way."

"Like the photographer missing the shoot?" I asked, cocking my head at her, and she went bright red. "You're not throwing anyone under the bus. I'm aware of the situation and taking care of it."

Charlie's shoulders slumped as she relaxed in the seat. "Thanks."

"If you're ever having issues with a vendor, please reach out to me. It's my job to straighten them out," I replied with what I hoped was a reassuring smile.

She smiled back, leaning forward to look at my cell phone. "So what you listening to? Let me guess, country?"

I blinked at her a few times before unplugging the headphones so she could hear. The sound of the announcer's voice filled the air.

"Welcome to Pandemonium Radio's Friday Night Freak Out where *we* get your favorite new bands on air, and *you* freak out– this week we have the up and coming band *Fade Burn* from the capital of metal music – Boston MA."

"Nice!" Charlie said. "I love Pandemonium and Fade Burn is incredible."

The room spun around me as I stared at the cell phone's screen and the announcer continued. "So we have the band here Adam, Mark, Joe, and Tony. It's great to have you!" The guys answered in unison, but I could still pick out Adam's voice. It was deeper than usual due to the situation. His voice always got deeper when he wasn't talking to someone he knew well. "We're going to hear a song called Faded Perfection off of their *On the Edge* EP. So who wrote the song? Alright, all of the guys are pointing at Adam. So is this about a girlfriend–tell us more?"

Adam wasn't the one who answered. Instead, it was Mark. "Not his current girlfriend."

"So you're taken?" the announcer asked, and I could imagine Adam rubbing the back of his neck.

"Something like that," he replied, and I felt my whole body go numb.

He has a girlfriend.

"Sorry ladies," the announcer began, and I finally came to my senses and hit the pause button.

"It's a shame," Charlie said with a shrug as she stood. "Adam's hot. I'd totally be his groupie." She stopped midstride, staring out the glass wall and before I could respond she continued; "Speaking of hot."

My eyes snapped up to see West making his way down the hallway. The numbness in my body was replaced with a racing heat.

"Is he yours?" Charlie asked as his gaze locked on mine, and he smiled.

Something like that. The irony of the thought wasn't lost on me.

"Just a friend," I replied as I stood and came around my desk.

Charlie blinked at me. "He's not staring at you like

you're just a friend." She pointed to my chin. "And you have some drool."

"Ditto," I hissed as West rounded the corner.

Charlie winked at me. "Have a good weekend," she said, and as she walked by West, she continued; "which I'm sure you will."

I put my head in my hands as I leaned back against my desk.

"You alright?" West asked as he stepped into my office, putting his hands on my bare shoulders.

"I'm going to have to have a conversation about inappropriate conversations with my employees on Monday," I replied as I looked up at him. "But you're here so it can't be all that bad. Speaking of which, why are you here?"

He stepped back, putting his hands in his pockets, so his arm muscles bulged beneath his black v-neck t-shirt as he leaned back on his heels. "I saw your car was still here, and I figured you could go for some friend time without puppies."

"That sounds good," I replied as I went to my desk and started packing up. When my hand reached for the phone on my desk, I paused, swallowing hard.

"It does?" West asked, and I looked up at him. "Because you look like it doesn't. Did I cross a line? I'm sorry..."

"No, it doesn't have to do with you," I replied, shoving my phone in my purse. "Just something I wasn't expecting happened."

"Something bad?" West asked as we fell into step next to one another.

I ran my hand through my hair. "I don't know."

West's eyebrows went into his forehead. "Things are usually either bad or good."

"Or they're bad for one person and good for another," I replied as West held the door for me. Our eyes locked and he ran his teeth over his lower lip, letting it out slowly.

"That's a bit vague," he replied.

"My ex has a girlfriend," I said, and I watched as his jaw clenched. He was quiet as we walked to his car. I turned to look at him, and his eyes avoided me. I cocked my head and managed to put a smile on my face. "Probably bad news for her."

West's eyes rose from the ground to my face. "Are you sure that's what you were thinking?"

"I just wasn't expecting to find out the way I did– that's all."

As my eyes locked on West's, I wondered if Adam having 'something' was a bad thing, especially if that 'something' made him as happy as I was right now. Butterflies rioted in my belly as West's eyes lightened, lips tipping up just enough to show some of those amazing dimples.

West nodded before asking, "So did you date a long time?"

"About a year, but we knew each other for a lot longer than that. We grew up together," I said as I leaned back against his car.

His eyes raced over mine. "Is that what you were running from? Did you get cold feet?"

"No...things went wrong fast, and it's kind of hard to go back once you've come so far." West's hand went to the back of his neck, and his eyes fell to his feet. I stepped forward, putting my hand on his bicep and pushing his arm down so I could intertwine our fingers. His gaze met mine as I smiled at him. "Besides an amazing man once told me you have to be strong for yourself and reminded me I needed to find myself on my own."

"Amazing man?" West asked.

I could've said amazing friend, but I didn't. I nodded.

"Sounds like he's a real catch," he replied, winking down at me.

I wrinkled my nose. "My employee seems to think so."

West tipped his head back, his chest rumbling with laughter before he let his chin drop to it and his head lowered, so his lips were only inches from my own. "Do you agree?"

Yes. I thought as his breath washed over my lips, sending tingles them to every inch of my body. It was already hot enough outside as it was and West being so close was making me sweat in a way that I didn't think was all that bad.

I managed to settle my attraction to him enough to pull away and open the passenger door to his tiny car. As I slid inside, I replied, "You're pretty good with animals and tattoos."

"And my hands." He added when he got in the driver's side. My eyes widened, and West shrugged as he put his arm over the back of the seat so he could see as he backed out. His fingertips grazed my shoulder as he looked over his shoulder, smirking. "I meant for tattoos. You have a dirty mind."

"Influenced heavily by you," I shot back, and my face immediately burned.

If that didn't say I thought he was hot, I wasn't sure what did.

"I can't help it if you liked seeing me shirtless and wet," he replied, and his teeth ran over his lower lip in a way that made the tingling start all over again from a place a bit lower down. Even if he hadn't done that I was pretty sure every part of me would be on fire just because of the thought and the way *he* looked at me wasn't helping matters.

"I think you enjoyed yourself too," I replied, narrowing my eyes at him even though I knew my face had to be red.

He reached over and squeezed my knee, and his touch sent a pleasant tingle up my thigh. "Why wouldn't I? I am a guy."

I laughed and how shitty I felt before drifted away like it always did when I was around West. I didn't feel like I was running. I didn't feel overwhelmed. I didn't feel not good enough.

I just felt like me– a me I actually liked.

Chapter 48

I concentrated on the puppy standing in front of me; his head cocked as he stared at the treat in my hand.

"Sit, Bagel," I said, signaling to his bum with my hand. I held my hand up. "High Five."

Bagel did as he was told. I moved my hand and placed my arm in front of him. "What do we do before we go to sleep?"

He lifted his paws to my arm and then tucked his head down between them as if praying.

"And how do we go to sleep?" I asked as I stood, signaling to the ground with my finger and then circling the finger. Bagel laid down and then flipped onto his back."Good boy!"

Dad chuckled on the porch behind us. "You're quite the talented bunch, aren't you?"

I smiled as I walked back up and sat down across from him. Bagel jumped into my lap.

"West's better than I am. He already has Sadie and Walter speaking on command. I'm afraid if I teach him to bark he'll never stop," I replied as I scratched between Bagel's ears and his leg thumped against my thigh. He sighed happily.

"Sounds like West's just braver than you are, teaching

a beagle to bark!" Dad said, and my eyes moved up to his as my pulse spiked and my throat constricted. I mentioned West. I never mentioned him to Dad before. Dad's brows rose as he sat back in his chair smiling at me.

"Brave's one word for it," I managed to say, but my voice was a breathless squeak.

I looked down at Bagel and the air in my lungs seemed to catch there, not wanting to come out.

"I'm proud of you, Riv," he said, and his voice was soft.

I let my gaze drift up to his. "For training a dog?"

He laughed, looking down at his hands on his knee before biting his lip and then answering, "That's cool, but that's not what I meant. I'm sorry I doubted you– that I said you'd be lost without Adam. You're not, and now I see I was wrong. You needed to do what you did, and I'm glad you did."

My jaw dropped before a smirk pulled at the edge of my lips. I leaned forward. "Did the great and wise Joel Ahlers actually admit he's wrong?"

Dad scratched the edge of his nose as he shook his head at me. "I'm glad to be wrong this time. So tell me more about this West gentleman?"

I ran my fingers over Bagel's coat, tracing the spot that looked like a heart when he curled up just right. "He's just a friend. We met at the beginning of July. He actually did my tattoos, and it turned out he's Maggie's cousin. He also works at the shelter I got Bagel from... He adopted his brother and sister."

"The woman you did wedding pictures for and became friends with?"

I nodded.

"Sounds like you've been seeing a lot of him?" Dad asked, and I let my eyes lift to his.

"A few times a week to bring the dogs to class and sometimes just to hang out," I replied and my muscles tensed as I waited for his eyes to shift from interested to dark and disapproving.

They didn't. Instead, he leaned forward on his forearms, forehead wrinkling with lines of concentration. "Do you like him?"

My whole body flushed with heat as I thought about that question. Did I like him?

Yes. A lot.

Dad chuckled, and I realized it must be written on my face. He reached across the table, taking my hand and squeezing it. "Then let him in, River. You've been different these past few weeks, and I thought it was just Bagel, but I see it's more than that. You've found yourself again."

My chest rose as I breathed in, locking eyes with him. "I kind of feel like I never really knew myself before this. I wish things had been different, though."

"You miss them both?" Dad asked, cocking his head.

I sighed, biting the inside of my lip. "I guess I feel like there's just a part of me that will never be whole."

Dad's lips pursed causing the wrinkles at the edge of his eyes to deepen. "Have you told him?"

My eyes drifted down to our hands as I shook my head.

"He knows I lost a friend and recently broke it off with a boyfriend—but he doesn't really know."

And he knows Adam.

"Are you still in love with Adam?"

The question caught me off guard, and I leaned back as I struggled to get air into my lungs. I thought the answer would be a resounding yes, but suddenly I didn't know. If I had feelings for West, could I still be in love with Adam? And how was that fair to West?

"I don't know."

Dad's eyes dropped from mine, and they stared down at the table as he contemplated something. Finally, they rose up to mine. "I think you do know. Just remember, River, you need to do what's best for you. Obviously, you know that better than I do."

I smirked at him. "There you go, admitting you're wrong again."

He laughed. "Don't go telling your mother."

The thought of Mom tore the smile from my lips, and my mouth went dry. "I think you'll be okay. If she ever sees me again, she'll be more hell bent on my new tattoos than anything else."

"I think she'll just be glad you're talking to her," Dad said, and I grit my teeth looking at the ground.

"She hasn't said sorry."

"Because she doesn't think you'll listen."

I looked up at him. "She'd have to try to find out."

Dad shifted in his chair, rubbing the back of his neck. "Maybe you should *both* try."

My chest rose as my lips parted and I thought about staying firm, but in the end, it did make sense. Life was too short to let petty things get in the way– as long as she changed the way she treated me.

"I will — just not quite yet," I said, and Dad blinked at me hard.

"I never thought I'd say this, but I'm actually liking not being right," he said with a chuckle as he took a cookie off the plate in front of us.

I leaned forward and took one too. "*When* Mom and I start talking again, I'll be sure not to mention *that*."

We both laughed.

"I'd appreciate that," Dad said with a smile.

Chapter 49

I stared at the guitar on the wall, my heart hammering against my too tight chest. All morning my mind had been stuck between the situation with Mom and the question of if I still loved Adam. I'd been caught off guard when I heard Adam was dating someone else through a radio station– but in truth, as soon as West walked in the door, I forgot. It just didn't seem to matter as much as I thought it would, and in the end, that was the thing that bugged me the most. It *didn't* bother me that he might have someone else and shouldn't it? I thought I was in love with him for ten years– and now for the first time, it didn't bother me he was with someone else. I squeezed my eyes shut, tipping my head back against the couch. Loving someone was supposed to make you feel whole, but with Adam, I never really felt that. The second we started dating our relationship started pulling down all my other relationships and all of his other ones. I felt the tears building in the corner of my eyes. I thought we were meant to be, but all we did was self-destruct ourselves. My muscles tensed as my stomach danced. I only wanted one thing: to talk to West. I looked down at my phone with a picture of Bagel pointing at a scent he caught in the air on the screen saver.

West was the one who helped me feel whole — he didn't make me whole — he helped show me how I could do it on my own. Did that mean I– *not possible.* I shook my head, but my hand went to my phone, moving past the lock screen to the main screen, which had a background of the very person I wanted to speak to right now.

What did West say he was doing today?

My head hurt too much for me to remember. I swiped my finger across the screen and found the good morning text he sent me, which I hadn't answered and hit the phone button. It rung a few times before a breathless West picked up, "Hey–what's up?"

My voice cracked as I replied, "What are you doing today?"

"Riv, are you okay?" he asked, and he was panting like he was working out. My pulse quickened. I hoped that's all he was *doing.* The headache deepened, and I fought the urge to vomit. The idea of *him* with someone else didn't cause a pleasant reaction, and I certainly reacted to the idea.

"This is going to sound crazy," I said as I pressed a shaky hand to my forehead. *Say it.* "I miss you."

West's breathing stopped for a second, and nausea hit me hard this time. Maybe he wanted the friend zone more than I did. Maybe I was misreading everything.

Shit.

"We can fix that by being together–I mean by hanging

out," he replied, and the breath I didn't realize I was holding came out in a whoosh. "I'll take that as a yes."

I was nodding, but he couldn't see me nodding. I found my voice, "I'd love that."

"Here's the thing–," he said, and my mind spiraled. *Here it is–he's with another woman.* "I'm kind of in the middle of running a 5K right now. I would've asked you to join me, but I know how much you love running." I laughed at that. I hated running. "And I'm sure you don't want to smell me after this. So how about a late lunch? There's this great organic cafe slash juice bar that I've wanted to bring you to. It's my favorite place."

I laughed, looking up at my ceiling as a smile warmed my face. The pressure in my head eased with each passing moment. "And why haven't you asked me until now?"

He must have started running again because I could hear his breathing picking up. "I didn't want to cross that imaginary line we have going on here...but seeing you called to say you miss me, I figured I'd jump over it because I miss you too."

Hearing his words made the tightness in my chest release. "I'm glad...otherwise, this phone call would've been hella awkward."

West chuckled through his paced breathing. "I'll text you when I'm on my way. I have to run–literally."

"Okay– one last thing — if you're running why did you pick up?" I asked.

"You just want to hear it again, huh? I missed you," he replied, and I could hear the smile on his lips.

"Well, have fun running. See you soon."

"Mhmm," he said, and I knew he was picking up his pace.

I hung up and looked down at Bagel, whose eyes were wide as if to say, *what took you so long?* I shrugged as I reached across the couch and grabbed my book, settling in to read. At some point during my reading, I ended up *sleeping*, only to be woken up by the feel of my cell phone buzzing against the couch.

West – Be there in twenty

I shot up, and Bagel groaned, narrowing his eyes as he cuddled back against me. Twenty minutes? I hadn't even showered. I managed to shower, get dressed and throw on some mascara before the doorbell rang.

"You look like you just showered," West said, nodding at my wet hair.

I blushed, running a hand through it and pulling it into a tiny ponytail. "I kind of fell asleep with a book."

West laughed as he tipped on his toes, and I was sure he could see completely behind me or down my shirt from the angle. I tilted my head up, and he laughed, scratching his chin. "That's adorable."

"What?" I asked, narrowing my eyes at him. I hoped he didn't think my breasts were adorable. My face burned at the thought. They weren't big, but I didn't think they were small enough to be called *adorable*.

He pointed to the back of my head. "The ponytail. I'm pretty sure I could make a bigger one with my hair."

He ran his fingers through the top length of his hair until

he reached the back and then turned, showing it to me. It was definitely longer by at least an inch. He turned back around, and I crossed my arms.

"You're a guy let me remind you. Exactly why are you proud of that?" I asked as I narrowed my gaze at him.

He blushed for a moment before regaining his confidence. He ran his hand through it again, his bicep flexing as he did. "You know you like my hair."

I rose an eyebrow at him. "And you don't like mine?"

He looked at my hair and then back to my face, a crooked smile pulling up the edge of his lips. "I love your hair." His arm reached around me, pulling the tiny ponytail out, his face lowering to mine. "But I prefer it down."

I swallowed hard, my mouth watering. His eyes searched mine, and my pulse spiked as our lips lingered over one another. It was incredible how a few simple words changed the dynamic made by that invisible line, which was far less visible now.

"If you insist," I replied, shrugging my shoulders and pulling away to grab my purse from the table next to the stairs. I didn't want to pull away, but my bedroom was way too close to where we were now. "So where's this fantastic cafe?"

"You'll seriously wear it down for me?" he asked, his hands now firmly planted in the front of his pockets with his thumbs sticking out. The position flexed his chest muscles beneath his gray t-shirt.

"I'm not wearing any makeup, so why the hell not?" I replied.

"I didn't notice," West said as he opened the door for me.

I shook my head at him and his grin. "Now that's a bold-faced lie."

His brow furrowed over his eyes. "No, it's not. The first thing I notice about you is your smile– and you don't usually wear that sticky shit on your lips, so this is no different. Then I notice your eyes– the way they turn an almost turquoise color when you're happy or a stormy gray when you're upset."

I stopped in my tracks, and he turned to face me, lips pursed. "What color are they now?"

"Turquoise," he replied stepping forward. My lips parted as I stared up at him. His eyes were lighter now—like green sea foam– something I recognized as him being happy. They shifted to a bluer hue when he was upset. The fact he knew the same thing about me made my body tingle.

"I'm also hungry– so maybe you're mistaken–maybe they're just this color because of that," I replied, finally finding my voice.

He coughed, rolling his eyes. "Yeah, that's it. Apparently, you're hungry ninety-nine percent of the time you're around me."

We fell in step together.

"It's possible," I replied as he opened the door to the car for me.

He raised an eyebrow. "Which begs to question what exactly you're hungry for."

You.

I got into the car without responding, and when we

began to drive the conversation moved to something less filled with sexual innuendos and thinly veiled attraction. Throughout lunch, we laughed, and when there was no food left I looked around the now empty cafe biting my lip.

"What's on your mind?" West asked, and his eyes flicked across my face.

"I don't want to go home." I bit my lip, and his eyes fell to them, causing his jaw to clench.

"Then I won't bring you home," he replied, standing and holding his hand out to me.

I hopped off the stool, placing my hand in his and let it stay there as we walked out. "Where are you going to take me?"

"Cloud watching," he replied as he unlocked his car, staring over the roof at me as I blinked at him. "I promise it's fun."

We drove in a comfortable silence, and I watched as the crowded houses disappeared, getting farther and farther apart until we drove up to a small ranch.

West put the car in park and smiled over at me as I narrowed my eyes at him. "What? You said not to take you home– this is my home– I assume that's okay?"

I got out of the car and stared at the little house. "I imagined it to be bigger."

"Why?" West asked. "It's just me and the two pups."

"Well, being on television and famous and all," I replied as I glanced around the well-manicured yard.

"I'm not very flashy," he said, and I blinked at him as

I turned and looked at his orange Audi. "Well, other than that."

"Mhmm." I rolled my eyes, and he laughed as he nodded inside.

"Try to be quiet — I don't want to wake the pups up. They'll get in the way of the cloud watching," he said, and I stifled a giggle as we snuck into his house. He grabbed a throw from over the couch and then lead the way to the backyard. He laid out the blanket and then sat on it, looking expectantly up at me. I gave in and sat down next to him.

"So how does this work?" I asked as we laid down to look up at the sky.

He looked at me from the corner of his eyes. "We watch the clouds and tell each other what we see."

"Cat," I said, pointing. He narrowed his eyes, looking in the general direction I was pointing and then frowned shaking his head. I moved closer to him, so our heads were barely an inch apart. "There."

"Ah," he said, his eyes moving to look at me from their corners again.

"Your turn," I said, and he pointed to the sky.

"Heart," he replied, and I shook my head, even though I saw it. I put my hand up as if I was trying to use it to pinpoint it. He laughed and put his hand over mine, taking it and moving it to where the cloud was and tracing its shape.

"Mhmm," I managed to get out as I let our fingers weave together. A jolt rushed through my body as I turned on my elbow and he did the same. "Tell me something," I said looking at our hands together.

"What?" he asked, and his voice was low and deep. The color of his eyes deepened as my gaze rose to his.

"Are the rumors true?" I asked as my heart pounded in my chest so much it hurt. I wasn't sure I wanted to know the answer.

"Which ones?" he asked, and when my eyebrows rose he swallowed. His tongue ran over his lips before he replied. "Ah, those *ones*. Sure, I've had a lot of girlfriends in the past few years." His jaw clenched, and his hand loosened from mine, going to my face. The back of his fingers brushed against the curve of my chin, and I fought the urge to close my eyes. "That's not who I am, though."

I put my hand over his, and his palm flattened against my cheek. Tingles spread throughout my body as I locked my eyes on his. "You don't seem like that kind of guy."

His forehead dipped towards mine, and our lips were only separated by his thumb. "I'm not. I wish I could explain, River–just things happened, and I pushed everyone away–but I don't want to push you away. I want to take you into me and never let you go."

My voice was barely a whisper as I replied, "Then don't. Please don't."

His eyes raced over mine as we sat up and his other hand found my face. His thumb moved, and his lips danced over mine, soft and tentative. My hands slid up his arms to the back of his head as the kiss deepened, and despite the undeniable heat between us, it didn't become physically driven. He pulled me into his lap as his lips parted mine, his tongue moving into my mouth and my body trembled against him.

He pulled away, and I pressed our foreheads together as I looked down at him.

"It took you long enough," I said, biting my lip as I raised my eyebrows.

His hand moved up my spine, coming to cup the back of my head as he leaned up and kissed me again. "I've wanted to do that since the moment you fell into my arms at my shop." The words were playful, but his eyes were serious as he moved my bangs from my eyes. "I just wanted to make sure this was different."

"Is it?"

His lips reached for mine again and behind the softness of the kiss was a passion I never felt before. Where with Adam it always felt like yearning kept in too long, this was a friendship overcast by a stronger emotional and physical pull. My chest tightened with the feeling of it, and his mouth trailed down my chin as his hand moved my hair away from my neck so he could kiss the vein that pulsed with the way my heart was beating out of control.

His lips moved up to my ear, and he whispered the words I needed to hear, "Yes."

Chapter 50

When I came in later than usual on Monday, Charlie turned in her chair and narrowed her eyes at me. "Tattoos, huh?"

I stopped, cocking my head at her. "Excuse me?"

She signaled to her arms. "Tattoos—not just a friend."

"I'll have you know that's not why I'm late," I replied, and I knew my face was a bright red from the burning of my cheeks. We only kissed...until the stars came out and Sadie and Walter started howling their heads off, which reminded me I needed to get home to my beagle baby. This morning I woke up to my favorite thing— a text from West. It was a simple *good morning, Beautiful,* but that didn't matter. The fact he woke up thinking of me was what did. She wiggled her eyebrows at me, and I pulled my cell phone out of my purse. I placed it on her desk and tapped the screen, so the screensaver showed. West shirtless with the beagles.

Her mouth dropped as she cocked her head, pen going into the corner of her mouth as she said, "I'm totally jealous."

I smirked as I turned and winked at her over my shoulder. When I got back to my desk, my phone vibrated.

West – Think I could pull you away for lunch today?

I sat back in my chair and smiled.

Only if I can get a veggie Ruben.

I opened my MacBook and typed in my password, glancing down at my cell phone to see the response.

Your wish is my command.

I logged into my email first, stopping on the HR job posting. It was for Boston, Jesse's district, but I was still curious who it was. Jobs rarely opened up here, and it was even rarer that someone gave one up. I opened the job description, and my stomach twisted into angry knots. *Social Media Manager*– that was Tara's job. I pulled up IM and typed in her name, staring at the green "Available" icon next to a picture of her, but I couldn't bring myself to ask. Instead, I typed in Jesse's number and picked up my phone.

"Hey...so you saw?" Jesse asked, and his voice was low. I wondered if the tone of disappointment was meant for me calling about it or for her quitting.

"Yeah...am I allowed to ask?" I tapped my finger against my desk as I swallowed.

"Yes, but I'm not sure you'll really want to know."

I considered his words for a moment. "I'll be fine."

"She's quitting. She's going on tour with Adam and Fade Burn as their manager," he replied, and his tone softened. "Are you okay?"

My mouth opened and closed, but nothing came out. Adam on tour with Fade Burn. Tara their manager. Somehow I managed to reply, "Sure. Good for them."

Are they dating — is she the 'something like that'? Surprisingly, my heart beat didn't quicken, and I realized I just wanted them to be happy– even if that meant they were together.

"The bad news, well, worse news, is that she gave her notice today and *today* is her last day."

"She's leaving us high and dry?" I asked, putting my head in my hand. "She's going to be hard to replace. She knows social media better than anyone."

"There's already some interest from a few individuals in your district — Jared and Ally."

I looked at the time on the email. "It's only been an hour — you'd swear they were running away from me or something."

Jesse chuckled to himself. "I don't think that's the case. It's a good opportunity, one that only comes once in a great while. We need to fill the spot quickly, though. Do you think you can reach out to them and arrange interviews today? I want to make a decision by Friday."

"Sure. I'll have two hours today that are free, so I'll get them in then," I said as I pulled up my calendar; so much for lunch.

"Great, and why are you in at such a normal hour?"

It was my turn to laugh. "When you're happy you tend to sleep better."

"I'm glad to hear that, River. You deserve to be happy. Benefit, I was totally right."

"Oh, really? I swear you're the one that told me to stay away from him."

"Knowing you'd go right to him."

"Let me remind you I knew him before you even mentioned it."

"Good point. Either way, I'm glad to hear you've let him in." I could hear the smile on Jesse's face. "You both need something good to happen."

Things happened. West's words rang in my head, and I wondered what that meant.

"Let me know what you think of our candidates."

"Sure thing," I replied before hanging up the phone and staring at my packed calendar. At that moment, staring at the blue blocks over most of my week, I was overwhelmed. I sighed as I picked up my phone.

Looks like lunch will have to wait. My free time just got booked.

My phone buzzed a moment later as I pulled my notebooks and files out of my briefcase.

How about I bring lunch and we can eat while you work?

Before I could respond another text came.

Not trying to be pushy. You should eat, though and I know if you get too busy you'll forget those strawberries and only eat the granola bar.

I laughed to myself, shaking my head. He nailed it.

I'd love a sexy delivery man for lunch.

My face burned as I realized that did not say what I meant. Although...

I mean to have a sexy man deliver my lunch.

I watched the three dots showing he was responding.

You could always have both.

I glanced around my office, open glass everywhere. Yeah,

that was not happening. Still the thought of more than kissing with West made my whole body tingle. I put my head in my hands as I breathed in slowly. I hit the reply button.

If only.

Between interviewing Jared and Ally and my normal tasks the morning flew past. When West walked in the door with the brown paper bag, my head was spinning, and my mind drifted back to Tara. West sat across from me, handing me an amazing drink concoction of pomegranate, chocolate and other amazing things that made my tongue tingle when it hit it.

"I got you the veggie Reuben like you asked," he said as he handed it to me, and I gave him a smile. As I unwrapped the foil, my eyes drifted back to my computer and the IM screen I'd been staring at for hours. Tara's smiling face looked back at me, and I chewed my lip before looking down at my sandwich.

"You okay?" West asked, and my gaze lifted up to his. He sat back in the chair, wiping his hands with a brown napkin. His eyebrows hovered over his green eyes as they raced back and forth over my face.

I looked back over at the IM. "I just have something on my mind."

"Which is?" West leaned forward onto his tattooed forearms, and I fought the urge to sit in his lap.

"My ex-best friend gave her resignation, and she's leaving today. I just keep wanting to say something, but I don't know what to say. I know what I want to say, but I doubt she'd listen."

West chewed on the inside of his lip, his fingers stretching out in front of him. "You never know until you try."

"It's complicated," I said before sighing and glancing back at the computer screen. She was still showing as available.

"Ex-boyfriend complicated?"

I inhaled, nodding at the same time. I didn't know how he knew, but it made it easier to explain. "She was –is– friends with him, and she didn't agree with my choice."

"It wasn't her choice to make, but she made the choice not to be your friend any longer because of it," he replied, tapping his thumbs against the desk before looking up at me. "Still, I think you should at least try to talk to her before she leaves. Especially if it's going to bug you if you don't."

I put my hand to my forehead. "I'm scared."

West's hand reached across the desk, moving my own down so he could weave his fingers between mine. "Why don't you call her now– that way, no matter what happens, I'll be here for you."

He squeezed my hand, and I picked up the receiver, clicking on her phone icon. It rang a few times, and then just when I thought she was going to send me to voicemail and never return my call, the phone picked up. It was silent on the other end for a moment before she spoke, "Hi."

Her voice was flat and definitely unamused.

"Hey," I replied, and my voice cracked. West squeezed my hand again, and I squeezed back.

"I guess you saw the posting."

"Yeah," I said, looking over at West as I struggled to

breathe. Stars popped in my vision, and I remembered to inhale as he gave me a soft smile. "I didn't want to leave things the way they've been."

"It's been three months, River. Why now?"

"I don't know if I'll ever have the opportunity again."

She scoffed on the other end. "You're lucky I picked up the phone."

"I know, and I'm thankful for that," I began, and I ignored the secondary scoff. "I just...please stay safe." I closed my eyes, afraid of what West's expression would be for the next thing I was about to say. "And keep him safe."

Another scoff. "Sure, I'll do what you couldn't."

I bit my lip hard, my head tipping back so when I opened my eyes I was looking at the ceiling. My voice was weak as I replied, "Don't you think Bobby would've wanted us to be happy?"

"You're happy without your soul?"

I didn't respond as I brought my head back down to face West. Our eyes locked as I replied, "I *am* happy. For the first time, I feel like my soul is my own."

"Right."

My chin trembled, and I sucked my cheeks in as I fought the tears in my eyes. "I still care about you both, Tara. I just want you to be happy– the both of you."

"We will be–*together*— like you should be."

With that the phone line went dead, and I put it down. I ran my hands over my face and then ducked my face in between my arms as the sob rolled over my body. It didn't have anything to do with the way she said they were together– it was the way she seemed to think I was the worst person in the world for not caring. I did care — I wanted them to be happy, but that didn't seem to be enough. I'd lost the both of them forever.

I didn't hear West stand, but suddenly I was in his arms. His lips pressed against the top of my head as I cried into his shoulder. We stayed like that for a moment until West pulled away slightly and put his hands on either side of my face, rubbing away the wet streaks on my cheeks with his thumbs.

"I'm sorry," he whispered before placing a kiss on my forehead.

I closed my eyes as I shook my head. "I miss them, but I know they both hate me–so many of my relationships were destroyed all for the sake of one that didn't even last — that I don't think was meant to last."

"Is Bobby the one who died?" he asked, and I watched as his chest rose, pressing against his thin cotton t-shirt.

"It's all connected...it's just a giant mess. You probably think I'm a coward for running...leaving shit the way I did," I said as I put my hands on his wrists.

"Look at me, Riv," West said, and when I did his eyes were locked on mine. "You carried too many burdens. You're not a coward for knowing you couldn't do that any-more. You said it– your soul is *yours* now. Without it, you're breathing but not living. How does it feel to live?"

I leaned up on my toes and kissed him once, pulling away slowly, our noses touching as I said, "Thank you."

"I hope someday you'll trust me enough to let me in all

the way...to tell me what happened," West said as he pulled away and went to sit back down across from me.

I glanced over at him, and he nodded to my sandwich. "Eat."

I picked up the food with shaky hands. Why couldn't I just tell him the truth?

Fear.

He knew Adam. What would he think? What had Adam told him?

My appetite was gone, but I still bit into the sandwich and chewed, not tasting it as I swallowed. I looked up and our eyes locked; West's were a darker green than I'd ever seen them, and his lips were dipped down in sadness. Like he knew something more than he was saying.

He knew Adam. Did he know Bobby was his brother? Had he connected the dots? My whole body flushed with heat, and I fought hard against the nausea rushing over me in waves.

"I guess I should get going," West said, crumbling up his empty foil. "I'll see you tomorrow."

He stood and leaned over the desk, kissing my forehead. When he reached the door, my voice finally kicked in, "West."

He stopped, hand on the door frame, and glanced over his shoulder at me. "Yeah."

"I'm scared to tell you."

He closed his eyes, running his teeth over his lower lip. "I get it."

"You're not mad?"

His eyes opened, and he shook his head. "That'd be hypocritical."

I nodded, and he gave me a smile before leaving.

The headache from before returned and only worsened when I looked at my cell phone and saw I missed a call from Alec. I figured he was going to tell me about Adam's tour, but I already knew so I cleared the call, then cleared my calendar and went home to sleep off the pain.

Chapter 51

The next few days West seemed on edge. I figured it had to do with the fact his show was filming again, and the fact one of us usually fell asleep before anything more than kissing could happen. Sometimes I wondered if that was on purpose.

I swallowed as I thought of that, glancing over at West waiting in line to do the obstacle course with Sadie. He wore a heathered green Henley pushed up to his elbows. The cut of the shirt accentuated his body, and the unbuttoned front showed the tattoo across his chest.

My soul, yours forever, to keep.

The breath in my throat stuck as West's eyes caught mine. They were more green than usual against the shirt, and he gave me a smile–but I couldn't return it. Those words– there had to have been someone else. A tattoo was a pretty permanent way to show you cared. My eyes dropped, and I swallowed as heat rushed over my body as my own tattoo burned. It was the one Adam, and I shared, but that was accidental. Those words couldn't be accidental–scrolled just above his heart. The heart I desperately wanted to be mine. The floor seemed to shift below me as the realization hit me hard. I was– no I had– fallen hard. That was the reason Adam being with someone else didn't bug me. A buzzing in my back pocket made me jump, and I pulled my cell phone out to see Alec's name on the screen.

I shook my head, breathing hard as I stared at the name.

"I can handle Bagel for a second if you want to get that," West said as he jogged up next to me, finished with his round.

My eyes lifted up to his, and I realized my mouth was perched open. I shut it and put my cell phone back into my pocket. "I'm good. Nothing urgent."

I went through the motions with Bagel, but my heart wasn't in it. My phone rang again at the end of the session, but I didn't even bother taking it out of my pocket. West glanced over at me, hearing the vibrating, and I looked at the instructor, acting like what she was saying was the most interesting thing I ever heard. After class, we drove in silence until West's hands squeaked against the steering wheel and he spoke, "So who keeps calling that you're ignoring?"

I looked out the window, my chest tight. How could I explain Alec without telling him everything?

"No one," I replied as I glanced over at him.

West's hands went tighter on the steering wheel, and his knuckles turned white. "Judging by your reaction it's not no one."

"It's fine. Don't worry about it," I replied, reaching over and squeezing his leg. I didn't know if I could speak to Alec when my head was spinning with what ifs. What if West loved someone else? What if I didn't love Adam anymore? What kind of person did that make me? What if I loved West? I thought Adam was a wall preventing whatever this was from truly happening, but what if the person that tattoo was for was too?

West glanced over at me, and I managed to pull myself from my thoughts to give him a smile. I put my hand in his lap and blinked until he gave in, dropping his own into mine.

Then the buzzing came again, and West glanced over at me from the corner of his eyes. His fingers tightened around mine and his voice lowered as he asked, "Is it him?" There was a pause and for a moment I thought he'd pull his hand away from mine, but he didn't. "The ex?"

I almost said Adam's name as a question, but somehow managed to stop myself. "No."

"Is it the ex-best friend?"

"No."

His jaw clenched, but he didn't push for more. Just like I didn't push for information on the tattoo, but God I wanted to. When my phone rang again at the dinner table, West closed his eyes, pinching the bridge of his nose.

"Just answer it, Riv. Go outside if you don't want me to hear it," he said and when I opened my mouth he shook his head and nodded to the deck.

I heaved a sigh before sliding my finger across the screen and standing. "Hi."

"You're a hard person to get a hold of," Alec said on the other end, and his voice was thick with relief.

I slid open the glass door, and the sticky summer air hit me, choking the air from my lungs as I stepped outside. I closed it behind me, and my eyes landed on West sitting at the table with his head in his hands. I turned my back to him.

"Bad timing, I guess," I replied as I walked forward and sat down on the steps. A thin bead of sweat was already forming between my shoulder blades, despite the crispness of the Fall air.

"Sorry to hear that. How have you been?"

I glanced over my shoulder to see West clearing the dinner table. "Good for the most part. You?"

"Decent. It's weird living on my own again, but I've been coaching hockey."

"You?" I asked, and the thought made me laugh. It wasn't a laugh of spite, but of amusement. Bobby would love that his dad was following in his footsteps.

"I'm not as good as Bobby," he replied, and I heard the smile on his lips. "But I guess that's to be expected."

"I'm sure you're great," I said, rubbing my hands against my skinny jeans. "I'd love to see a game."

"Actually...that's kind of what I was calling about. I had some money set aside, and I donated it to Bobby's old rink—you remember the one you guys learned to skate in? It was in pretty bad shape, and they were going to close it. I couldn't stand to see it happen. They're changing the name to the Robert Beckerson Memorial Ice Hockey Ring."

Tears pricked in my eyes and I put my head between my

knees. "That's awesome," I replied, and I knew Alec could hear the tears in my voice.

"Don't be sad, Riv."

"I'm not," I replied, my voice choked. "I just think he'd love it, and that makes me happy."

"I want you to be there for the grand opening. It's October tenth at two. Adam can't go since he's on tour..." Alec paused, and he cleared his voice. "Along with Tara."

"I know," I replied as I looked at the sky. I blew air out through my cheeks, puffing them.

Alec's voice was soft as he continued, "So you could bring a date if you wanted."

So Dad told him. I didn't mind, because at least I wouldn't have to. "Okay."

"I can count you in?"

I glanced over my shoulder to see West sitting on the floor playing with the puppies. His eyes darted to me and then back to them. "Of course."

"Great," he replied and his voice again filled with relief. "I was afraid you'd say no."

Another thought struck me, and I felt my whole body tense. The words were breathless as I asked, "Will my mom be there?"

Silence filled the line, and I wondered if I accidentally hung up, but then Alec took a long inhale. "Yes, but please, River, it'd mean the world to Bobby and me if you went."

"It's fine."

My body was shaking. I needed West to be there, but what would Mom think of my new tattoos, of West's? Of his career. The world became too hot, and the air around me seemed to thicken, its molecules too big to get into my lungs.

"Great, see you in two weeks," Alec said, and the phone line went silent.

I felt my lashes flutter against my cheek as I put the phone down, and my head went to my knees again. The slider opened behind me, and I expected to be bounced by beagles, but instead all I felt was West sit down next to me.

"That good?" he asked, and his voice was quiet against the peep frogs chirping in the background.

I tilted my head to look at him, and his eyes rushed over my face. Bobby's voice echoed in my mind. *You need to be honest with him.*

I looked straight ahead before replying, "No."

"Tell me?" he asked. I wanted to, but fear held me back and those nasty what ifs. I shook my head. He stood, putting his hands behind his head, so they formed muscular triangles. When he turned his brows were furrowed, causing hard lines to stretch across his forehead. "Please, River. Let me in. Why can't you let me in?"

"I'm sorry."

"I am too–you're in pain, and I can't do anything about it."

"It's not that easy to explain."

He looked at the sky before locking eyes on me. "I know pain as deep as yours, River. I promise you," his voice broke, and he shook his head before continuing; "Not everyone wears their pain as a challenge, some people bury it so deep no one knows. That's where we differ, but both methods end up the same. We push people away. We drown. God, I was drowning before you, River." His eyes sparkled with tears, and I stood.

"Tell me," I whispered, and he crushed his eyes shut.

"Let me show you." His hands went to the edge of his shirt before lifting it over his head. He turned before I could fully take in his front, and my eyes moved up from the dimples in his back to a scar that ran up his spine. I couldn't believe I hadn't noticed it before. "There's newspaper articles under my bed...a gravestone with her name on it."

He turned back around, and my eyes ran over the tattoos that seemed to show his story. The pain and anger he hid so well seemed to dance within the beautiful lines. Waves of pain crashed against the Japanese demons, and I wondered if they symbolized his own. My eyes moved to where flower petals littered their inked beauty from their tree that was collapsing under the weight of the water. The water rushed across and formed the words scrolled over his chest, flowing into wisps of the wind that connected the tattoo to his other arm where another battle raged. There, swallowtails fought against clouds, wind and Japanese maple leaves. It was beautiful in the anger and pain it showed– a battle I hardly understood from his perspective, but one I knew entirely of my own.

I stepped forward, placing my hand over his heart and his fingers came to cover mine. His chest rose and I looked up at him to see he was struggling with the words to explain.

His eyes crushed closed, and I knew I needed to explain my pain so he could let me into his.

"Bobby Beckerson was my best friend," I began, and West's eyes opened, locking on mine. I continued, "He fell in love with me...but I fell in love with his brother, Adam." I watched as recognition flitted in his eyes, but he didn't interrupt. "The three of us...we made an interesting crew. Bobby in love with me, me in love with Adam and Adam in love with himself...or so I thought."

"He loved you, though," West said, and his jaw trembled as he bit his cheek. I nodded. "I know him."

"I know– that's why I didn't want to tell you." He nodded but didn't say anything else.

I took a deep breath before continuing because I needed to explain that I had been wrong, and I knew it more than ever as I stared at West now.

"Adam and I started dating around the time Bobby started dating the only girl friend I had–, Tara. We thought it would make it easier, but when Bobby found out he blew up. Things just kept getting worse from there. I sparked some war between the two of them and Bobby was a sore loser. He took some cheap shots– exposed some things to our parents that shifted and broke those relationships," I paused, shaking my head. "But somehow we made it through all of that. And then one night Bobby saw how crappy his parents treated us, and he was coming home...there was a patch of ice. I lost everything that night." My lips shook, tears gliding over them as I locked eyes with West. "I always thought Adam was the one. That we made each other better, but we never did. We destroyed each other. And when Bobby died, there was nothing to hold us together. Adam became a drunk, and I just faded until I couldn't take it anymore. Tara was collateral damage. She thought I was awful for leaving, and I believed her. But she's wrong. For once in my life, I feel like I'm enough."

West's jaw clenched, and his eyes looked passed me as a tear dripped down the curve of his nose, and I reached up to push it away. My chest tightened painfully as I waited for any response. When his eyes came back to mine, he finally spoke, "I don't want my pain to change whatever is going to happen. Your heart is yours. When you make your decision, I want it to be yours without the weight of mine. I never want my heart to weigh you down like his has."

"My decision?" I asked, and my voice was barely audible.

He put his hands on either side of my face, and he ran his tongue over his dry lips before replying, "Him or me."

"There's no decision to make."

"You won't be able to leave things like you did, River. You'll need some closure...from one of us," he said, and the tears weighed his lashes down.

"I won't let you drown," I said as I put my hands behind his neck and his forehead dipped to mine. "No matter what."

He took a shaky breath. "I was engaged once...I was in love and stupid...God, was I stupid. Twenty-two wasn't a good age for me. I drank too much...and one day we paid the price. We slammed right into the tree. Sophia died on impact. I haven't gotten drunk since then– a drink here or there, but nothing like that. Art was my way out. I buried my pain with every tattoo I got– and then with every one I gave. But it was always on the edge threatening to drag me down."

"Until?"

West's eyes locked on me. "Until now. But River, I don't want you to drown for me. Never do that."

"You're the reason I'm not drowning," I whispered. "I thought I needed Adam to find me." West's eyes dropped, and I leaned up on my toes to press my forehead to his. His eyes rose back to mine. "But I needed to find myself, and I have. I'm not leaving."

West's hands came up to my face, cupping it as his lips met mine. The kissed deepened as the walls we formed around our hearts fell. My lips slid from his, down his chin to his collarbone and his head tipped back as he gasped. He let his hands fall to my ass, where he lifted me, parting my legs around his waist. I continued kissing across his tattoos as he made his way up the deck and back into the house. He put me on the table to lift my shirt over my head, and his head ducked down, kissing my chest as his hands worked the clasp of my bra and it came away. I put my hand under his chin and tilted his mouth back up to mine, pulling our bare skin together. His warmth spread over me, and my lips parted, a moan drifting from the pleasure of his skin against mine. West pulled me back into him, his arm muscles tensing under my hands as he lifted me back up. He managed to get past the sleeping dogs without waking them and stopped at the stairs. His kisses slowed as his eyes opened to look up them. He was strong, but walking up a flight of stairs caring me and making out was dangerous. I smiled, sliding down his body and intertwining our fingers as I led him up to the bedroom. I closed the door behind us, and his bare chest heaved as he put his forearms on either side of my head. I tilted my face to his arm, running kisses over his tattoos and leaving a trail of goosebumps as I made my way up to his lips. His head tipped back.

"I'm not sure that's fair," he said between breaths. My hands fell to his belt, and his body stiffened. Our lips met again as his pants fell and he stepped backward out of them. By the time we made it to the bed, there was no clothing separating us, just thin air and protection. West laid me back on the bed, one arm under my waist while the other held his body above me and our lips hovered over one another as we stared into each other's eyes. Something clicked then and when our lips met it was with a new emotion, deeper and stronger than before. His body moved into mine, and my back arched, fingers digging into his shoulders as my lips left him to gasp, and the name that left my lips was the one I knew held my heart, but set my soul free. "West."

Finding Perfection
(Beautifully Flawed, #3)

The conclusion to the Beautifully Flawed Series

Find me.

Those were the two words I wrote half-cursive on a sheet of paper and left on the island for Adam. The two words I said to him, although he couldn't hear it before I walked away.

Find me.

Then I thought when you lose everything, you're sure to lose yourself and never be able to get it back. I was wrong. Adam couldn't find me if he tried. The only one who could find me was me.

And I had.

Despite the mess, my life became after Adam kissed me; after Bobby died. After I ran.

I somehow found myself.

As I lifted my eyes to stare at the life-size statue of Adam, Bobby and I skating, I found a smile tugging at my lips. West squeezed my hand, and I looked up at him, green eyes soft, caring and worried as they raced across my face. His eyes fell to my lips, and his own tugged upward as he nodded up to the statue.

"You three look like you were thick as thieves," he said, and his voice cracked. There was worry layered into the deep cadence of his voice.

My eyes moved up to the statue– us skating and laughing, me in the middle of the two boys. We were teenagers then, Adam and I sixteen and Bobby eighteen and I was oblivious to how in the middle of them I was. My throat thickened as I stared between the two of them. They were opposites in every way. Adam thin, swimmer body, a full head and a half shorter than broad and chiseled Bobby. Even their eyes were opposing; Adam's a brown of mud with grass flecks while Bobby's were blue like the sky. West's body tensed beside me, and I realized I was so lost in my thoughts I hadn't answered.

"We were," I said, biting my lip. "But there was just as many fights as there was laughter."

And I was in the middle of those fights– the reason for them. Even after Bobby's death I felt like I was still locked in a war with them. The thing was, no one ever won.

Not Bobby.

Not Adam.

Not me.

We all lost ourselves in that war, and none of us were connected anymore–at least not on the mortal plane. We were here because nine months ago Bobby died in a car crash and now his father paid to restore our old ice rink in memory of him. Adam wasn't here; we hadn't spoken in over three months, and he was somewhere in the world on tour with his band and Tara. I grit my teeth at the thought of my ex-best friend. We spoke on the day she quit her job to go on tour with the band. It hadn't ended well, but my boyfriend West was there for me then. He was here for me as we stood staring at the statue of my dead best friend and my ex-boyfriend. I readjusted the guitar case in my hand as I looked away from the bronzed version of my teenage self to West. His eyes were locked on Bobby.

I elbowed him. "I know it's weird he doesn't look anything like Adam."

West's eyes fell to me and his brows furrowed, causing a shadow to fall over his eyes. "Why don't you have any pictures out?"

I didn't have any pictures or anything besides the guitar in my hand to remind me of Adam or Bobby. My shoulders rose as I bit my lip before answering, "It was hard after I left Adam– every picture is of the three of us. Don't you think that would be awkward now?"

"Umm," West began, his head jerking back as he laughed. "Yeah, maybe– they have photoshop for that, don't they?"

I rolled my eyes as we headed past the statue and to the front door. "I'm not that good with photoshop."

West squeezed my hand. "There's none of just you and Bobby?"

"I'm sure there's some, although Adam probably burned them," I replied, looking over at him.

"That jealous?" he asked, cocking his head at me.

"You have no idea–"

The doors swung open just before we reached them and Alec pulled me into his arms before I could say anything. "River! I'm so glad you agreed to come...and to sing."

He held me out at arm's length, and I looked around at the renovated building and back to the statue before looking at Alec's eyes– a bright blue I memorized in his son's eyes. "Bobby would've loved this. The statue is a bit much, though."

Alec laughed and his broad shoulders, also a mirror to Bobby's shape, lifted. "Yeah, but Bobby was all for bigger is better. You remember that truck?"

I swallowed, and Alec's eyes shut as he put his hand on his forehead. I could tell by his response he knew what I was thinking. *The truck he died driving.*

"Yeah," I replied, forcing a smile on my face to let Alec know it was okay. "He always teased me about not being able to get into it. I figured he bought it on purpose so he could get a little closer to the girls he drove in it."

Alec's brows rose. "You're probably right about that — at least on one account."

I bit my cheek, knowing he was referencing me before turning and looking at West. He was looking down at the toes of his navy blue suede shoes. I took his hand into mine and turned to face Alec again. "This is my boyfriend West — West this is Bobby and Adam's dad, Alec."

Alec reached out to shake West's hand and put his other hand on the top, eyes locking on West's. "I'm so glad River brought you. Her dad has told me how amazing you've been for her." His eyes drifted to me. "You can imagine how special she is to our family."

My chest tightened as Alec gave me a soft smile before letting go of West's hand. He was sincere and had changed so much over the last few months. Despite the loss of one son, the distancing of the other and the dissolution of his marriage he seemed to have found himself. It was ironic that one of the worst things in our lives had pulled things together.

"Pleasure to meet you too, but I'm afraid I haven't met River's dad yet," West said as he glanced over at me, his forehead creasing.

"Well, we can fix that! He's right inside," Alec replied as he glanced down at his watch and then back up. "The guests should start arriving in about fifteen or so minutes, but River's parents and my ex-wife are already here."

He turned and held the door open for us, and I watched as West's face paled. It was my turn to squeeze his hand. We followed Alec inside, and West leaned down as much as he could without being obvious to whisper, "How can they like me already? What did you say about me?"

I leaned up and kissed his cheek. "I don't think I had to say anything. It's just the way you make me feel and act–like me."

Acknowledgements

Nine. This is my ninth published book, my seventh full-length novel– in only a handful of years. You'd think that writing acknowledgements would be easy by now, but it never is. There's so much that goes into writing a novel and while you'd think it's a solitary endeavour, it's not– at least at this point. It's been awhile since I published the first book in the Beautifully Flawed series, in fact, it's been over two years. For that, I must apologize to my readers. If you're one of the ones who stood by me while I published several other books and wondered what the heck I was doing, then I must absolutely thank you for your patience and for sticking around. If you're new to the series, then I want to thank you, too. All of you make this journey worthwhile.

That's what writing a series, or a novel is. It's a constant journey of growth and getting to know yourself, your characters, your readers, your editors, bloggers and your fellow authors. All of those people make this journey epic.

Last, but certainly not least, thank you to my family for supporting this dream. Especially to my tolerant husband. I can't imagine being married to an author is easy, but somehow you get it. Maybe, someday, we'll hit the author lottery, and I'll be doing one job instead of a million. Until then, thank you for tolerating me coming home and sitting on the couch to work some more, and for always telling me it takes just one book–and this *one* might just be it.

Always,
Cassie Giovanni

About the Author

Cassandra doesn't remember a time when she wasn't writing. In fact, the first time she was published was when she was seven years old and won a contest to be published in an American Girl Doll novel. Since then Cassandra has written more novels than she can count and put just as many in the circular bin. Her personal goal with her writing is to show the reader the character's stories through their dialogue and actions instead of just telling the reader what is happening. Besides being a writer, Cassandra is a professional photographer known for her automotive, nature and architectural shots. She is happily married to the man of her dreams and they live in the rolling hills of New England their dogs, Bubski and Kanga.

Cassandra can be found on Goodreads, Facebook and Twitter.

For regular updates visit Cassandra's website and sign up for her newsletter.

Other Novels by the Author

Adult
Love Exactly – Contemporary Romance
Finding the Cure – Contemporary Romance
In Between Seasons – Post-Apocalyptic Romance
Young Adult
Walking in the Shadows – Romantic Suspense
Children's
The Adventures of Skippy Von Flippy
Mystic Mayhem (Finding Freckles, #1)
Bermuda Bounce (Finding Freckles, #2)
COMING SOON
City on Fire – Adult Fantasy
Finding Perfection (Beautifully Flawed, #3) – Adult
Contemporary Romance

www.ingramcontent.com/pod-product-compliance
Lightning Source LLC
Chambersburg PA
CBHW070634180626
46817CB00006B/2118